Dear Reader,

I did a fair amount of my growing up on a small farm in Hamilton County, Texas. When I wasn't hoeing squash or picking okra (my father and I have differing opinions as to how much of this I actually did) I was reading. Fred Gibson set his stories a couple of counties over from the very ground I worked, so *Old Yeller* and *Savage Sam* were some of the first books I read. I watched "Gunsmoke" and "The Rifleman" with my grandpa and listened to him talk about his boyhood trapping and hunting in central Texas. To me, the West was real and it was right outside my door. From my bedroom window, I could make out the ghost-white limestone markers on the neighboring ranch where a Comanche raiding party had massacred a young school teacher and her five students only a few generations before. My local librarian told me the Texas Rangers had played a large part in chasing down the renegades. So, I read everything I could get my hands on about Indians or Texas Rangers.

When it came time to choose a career, law enforcement seemed like the only choice—and early on, when I realized I wanted to write, Western stories came naturally to my pen.

When I was a young-pup detective, it was a savvy Texas Ranger who gave me some of the best advice I've ever heard—on police work and writing.

It was my first homicide investigation, and I was twenty-six years old. The victim was a pretty college coed. The poor thing's body had been dumped in a weedy ditch along a lonely gravel road, where we found her three days later. Everything I knew to do, I did twice and had a good start on a stomach ulcer by the time the Ranger pulled up in his dark blue Crown Victoria and strode over to where I stood a couple of feet upwind from the corpse. Without speaking, he hunkered down on the heels of his lizard skin boots to take a closer look.

I squatted beside him. "Billy," I pleaded. He'd have slapped me if I'd called him "Ranger" like they did in the movies. "I'm not sure what to do. You've investigated dozens of murders. Teach me."

Billy nudged the straw hat back on his head a few inches and picked at his teeth with the flat wooden toothpick he never seemed to be without. "Well, Markus," he said, fooling with the toothpick as he spoke. "Just write down everything you see . . ."

At that moment a tiny pupa, which had only recently been a wriggling critter feeding on the decaying body, hatched into a sticky, green-backed fly and flew straight into the Ranger's mouth. I looked on in horror but he never missed a beat. He picked out the fly with a thumb and forefinger, returned the toothpick to the corner of his mouth and gave me a wry smile.

"Just write down everything you see . . . and watch out for the blow flies."

Over the years, I've been fortunate enough to work with beat cops, detectives, Rangers, deputy marshals, and a whole alphabet soup of federal law enforcement agents who exemplify those standards set by the lawmen I read about as a boy. The spirit of the Old West lives in them—and most are far more interesting than any character I could ever dream up. We've had some hellacious adventures together, and through it all, I've tried to follow the Ranger's advice and keep good notes.

I'll apologize now if my comrades-at-arms find any piece of themselves reflected between these pages. You see, they may have different names, but I've had the privilege of riding with Trap, Clay, Hezekiah, and many of the others.

I only hope I can make their stories as gritty and real to you as they are to me . . . so enjoy the adventure—and watch out for the blow flies.

Respectfully,

Mark Henry
Anchorage, Alaska
May 2005

THE HELL RIDERS

MARK HENRY

PINNACLE BOOKS
Kensington Publishing Corp.
http://www.kensingtonbooks.com

PINNACLE BOOKS are published by

Kensington Publishing Corp.
850 Third Avenue
New York, NY 10022

All Kensington Titles, Imprints, and Distributed Lines are available at special quantity discounts for bulk purchases for sales promotions, premiums, fund-raising, and educational or institutional use. Special book excerpts or customized printings can also be created to fit specific needs. For details, write or phone the office of the Kensington special sales manager: Kensington Publishing Corp., 850 Third Avenue, New York, NY 10022, attn: Special Sales Department, Phone: 1-800-221-2647.

Pinnacle and the P logo Reg. U.S. Pat. & TM Off.

First Pinnacle Books Printing: February 2006

10 9 8 7 6 5 4 3 2 1

Printed in the United States of America

ACKNOWLEDGMENTS

The list of good people who helped me and buoyed me up during this adventure is almost without number. I should take the time to thank my fellow trackers and gun-toters for watching over me when my mind was somewhere else: Holland, Sonny, Kevin, John, and Wanda—and especially Ty Cunningham, a superb comrade at arms and a tracker who knows no equal.

Further, I ought to thank the librarians and teachers in my life: Lou, Al, Julie, Lola, Billie, and Irene—the only people who are sure to read this story and tell me they like it—no matter what they really think.

AUTHOR'S NOTE

On rare occasion, when enlisted men in the United States Cavalry desired to bestow the highest honor on a particular officer, they gave him the gift of a sword. By this token, these leaders were inducted into an exclusive order of fighting men, an order of absolute respect and devotion from their subordinates—the Order of the Saber.

PROLOGUE

October 5, 1877
Montana
Alikos Pah—*The Place of Dung Fires*
Thirty miles south of the Canadian border

Looking Glass was dead. Ollokut, Poker Joe—most of the young warriors were dead or dying in the freezing mud.

Maggie Sundown, of the Wallowa Nez Percé, struggled against the stiff rope that bound her wrists and ankles and wished she was dead as well.

The once-beautiful fourteen-year-old was covered in mud, her fingernails blackened past the quick from frantic digging in the soggy prairie muck in advance of Colonel Miles's unrelenting army. Dirt and bits of grass matted her waist-length hair into a tangled nest.

Only hours before, she'd been reloading rifles for Broad Hand in a hastily dug pit, while he poured fire down on the blue-coats. Now, the blood of her childhood friend mingled with the grime on the side of her face.

In the ghost-gray fog of early morning, a group of soldiers had flanked their position and shot her brave friend in the eye with a big-bore rifle. He was only fifteen.

Maggie had taken up one of Broad Hand's Sharps to

continue the battle. Tiny crystals of snow spit against the barrel, sizzling and evaporating on contact from the heat brought on by heavy fire. She fully expected to be shot at any moment. Instead, a blond soldier with freckles across his nose like the spots on an Appaloosa pony leapt into the sodden hole. He clubbed her in the head with his pistol before she could turn the big gun back toward him.

When she awoke, Maggie found herself bound hand and foot with rough hemp, slumped against the wheel of a supply ambulance. A searing pain, made worse by the earlier blasting of the soldiers' artillery, roared in her head. The copper taste of blood cloyed, hard and bitter, in the back of her throat.

The battle had fallen off to a lull of sporadic pops and hollow shouts of distant skirmishers. Yellow-tinged gun smoke drifted like soiled cotton across the rolling plain and hung in blurred layers. Dead horses and fighters from both sides, corpses tight from the cold, littered the frosted grass. Gossamer flakes of snow drifted down through the haze in serene indifference to the murderous landscape.

Dozens of soldiers milled about in small groups. Phlegmatic coughs rattled their chests and they stomped their feet against the chill. Some wore capes; others pulled wool blankets tight around their whiskered necks.

Maggie thought little of the cold. She felt nothing but a hot, seething anger—tight in her breast—a fist around her heart. All around her, the air was filled with the drawn-out twang of the white men's chatter. The foreign whine of it bit at her nerves like a swarm of mosquitoes in her ears.

The Nimi'ipuu—her people—were silent.

A Crow Army scout with a pockmarked face and a mean scar from chin to ear squatted on his haunches beside her, leering with rheumy, black eyes and a cocked head. He touched himself lewdly, then licked his lips and reached out for the hem of her muddy calico skirt.

A swift kick from the freckle-nosed soldier sent him sprawling. It was Broad Hand's killer.

"Get from here, you heathen cur." The blond soldier drew his pistol and thumbed back the hammer. His pale fingers were blackened from putting the gun to much use during recent hours. "Do you understand me, you miserable wretch? Touch her again and you'll not leave this place alive."

The Crow gave a sullen shrug and padded off out of pistol range in search of an unguarded prisoner.

"You understand English?" Maggie's savior took the Indian scout's place and squatted beside her, only inches away from her knee. She held her breath, not knowing what to expect from the young soldier. He had a yellow bar on his shoulder. She knew enough of the military to know this meant he was one of the leaders. There seemed to be a lot of men with such decorations. Joseph said that was the trouble with the whites—they had too many chiefs who didn't know what the others were up to.

Leader or not, Maggie planned to bite the nose off of any man who touched her again. This one kept his hands to himself. He wasn't too many years older than her. Not yet past twenty-five.

"Lieutenant Peter Grant." He pointed to himself as if she couldn't understand him, then wrapped his arms around his own shoulders and pretended to be shivering. "You need to warm up, child; you're soaked to the skin."

He disappeared into the gray mist for a moment before trotting back through the muddy grass with a wool blanket. Squatting, he moved to drape it over her.

"I'm not cold," Maggie grunted, focusing on the falling snow. She'd learned English from the Christian missionaries in Oregon who'd been intent on converting her people.

The lieutenant grinned when she spoke and clapped his hands together like a happy child. His eyes played over her in silence for a time as if he were coming to some decision. He opened his mouth, but a commotion behind him caught his attention.

"It's him," he whispered, rising to his feet. "Joseph himself, under a truce flag. Thank the Good Lord in heaven. I reckon it's finally over."

Maggie stared at the ground. At first it was pleasant to hear the words pour out in her own tongue, but the longer Joseph spoke, the more those words cut her spirit. Another soldier translated for Howard, the one-armed Bible General who had pursued her people almost two thousand miles—and for the colonel, who had finally caught them.

A tremor beset Joseph's voice as he spoke from the back of his tired pony. *". . . I want to have time to look for my children and see how many I can find. Maybe I shall find them among the dead. Hear me, my chiefs. My heart is sick and sad. . . ."*

The once-proud leader dismounted and with a nod from the Bible General, gave his rifle to Colonel Miles. Then, in shame, he pulled his blanket across his face.

A single tear, the first Maggie had shed since leaving her homeland in the Wallowa Valley, creased her dirty cheek.

Lieutenant Grant turned his attention back to her. He gave a thin smile. "Don't you worry," he said. "This is all for the best."

Whose best? Maggie thought, but she didn't say it. "Will you let my people return to their homes?" She refused to look at this soldier, refused to let him see her cry.

Lieutenant Grant remained silent, watching her. At length he shrugged. "I don't have any say in such matters. To tell you the truth, I'm not sure the general does either. I'm sure he'll try if he says he will."

He knelt down next to her again. His saber scabbard rattled when he pushed it behind him. "No matter what happens," he said, "I'll personally see to it that you're well taken care of."

Maggie was young, but she'd celebrated her womanhood a year before. She knew what it meant when a soldier said he would *take care* of an Indian girl. The old women often told bawdy stories of such things while they gathered camas bulbs in the spring.

The pale lieutenant's boyish face suddenly grew somber, a serenely benevolent look in his water-blue eyes. "There's too much sickness on the rez. You're so very beautiful . . . or at least you could be." He had the condescending look of piety about him, as if he were about to give money to a beggar. "My uncle sits on the board of a Presbyterian Indian school down Missouri way. They can help you there—teach you to be a

proper Christian American. Help you become civilized."
His wide eyes brimmed with youthful dreams. He spoke
slowly so she would understand him. "I've cleared it with the
colonel so you have nothing to worry about."

She shuddered when he put a gentle hand on her shoulder.

"Listen to me, now," he said. "I know this is hard. But take
my word for it. The folks at the school are good, solid
people. It'll be a darn sight more tolerable than any reservation." He smiled and took her hand in his. Rather than pull
away, she let it sag.

"I'll be up for a promotion to first lieutenant in three
months." He spoke to her as though he was convinced she
must share whatever dreams he held for their future. "I'll
look in on you then when things settle down some. Would
you mind that? If I came to visit you, I mean."

Maggie sat still. She could think of nothing but Chief
Joseph's words and her defeated people.

The lieutenant pressed on with his objective. "I know a
good number of men who made happy homes with Indian
women. Met a squaw man once down in Kansas who appeared to be a right happy fellow."

Grant gazed at her for a moment—locked in a daydream—
then shook his head as if to cast off the thought. He put both
hands on his knees and pushed himself to his feet with the
groan of a much older man.

"I just realized—I don't even know your name."

Maggie nodded, but didn't speak.

Grant smiled. "It's all right, I guess. We've got plenty of
time to get to know each other." He let his eyes play over
the pitiful groups of Nez Percé dragging in from the low
hills and brushy draws along Snake Creek.

"Poor souls," he whispered. "I wish I could send them all
to school." His pink face glistened in the flat light.

Maggie had seen the look before, back in Oregon. The
lieutenant was a missionary in a uniform, a man with an un-
bending surety of his own beliefs and righteous purpose.

He had the clear eyes of a man with no guile. His heart

was good—but at that moment, if given the means, Maggie Sundown would have gladly cut it out of his chest.

"There are worse futures than marrying an officer in the United States Army." The freckled nose wrinkled when he smiled. His eyes twinkled. "Don't you fret now." His mind made up regarding his future wife, other more immediate duties called him away.

Perhaps, Maggie thought, he should go wash the blood of her people off his hands before he takes me to his bed.

He turned to smile at her as he walked away. "They'll take good care of you at the school," he said softly. "I'll be there to get you soon enough. I promise."

PART ONE

CHAPTER 1

November 1910
Montana

The nine A.M. Great Northern train out of St. Regis rarely pulled away from the station before a quarter to ten. That gave Deputy U.S. Marshal Blake O'Shannon a little over an hour to make the trip that normally took twenty minutes. But normally, he didn't have to plow through stirrup-deep snow.

O'Shannon urged his stout leopard Appaloosa forward, into the bone-numbing cold. A fierce wind burned the exposed areas of his face above his wool scarf. Important news weighed heavy on his shoulders and pressed him into the saddle. He groaned within himself and prayed the train would be late in leaving—not so much of a stretch as far as prayers went, considering the rank weather.

Driving snow lent teeth to the air and gave the sky the gunmetal face of a stone-cold killer. The young deputy stretched his aching leg in the stirrup. He'd only been able to walk without a crutch for a few weeks. If not for the message he carried, a message his father needed to hear, he never would have attempted a ride in such frigid conditions.

"What's a hot-blooded Apache like you doin' up here in all this white stuff?" He mumbled. A bitter wind tore the words away from his lips. He often talked to himself on lone rides, letting the three aspects of his heritage argue over whatever problem he happened to be chewing on at the time.

His gelding trudged doggedly on, but cocked a speckled ear back at the one-sided conversation.

Blake pulled his sheepskin coat tighter around his throat. "Better not let your Nez Percé mama hear you talk like that about her precious mountains," he chided himself. White vapor plumed out around his face as he spoke. He wished he'd inherited his mother's love—or at least her tolerance—for the cold.

A weak sun made a feeble attempt at burning through the clouds over the mountains to the east, but the gathering light only added to the sense of urgency welling up inside Blake's gut. He had a train to catch.

He came upon the stranded wagon suddenly in a blinding sliver swirl of snow at the edge of a mountain shadow.

The driver, a sour man named Edward Cooksey, worked with a broken shovel to free the front wheel from a drift as deep as his waist. A flea-bitten gray slouched in the traces with a drooping lower lip. The horse was almost invisible amid the ghostlike curtains of blowing snow.

Blake reined up and sighed. St. Regis was less than a mile away to the west. He took a gold watch from his pocket and fumbled with a gloved had to open it. He was cutting it close.

Cooksey had a half-dozen arrests under his belt for being drunk and disorderly. Each time he'd gone in only after an all-out kicking and gouging fight.

Blake didn't have time for this. Still, he couldn't very well ride by and leave someone to freeze to death—not even someone as ill-tempered as Ed Cooksey.

The deputy cleared his throat with a cough. "Hitch up my horse alongside yours and we'll pull you outta that mess." Wind moaned through snow-bent jack pines along the road and Blake strained to be heard.

Cooksey had a moth-eaten red scarf tied over his head that pulled the brim of his torn hat down over his ears against the cold. He wore two tattered coats that together did only a slightly passable job of keeping out the winter air. Stubby, chapped fingers poked out of frayed holes in his homespun woolen gloves. The man was no wealthier than he was pleasant.

"Damned horse bowed a tendon on me. She ain't worth a bucket of frozen spit for pullin' anyhow," he grunted against the wheel. When he looked up from his labor, his craggy face fell into a foul grimace as if he'd just eaten a piece of rotten fruit. "Push on," he spit.

"You don't want my help?" Blake was relieved but not surprised.

Cooksey leaned against the wheel and wiped a drip of moisture off the red end of his swollen nose. He brandished the broken shovel. "I'd rather drown, freeze plumb to death, or be poked with Lucifer's own scaldin' fork than to take assistance from a red nigger Injun—'specially one who's high-toned enough to pin on a lawman's badge."

Blake caught the sent of whiskey, sharp as shattered glass on the frigid air.

"Suit yourself then." He lifted his reins to go.

"Twenty years ago, boy," Cooksey snarled, "you and me woulda been tryin' to cut each other's guts out."

"Twenty years ago, I was four years old."

Cooksey gave a cruel grin. "I reckon that woulda just made my job all the easier."

The Appaloosa pawed impatiently at the snow with a forefoot, feeling Blake's agitation through his gloves and the thick leather reins.

"I doubt that," the deputy said.

"I tell you what." Cooksey sucked on his top lip, an easy chore since there were no teeth there to get in the way. "I don't need any of your help, but I will take that horse off your hands."

"I said I'd be glad to hitch up the horse and pull you out."

"I don't want you to hitch the damned thing up." Cooksey's gloved hand came out of his coat pocket, wrapped around an ugly black derringer. "I want you to get your red nigger tail out of that saddle and let me ride back into town."

Like most derringers, Cooksey's hideout pistol was a large caliber, capable of doing tremendous damage in the unlikely event it happened to hit anything. Blake was less than ten feet away. At that distance, even the bleary-eyed drunk might get lucky.

"Think again, Cooksey." Blake gritted his teeth, racking his brain for a way out of this predicament. "You're not getting my horse." He'd had enough sense to strap his Remington pistol outside the heavy winter coat, but wearing gloves and sitting in the saddle made him awkward at best. Cooksey definitely had the advantage.

"Hell, you probably stole it from some honest white man anyhow," Cooksey sneered. "To my way of thinkin', that makes it more mine than it is yours."

A fat raven perched in the shadows of a ponderosa pine directly behind the gunman, hopped to a lower limb, and sent a silent cascade of snow though the dark branches. The bird turned a round eye toward the two men.

Blake's Nez Percé mother said the raven was a trickster. She'd often told him the story of how one had saved her life. He began to work out an idea that would have made her proud.

"Brother Raven," he said, in his best how-the-white-man-thinks-all-Indians-talk voice. "I am glad you could come visit on this cold day."

Cooksey's eyes narrowed. He raised the derringer higher. "What in the hell are you talkin' about?"

Blake pressed on, keeping his voice relaxed. "I need a favor, my brother. Would you fly over here and tell Ed Cooksey he cannot have my horse?" Blake gave a tired shrug for effect. "I already told him, but he doesn't believe me. It would help me a lot if you would make him understand."

"Shut up and clamber down off that horse before I blow you outta the saddle."

The raven winged its way over to the tree directly behind Cooksey. Wind whooshed off its great wings, and it began to make a series of loud gurgling noises like water dripping into a full bucket.

The would-be gunman's bloodshot eyes went wide.

When he snapped his head around to look, Blake put the spurs to his Appaloosa and ran smack over the top of him.

Cooksey let out a muffled screech and fell back to disappear in the deep snow. The derringer fired once, echoing through the snow-clad evergreens. Blake was off the horse with his hand around the gun in less than a heartbeat.

O'Shannon was a powerful man, tall and well muscled. Even with his healing leg, he had no trouble with the half-frozen drunk. Three swift kicks to the ribs loosened Cooksey's grip on the little pistol and diminished his appetite for a fight.

Blake snatched up the derringer and took a step back, plowing snow as he went. Snapping the pug barrels forward, he tugged the spent casing and the remaining live round into the snow. He flung the empty pistol as far as he could into the tree line. His hat had come off in the fight. A silver line of frost had already formed along his short black hair. He bent to pick the hat up, panting softly.

"You can come back and look for that in the spring," the deputy said. Huge clouds of fog erupted into the cold air as he spoke. "Wish I had time to arrest you, but I figure you'll give me all kinds of opportunity later. You're too mean-hearted to do everybody a favor and freeze to death."

Cooksey moaned and tried push himself up on an unsteady arm. He held the other hand to his chest. "You broke my ribs. . . ." His breath came in ragged gasps. "You redskin bastard."

"Better'n you had planned for me." O'Shannon caught his Appy and climbed back into the saddle, sweating from the exertion in all his heavy clothes. He winced at the pain in his injured leg. "I gotta move on." He shook his head and grinned. "I can't believe you fell for that Indian-who-talks-to-the-raven trick."

Wheeling his horse in a complete circle, he looked down at the sullen man who still lay heaving and helpless in a trampled depression in the snow. "My mother's the only one I know who can talk to ravens."

Blake turned into the wind again and urged the horse into a shuffling trot through the deep snow. He wanted to put as much distance as he could between himself and Edward Cooksey. Twenty yards up the trail he passed the raven, who'd taken up a perch in another pine after the shot. The huge bird fluffed black feathers against the chill. Its head turned slowly and an ebony eye followed the horse as they rode by.

"Many thanks, my brother." The young deputy winked and tipped his hat. "I owe you one."

It was a quarter to ten when Blake O'Shannon finally pushed into the outskirts of St. Regis. The wind had let up, but snow fell in huge, popcorn-sized clumps.

The train, and his parents along with it, was gone, shallow furrows in the snow the only sign it was ever there.

He slumped in the saddle, the news he bore for his father still heavy on his mind.

"Pulled out on time for once," a man with narrow shoulders and mussed gray hair said from a green wooden bench along the depot platform. He'd pushed the snow to one side to give himself room to sit and it formed a white armrest alongside his elbow. A light woolen shirt was all that separated him from the cold. Frost ringed his silver mustache and Van Dyke beard. "All the lines are down so I can't get word to Coeur d' Alene or Spokane to stop 'em." He wrung his hands and shook his head slowly as he spoke. "I assume you're looking for the train."

Blake grunted and slid down from his horse to work the kinks out of his sore leg. The snow came well over his boot tops. "Yessir, I was hopin' to get here before it left." He gazed down the deserted track and added under his breath: "Pa, I guess your news will have to keep."

"You have loved ones aboard?" The way the man said it caused Blake to go hollow inside.

"Both my parents. Why do you ask?"

"I tried to get here myself, you know," the man moaned in a brittle voice. "I'd have made it if that Bjornstead woman hadn't decided to have her baby at dawn. I have so many patients, you see. Especially since the fires."

"You're a doctor?"

"I am. Dr. Holier." The man suddenly stiffened and looked straight at Blake. "It's a providence you happened along when you did, son."

Blake shook his head. "And just why is that?" He realized he was squeezing the reins tight enough to cut off the circulation in his hand.

"Four cases this morning—miners at a camp east of town." The doctor groaned. "I'm ashamed at being so late . . . afraid one has made it on board . . ." He looked wide-eyed at Blake, as if struck by a sudden revelation. "It's imperative that you stop that train."

"Cases? Stop the train?" Blake dropped the Appaloosa's reins. All this talking in circles made his head ache. "Get to the point, man. What are you talking about?"

The doctor bit the silver whiskers on a trembling bottom lip.

"Pox," he said.

CHAPTER 2

Birdie Baker had a nose for things that were out of place. It was a hooked nose, perched on a wedgelike face, perfectly suited to horn in on other people's business. Born with a keen sense of order, she took it upon herself to set things right when she observed them to be otherwise—liquor where there should be temperance, wanton women where there should be fidelity, and most of all, Indians where there should be only God-fearing white people.

No one, least of all Birdie, knew the exact reason she hated Indians with such a passion. But hate them she did, and she made it one of her many missions in life to be certain the hotels, restaurants, and trains in western Montana were properly segregated.

Her husband, Leo, shared her feelings if not her zeal and generally backed her up—in a sullen, simmering sort of way. Birdie swung her husband's title like an ax, as if he was a general or Japanese warlord instead of the postmaster of Dillon, Montana.

Where she was tall with big hands and sharp, accusing eyes, Leo was more of a thick-necked stump. His wire-rimmed spectacles looked absurdly small on his wide face. Deep furrows creased his forehead and frown lines decorated the corners of his nose and down-turned mouth. People often wondered if it was the constant squint through the tiny glasses or the day-to-day burden of living with Birdie that gave

Leo his permanent scowl. Those who were familiar with the family knew his eyesight wasn't all that bad.

Birdie stood on the wide train platform and sniffed the cold air around her, testing it for nearby improprieties. She stomped snow from her highly polished boots and stared down at the balding top of her husband's head.

"Leo," she barked. "What have you done with your hat?" He was taking her to a postmasters' convention in Phoenix. The last thing she needed was for him to take ill and muck up all her vacation plans.

He tugged at a cart piled high with her luggage and his single leather valise. A chilly wind blew back his wool topcoat and revealed a short-barreled pistol with pearl bird's-head grips in a leather shoulder holster. He looked up at his wife and shrugged off her comment with a scowl.

Birdie was not one to be ignored. "Leo Baker! Your hat?"

"The damned thing blew off while I had my hands full with your blasted steamer trunks," he grunted. "You know, woman, this is a three-week trip, not an expedition to the Fertile Crescent. I see no reason to bring along your entire wardrobe."

"Get the bags on board and meet me in the dining car," Birdie said in her usual imperious manner. The porter standing beside Leo blinked his eyes at every word as if he were facing into a strong wind.

"I, for one, am hungry," Birdie blew on. "I want to make certain the railroad carries the things I eat before we pull out of the station."

Leo grunted around his scowl and passed the luggage up to the waiting attendant. "Wyoming has ruined it for us all," Leo muttered. "We'll be damned fools if the rest of us give women the vote."

Birdie watched for a moment before she stepped onto the train. The porter was a young black man, a bit on the scrawny side for handling such heavy bags, to Birdie's way of thinking. She supposed riding on a train with a Negro was acceptable, so long as he was one of the servants.

* * *

Looking after a body—even the body of a friend—was enough to give Trap O'Shannon a case of the jumps. Though he'd sent a fair number of people to meet their Maker in the course of his forty-eight years, he'd never been one to hover too long near the dead. But Hezekiah Roman had been not only his commander; he'd been his friend—and Trap had never had more friends than he had fingers on his gun hand. If Captain Roman wished to be buried in Arizona, then that's the way it would be. Even if it did mean days on board the same train as a corpse.

O'Shannon pulled the collar of his mackinaw up close around his neck and blew a cloud of white vapor out in front of him. Ice crystals formed on the brim of his black felt hat. His ears burned from the cold and he could hardly feel his feet. He kept both hands thrust inside the folds of the heavy wool coat. Leaning toward gaunt, he had very little fat to keep him warm.

A dull blue light spilled across the muted landscape. Up and down the tracks the snow was peppered with a wide swath of black cinders belched from the coal-fired steam engine.

O'Shannon's Nez Percé wife, Maggie, stood beside him on the cramped walkway that linked the dining car and the passenger compartments of the train. She wore only a thin pair of doeskin gloves and a light suede jacket with bead-work on the breast and sleeves she'd done herself. Her long hair was pulled back into a loose ponytail, kept together with a colorful, porcupine-quill comb her cousin from Lapwai had given her. The cold air pinked her full cheeks. Moisture glistened in dark brown eyes. She was virtually unaffected by the chill, and even appeared to thrive in it.

"Thought Blake might come see us off back in St. Regis." Her voice was husky-despondent.

Trap crossed his arms over his chest and stomped his feet to get some feeling back. "You know how it is in the lawman business. He was likely busy with some outlaw or another."

Maggie looked up at her husband and touched his cheek with a gloved hand. She never had been the brooding type. When she got sad, she got over it quickly, wasting no time fretting over things out of her control. "You about ready to go inside?" she said. "You got an icicle hangin' off your chin."

"Don't know why." O'Shannon's teeth chattered. "It's only fifteen degrees. Hardly what a body c-could call c-cold."

The smiling Indian woman let her finger slide to the tip of her husband's nose. "Let's go in." She winked. Her black coffee eyes held more than a hint of mischief. "I'll scoot up real close. That'll warm your bones."

Trap let her herd him through the narrow accordion entryway. The pink flesh on his hands and arms was still tender and tight from the devastating fires only months before. Maggie hadn't fared much better. She'd singed almost a foot off the waist-length hair she was so proud of, and the right side of her face still looked like it had a bad sunburn.

She'd stayed so close to him in the weeks after his return from the fires that for a time, Trap thought their healing bodies might grow together and become one person.

He didn't complain.

The warm air of the dining car hit Trap full in the face. The aroma of hot coffee and bread tugged him toward a table just inside the door. Maggie chuckled behind him, low in her belly, and leaned against his shoulder blades with her head, pushing him to the chairs. He helped her with her coat, and then took off his own before he sat across from her.

"You don't want to sit beside me?" Maggie raised an eyebrow and pretended to pout.

"I want to look at you for a while when my eyeballs thaw out." He also wanted to keep his eyes on the far door.

A big-boned woman two tables away was the only other occupant in the car. Given a bronze breast plate and a horned helmet, she could have passed for an opera singer. Trap attempted a smile, but she eyed him malignantly over a hooked nose. He reckoned her to be in her fifties—a few years older than him maybe—but she had so many frown lines around her deep-set eyes, it was difficult to tell for certain.

Maggie peeled off her gloves and laid them on the

table, taking Trap's hands in hers. Her face was passive. "She's looking at me, isn't she?"

Trap nodded. "Giving us both the once-over like we might have the plague. People like her have a way of getting my blood up."

"Don't let her bother you, husband. I'm fine, no matter what she does. The important thing is for us to get Hezekiah back to Irene. It's only right he should be buried where she can visit him from time to time. I would want to visit *you*."

O'Shannon sighed. It was just like his wife to think about others when someone was about to impugn her heritage. They traveled little and this was the reason.

Maggie rubbed his hands gently between her palms to warm them. "I'm a tough, old bird, husband. She can't say anything I haven't heard before."

Trap grunted. The fact Maggie had touched him in public seemed to send the woman into a purple rage. "She's about to bust her brain trying to get a handle on me," he said. "Probably sniff out an Indian from a mile away. Wonder if she'll be able to figure out I'm half of that wild breed of Apache who would have had her guts for garters just a decade or two ago."

Maggie gave the relaxed belly laugh that made him love her so much. "Garters?"

Trap rolled his eyes. "It's something Madsen always says."

"Where did he run off to?" Maggie toyed with the leather medicine bag around her neck. "I saw him talking to a handsome woman before we boarded. Surprising to see him flirt with someone his own age."

The train began to speed up, slowly at first, the car rocking enough to sway the draping edges on the white tablecloths.

"I'm sure he's back getting her settled in her compartment," Trap said. "Her name's Hanna something or another—a schoolteacher, I think he said. He's been seein' her for a few weeks now. Says they're really hitting it off."

"Every female I ever met hits it off with Clay Madsen," Maggie said, winking.

A waiter wearing a white waistcoat with a red rag sticking out of the front pocket of his black trousers came through the door nearest Trap and started for the O'Shannons' table. He was a young man with a wispy blond mustache and a matching attempt at side-whiskers.

The frowning woman cleared her throat and glared. "I believe I was here first," she hissed.

The young man shot a caged glance at the woman, then looked sheepishly at the O'Shannons. "I'll be right with you folks," he said, smiling. "Won't be a moment, I'm . . ."

"Did I mention I was seated before that little man and his squaw?"

Trap flinched at the cutting tone in the woman's voice. Calling his sweet wife a squaw would have earned another man a sound thrashing. Maggie released a quiet sigh, but held him in his seat with her eyes.

He wouldn't be able to put up with this sort of behavior all the way to Arizona.

"Can I help you then, ma'am?" The waiter stood back from the table a few feet as if the woman might strike if he got too close. "Would you like some coffee—or maybe some spice cake? Gerta, that's our cook—she makes excellent spice cake."

The woman shook her head. "I don't want any spice cake. My name is Birdie Baker. My husband is Leo Baker, the postmaster of Dillon, Montana." She waited as if the waiter might bow or otherwise yield to the influential status of her name.

"What can I do for you then, Mrs. Baker?"

Birdie lowered her husky voice, but kept it loud enough that the O'Shannons could hear every word. "Tell me your name, young man."

"Sidney, Mrs. B-Baker." He began to stammer. "If you'd like to order, then I'd be g-glad to . . ."

"Well, Sidney," she said, cutting him off and folding her hands as if she were passing sentence. "Here's what you may do for me. You may make certain that I have a decent place in which to eat my breakfast."

Sidney looked up and down the dining car and then at

the table where Birdie sat. "I swear, ma'am, this is the most decent dining car we have on the train."

"The car is just fine, young man," she said with an acid tone. "I'm speaking of the company." Birdie jerked her big head toward the O'Shannons. "You run along and fetch the conductor for me. There are laws of common decency, you know. Honestly, does the railroad expect me to have an appetite while practically sitting at the same table with this Indian slut?"

Trap crashed his hand flat against the table. The slap was loud enough to make poor Sidney jerk. The boy swayed on his feet in fright.

Maggie might be tough, but that wasn't the point. Trap was her husband, and though she was capable enough on her own, *no one* was going to get by with this sort of behavior—not even the postmaster's wife from Dillon, Montana.

CHAPTER 3

"What do you mean, pox?" Blake eyed the doctor. "Tell me exactly what happened."

Holier sighed, stroking his gray beard. "I apologize, young man. I suppose I am rambling. Can't remember the last time I slept."

Blake kicked a drift of snow off the peeling wood on the platform and rested his foot there. It took some strain off his aching thigh. "You say someone with smallpox ended up on this train?" He pointed down the empty tracks.

"It does appear that way." Holier shrugged. "His three friends have already broken out into sores. That's why you have to stop the train. Smallpox carries a hell of a lot of pain with it once the sores come. Double you over like an ax in the belly. Usually puts a body in bed straightaway. But if this fellow's able to move around by train, he could infect countless people who get on and off before anyone figures out what's going on. This could be the beginning of an epidemic."

The gravity of the situation hit Blake like a cold slap. As far as he knew, neither his mother or father had ever been exposed to full-blown smallpox. Many people in the West had had it in one form or another, but there were just as many who hadn't. One thing he knew for sure—when an Indian was exposed, the outcome was usually a horrific death.

"And the lines are down?" Blake looked up at the gray sky. It still sifted a steady powder of snow.

"Completely cut off, that's what we are," Holier said.

Blake climbed back into the saddle and tugged his hat down against the wind. "If anyone is able to get the lines repaired, get word to Coeur d'Alene to stop them. Use the Army out of Spokane if they have to, but keep everyone on board that train. I'll ride until I can either catch them or find a place to send the same message."

Blake tipped his head to the grim-faced doctor and spurred his Appaloosa into the snow. The news he carried for his father still weighed heavy on his mind.

CHAPTER 4

Raucous laughter erupted from outside and the door behind Trap swung open with a gust of cold air. Clay Madsen had his silver-belly hat thrown back in his normally rakish manner. He gestured high over his head with both hands and lowered his voice to finish his bawdy story as he came into the dining car behind the conductor.

Cold and laughter pinked both men's cheeks. Madsen smoothed the corners of his thick, chocolate mustache and wiped his eyes. Tears rolled down the conductor's round face.

"No need to stand on my account." Madsen nodded at Trap when he came up alongside the table. The big man's presence calmed O'Shannon, but not much.

Birdie Baker piped up like a pestered wren when she spied the conductor. His smiling face fell at once.

"I am so glad you arrived when you did," she keened.

"How can I help you, Mrs. Baker?" The conductor motioned an addled Sidney back to the cook car with a flick of his thick fingers.

"I assume there are two dining cars on board this train."

The conductor nodded. "That's right, one to the fore of the cook car and one behind it."

"Would not the Jim Crow dining car be up front?" Baker folded her arms across her chest, barely containing her huff.

It was the custom of the railroad to put higher-class

patrons in the cars further away from the ash and smoke of the engine. The dining car behind the cook car was usually considered preferable and reserved for the upper crust. Negroes, Indians, and other "undesirables" were supposed to use the forward car.

"I reckon it would, ma'am," the conductor said. "But the windows are busted out on the forward cars on account of an avalanche last week. There's no one riding up there on this trip."

"The railroad's broken windows are none of my concern. I have the right to take my breakfast without the presence of a filthy red savage nearby."

O'Shannon fought back the urge to stomp across the car and keep stomping. He seethed inside, but beating on women, even rude ones, gave him pause.

Clay let out a deep breath and shot a sideways wink at Trap. The big cowboy took off his hat and moved up next to the conductor.

"I see your predicament, dear lady," he said, giving a slight bow. "To tell you the truth, I was a mite surprised to see these folks here as well."

The conductor's mouth fell open.

"At last, a man who understands the laws of common decency," Birdie sighed.

"Perhaps I can be of service to you somehow in this"— Madsen shot a glance over his shoulder at Trap, who remained standing with clenched fists—"delicate matter."

"I'd be grateful for any assistance you could offer, sir," Birdie said, turning her hooked beak up at the conductor. "The railroad appears to have its priorities askew."

Clay nodded. His deep voice was soft and honey-sweet. "Here's what I propose. If the company in this particular dining car upsets your tender digestion, may I suggest you take your fat caboose back to your own compartment and have your meals delivered—or better yet, skip a meal or two entirely? Looks like it might do you some good."

He smiled to let the words sink in and twirled the handlebars of his dark mustache. "If you continue to speak rudely to my friends, I'll be compelled to pitch your broad ass off this train." He turned again and tipped his hat toward the O'Shannons. "Forgive the language, Maggie darlin', but I fear this woman will only respond to the harshest words."

Birdie blustered and looked to the conductor for help. He offered none.

"Well," she harrumphed. "Never in my life have I been subjected to this sort of . . ."

Clay cut her off. "Ma'am." He shook his head. "I believe we're done. I'm about to buy my friends breakfast. If you aim to perch here any longer, you best keep your pie hole shut."

"I must advise you that my husband is the postmaster of Dillon, Montana, and you, sir, shall hear from him on this matter." Birdie pushed her chair back and strode for the doorway.

"The postmaster, huh?" Clay shrugged. "Well, that's damned lucky. If he talks like you, I'll give him the whippin' he deserves, put a stamp on his ass, and mail him straight back to Dillon, Montana. I find it's a hell of a lot easier to deal with rude menfolk."

Clay sat down next to Maggie and tipped back his hat to reveal a forelock of dark hair.

A blond woman in a red shawl and with a matching smile on full lips came in as a fuming Birdie Baker left the swaying dining car. Her tea-green eyes fell straight on Clay and the smile became more animated. She was tall and lean with a strong jaw. Flaxen hair hung in loose curls at her broad shoulders, and a healthy crop of freckles splashed across the bridge of a button nose.

"I'd have been here sooner but there's a man in the next car looks like he's about to throw up on somebody. I was afraid to pass him until he sat down." She was in her early forties—just a few years younger than Clay and vibrant enough to make the air around her buzz. Clay and Trap both stood.

"This man, what did he look like?" The conductor shot a worried glance at the door. "I've had two reports about him already."

The woman shrugged. "I don't know. My age, maybe—a little taller than me, stoop-shouldered. Hard to get a good look at his face because he was so downcast. Look for the man who's green around the gills. That's him."

"Likely the postmaster of Dillon, Montana, drinking away his troubles at being married to such a"—Clay looked at both the ladies and changed his tack—"awful woman."

The conductor tipped his pillbox cap and strode off in search of his troublesome passenger.

"Have I missed something?" asked the blond woman. "The tension is thick enough in here to cut. Clay dear, did you just tell one of your rough-hewn stories?"

Clay took off his hat and gave the grinning woman a kiss on the cheek. "Nothing that exciting. That gal with her snoot up in the air is just going to get her husband to come back and have a go at kicking my tail. " He turned to the O'Shannons. "Maggie, Trap, I'd like to introduce you to Hanna Cobb, a schoolteacher who finds herself in-between appointments. She has a grown daughter in Phoenix, so I convinced her to accompany us on our little journey with the captain."

Trap took off his hat and smiled. It seemed that Clay Madsen could convince just about any woman of just about anything. Maggie reached across the table and offered her hand. "Won't you join us?"

Hanna took the seat next to Trap. "Sounds like you were all having another one of your adventures before I came in."

Clay scoffed. "I wouldn't call it much of an adventure. More like a case of prickly heat."

"Mr. Madsen has told me so much about the two of you," Hanna went on. "In fact, that's one of the reasons I looked forward to coming on this trip, to get to know the both of you better. He said the three of you, along with your poor departed Captain Roman, have quite a history together. Be-sides . . ." She looked at Maggie with a hint of mischief bud-ding on her full lips. "Mr. Madsen informs me he is a widower many times over. I understand he has the reputa-tion of being quite a scamp between marriages. Perhaps you could speak with me, woman to woman, a little later on that particular matter."

Clay raised a beefy hand. "You may ask Maggie anything you want about me, my dear Mrs. Cobb. I admit that I have been a rounder in my time, and may very well continue to be one. But I am honest about it. And if I may say one thing in my own defense, I never once jumped the fence while I was married."

Hanna grinned. "Ah, you never jumped the fence, but from what I hear, you were a bull that was all too happy to play with every heifer in the herd when the Good Lord opened the gate between engagements."

Trap had to hand it to this Mrs. Cobb. It looked like Madsen had finally met his match.

Clay took her hand across the table and gazed at her as if she was the only woman in the world, his hat thrown back on his head like a lovesick puppy. "What you say is a fact, my dear. But I do believe I feel that gate swinging shut again."

The Widow Cobb narrowed her eyes. "Oh you do, do you?" She withdrew her hand and turned to a smiling Maggie, who sat enjoying the show. "I hear you all met when you were quite young."

"I was fourteen."

"And you've been married how long?"

"Thirty-two years," Maggie whispered.

"Thirty-two years with this little wart?" Clay shot a grin at Trap. "I reckon I've known you for all of that but a day or two. I was just tellin' Hanna how we got started, the three of us. It makes a mighty good story when you think of it. The country was still so fresh back then. . . ."

Hanna rested both elbows on the table in front of her and leaned her chin on her clasped hands. Her green eyes twinkled and she suddenly looked more like a schoolgirl than a teacher. "I don't mean to pry, but we have a long trip ahead of us while we wait for that huffy woman's husband to come challenge Mr. Madsen."

Trap chuckled in spite of himself. "The way Clay spins

CHAPTER 5

April 1878
Near Lebanon, Missouri

Patrick "Trap" O'Shannon was about to leave the only woman he'd ever love, except for his mother, before he even met her.

He slumped in a high-backed wooden chair and stared at the buds on huge white oaks outside the rippled glass of the second-story window. His father, the Right Reverend James B. O'Shannon was a head taller than him, lean and wiry of build with the keen eyes of a boxer. He had a ruddy complexion with thick, sandy hair. More often than not, he showed at least a day's growth of dark red beard when he became too engrossed in his studies to remember to shave.

Though in coloring and complexion they were complete opposites, both father and son shared a short button nose and the propensity to grow a heavy beard if left unattended by a razor. They also shared the same intensity, albeit about different things. When he wasn't doting on his wife, the Reverend O'Shannon spent his days at study of the Scripture and other zealous pursuits in better understanding the ways of God. Trap had inherited a love for the outdoors from his mother, and preferred the woods and what they had to teach to any book or chapel.

The reverend broke the news in his customary way. A Scots-Irish Presbyterian, he believed a sharp knife cut quickest and always went directly to the meat of the matter. His Apache wife, Hummingbird, was spirited but tender-hearted, so he always followed his direct pronouncements with quiet explanations, allowing room for understanding if not debate.

The elder O'Shannon sat across from his son in an equally uncomfortable chair, his hands folded across his lap. Trap's mother once confided that when his father folded his hands in his lap, his mind was made up for good. In all his sixteen years, Trap had never known his father to change his mind once he'd voiced an opinion, so he doubted any hand-folding made much of a difference.

"It will do your mother good to be nearer her family," the reverend said. His voice was soft and sure as if he was trying to calm a frightened horse, but his green eyes held the same passionate sparkle they had when he preached. "God wants us in Arizona."

Trap had been to Arizona once before when he was very young. He still remembered the oppressive heat and bleak desert. If God sent a person to a desolate piece of ground like that, they must have done something particularly bad to displease Him.

Trap stood and stepped across the polished hardwood to the window, looking out but seeing nothing. "Is she unhappy here?" He could force no spirit into his words. The thought of leaving behind the rivers and oak forests of Missouri caught hard in the boy's throat. His mother often walked with him and taught him the ways of her forebears— how to hunt and track and make his way in the woods. He'd always believed she liked it here. It didn't matter. His father hadn't called him to the office to ask for his opinion. To James O'Shannon things were as they were, and that was that.

"No, she is not unhappy," the reverend said. He moved to the window beside his son. Coach wheels chattered across the stone drive below. "But she could be happier. My duty as a husband is to see to her complete happiness.

You're what now, sixteen? Nearly a man. One day you'll meet someone—and nothing else in the world will matter. Everything you do, down to the very breath you draw, will be meaningless unless that person is content. . . ."

Trap's head felt numb. His father's words hit his ears but went no further. Arizona was a world away from White Oak Indian Academy and the place where he'd grown up—the place where he thought he would live for ever.

He watched as the door on the newly arrived coach—a refit Army ambulance—opened slowly. Three Indian girls in their early teens stepped timidly onto the drive, a toe at a time, as a doe might enter a clearing from the safety of the dark wood line.

Four horses of mixed size and heritage pranced in the morning mist, tugging at the harness. The heavyset driver hauled himself out of the seat and climbed down to grab the lead horse, a thick roan, by the headstall. His presence only seemed to irritate the animal, and the entire team began to rock the coach back and forth in an effort to move forward.

A flicker of movement inside the dark ambulance caught Trap's eye. A moment later, a fourth girl appeared at the door. She was young, no more than fifteen, but had the sure movements of a woman who'd seen a great deal of life. A loose, fawn-colored skirt covered her feet and made her appear to float in the air.

All the new arrivals, including the fidgety driver, wore various designs of frock or coat, but not the floating girl. A loose white blouse fell unbuttoned at the neck and hung open enough; Trap could see the bronze lines of her collarbone and the smooth beginnings of young breasts. Despite the morning chill, she'd pushed her long sleeves high on her arms. The garment was an afterthought, something she'd be more comfortable without.

The horses kept up their jigging fit while the driver continued to make things worse by facing them and shouting. The new girl hopped from the rocking coach and floated up next to him. There was a liquid grace in the way she moved that reminded Trap of a panther. For a moment he wasn't sure if she intended to melt into the shadowed oaks or pounce on the horses and kill them all.

The animals knew, and calmed immediately at her presence.

The big driver cocked his head to one side, scratched his belly under a baggy wool cloak, then walked back to check the brake.

Vapor blew from the horses' noses. Steam rose from their backs. The floating girl rubbed the big roan's forehead. Then, without warning, she turned and looked directly at the window—and Trap.

Trap felt a sudden knot in his gut. His face flushed and he glanced up to see if his father had noticed.

The reverend spoke on, his hands clasped behind the small of his back; touching on the varied reasons the move to Arizona was inevitable, sprinkling his discourse as always with liberal points from the Scriptures.

Trap turned his attention back to the girl. He was at once relieved and disappointed that she was no longer looking at him. She'd calmed the spirited horses, but even from the second-story window, Trap could see there was nothing calm about her. Where the other girls looked small and frightened in their new surroundings, this one looked around the brick and stone buildings of the Indian school as if sizing up an opponent—an enemy she had no doubt that she could beat.

Thick, black hair flowed past full hips in stark contrast to the bright material of her blouse. Trap felt his mouth go dry. He'd never seen such long hair; so black in the morning light it was almost blue.

Mrs. Tally, the mistress of girls, waddled out like a red-headed hen to welcome her new charges. She spoke briefly to the driver, then turned her attention to the newcomers, three of whom huddled around the floating girl with the long, blue-black hair.

Mrs. Tally's shrill voice made the second-story windows buzz. She never could get it through her head that English spoken succinctly and at a great volume did not automatically translate into every other language in the world. He could see the girls flinch at the well-intentioned but earsplitting words the heavy woman hurled at them as she pointed toward the double doors that led into the main lobby.

The wild girl appeared to ignore the barrage, and let her eyes crawl back up the red brick face of the building until again they settled on Trap. She cocked her face to one side and ran a hand over the top of her head, sliding her fingers through the black mane. Her eyes caught his this time, and held them while she gently fingered a small leather bag that hung from a thong at her breast. The tiniest hint of a smile twitched at the corners of her mouth, and then vanished as quickly as it had appeared.

Mrs. Tally interrupted the moment and shooed her new charges in the front door and out of sight.

Trap blinked to clear his head. He felt an overpowering need to flee his father's study and rush headlong down the stairs to see the beautiful apparition again. As far as he knew, no girl had ever singled him out for a smile.

". . . and you should remember, the Chiricahua Apache are your people as well," his father was saying. Reverend O'Shannon stared at the window at his own reflection. His hands were still clasped behind his back. "Someday, you'll meet someone. When that day comes, you will see what I mean. Nothing else will matter but her."

Trap looked at his father. His mind filled with the vision of the floating girl with blue-black hair. Now, more than ever, he understood what his father meant—and they were moving to Arizona in five days.

CHAPTER 6

"Carpe diem," Trap's father would often say. "Seize the day and worry not for the morrow; the Lord has your future well in hand."

Mrs. Tally had the new arrivals shuffled off to the girls' dormitory behind the main building by the time Trap was able to escape his father's study and make it downstairs. She would keep them busy settling in and getting them fitted for uniforms until lunch, so Trap resigned himself to a dry morning of lessons and pretended study.

Trap had never been the kind of boy to make long-range plans. He walked for hours in the woods with his mother, enjoyed yearly hunting trips with his father in the fall, but the future and the world of adulthood rarely came up. Each day provided a new sort of adventure, and he was happy to tend to each one as it presented itself. *Carpe diem* indeed.

The arrival of this mysterious girl who floated across the ground sent a sudden whirlwind of thoughts spinning through the boy's head. For the first time in his life, Trap thought about the eventuality of providing for someone else, and came to the sad realization that he didn't have many marketable skills. This thought alone put him into a quiet stupor, and he spent the morning brooding into his arithmetic primer, seeing nothing but a blur.

At sixteen, Trap was among the oldest of the twenty-five students at White Oak. Girls of any age outnumbered boys

six to one. The only other boy close to his age was Frank
Tall Horse, a gangly Ogallala Sioux. None of the other male
students was older than twelve.

When he was ten, Trap had asked his mother why there
were few other boys his age to play with.

"Indian boys of all ages are fighters," she'd told him.
"Most are killed in battle. A few more of the girls survive. If
they aren't taken as slaves by other tribes, well-meaning soldiers sometimes bring them here." Hummingbird was a
quiet woman, but she wasn't one to beat around the bush.

Morning classes ground by with a glacial lack of speed.
When it came time for midday break, Trap felt as if he
might jump out of his skin if he didn't get another look at
the floating girl.

A bright sun filtered through the new foliage on the tall
oaks and cast dimpled shadows around the spring grass in
the exercise yard below.

Mrs. Tally was in the habit of having what she called an
early lunch, which everyone knew was a nap. Trap was
certain she would let the new girls out for some fresh air
while she retired to her quarters for an hour or so.

Knowing the new girl would likely come out the large
double doors off the front hallway, Trap resolved to station
himself in the grassy area nearby.

Frank Tall Horse was a quiet boy, a head taller than
Trap. He'd been orphaned at three—too young to be a warrior when he was brought to White Oak. Prone to spending hours with his nose stuck in fanciful tales by someone
named Jules Verne, he knew little of his native ways except
for what Trap's mother had taught him. He liked to joke
that he'd been raised in captivity.

Trap stared at the door and bounced with nervous energy.

"How about a leg-wrestling match?" Tall Horse suggested.
He had a new book, but sensed his friend's anxiety and genuinely wanted to help.

Trap watched the door while he spoke. He'd wrestled the
long-legged Sioux at least two dozen times over the years,
and bested him every time though he was over a head
shorter. Suddenly, the thought of this new girl seeing him

doing nothing but standing around waiting seemed foolish. It would be better if he were engaged in some sort of contest. Especially a contest he was likely to win.

"Sure," Trap said, trying to sound disinterested. "A game might be good."

The two boys lay down on the grass elbow-to-elbow, Trap's feet toward the building and Tall Horse's toward the trees. In unison they counted to three, then raised their legs to hook each other at the knee. Locked together, each struggled to roll his opponent backward over his own head.

Trap beat the taller boy soundly on the first round.

"Two out of three?" Frank picked bits of grass and twigs out of his close-cropped hair.

Trap shrugged. "All right by me," he said resuming his position.

"I've learned your trick, Apache," Tall Horse said as he raised his leg the first time. "This time the mighty Sioux will be victorious."

On the count of two, the front doors of the school opened. Trap felt the strength leave his legs when the new girl floated out in her crisp blue uniform dress. The sight of her hit Trap like a bucket of springwater. The ability for all concentration drained from his body. She looked directly at him. A smile crossed her oval face.

Tall Horse took advantage of the momentary lapse and sent the befuddled Trap flying backward into the grass. When he rolled to his feet, the girl was gone.

The Sioux boy ducked his head and gave an embarrassed grimace at having won the contest. He never won at anything physical, and seemed uncomfortable with the thought of it.

"Want another go at it?" Tall Horse grunted.

Trap popped his neck from side to side and grinned. "No. It was fair."

He left a beaming Tall Horse to his book and moved immediately toward the place where he'd last seen the floating girl.

The other new arrivals milled around at the edge of the yard, bunched in the same nervous group. Two of them looked as though they might be sisters; all were surely from the same tribe.

It was easy to find the girl's track. The stiff leather soles of her newly issued shoes couldn't hide the soft, toe-first way her feet struck the ground with each step. His mother walked the same way, and Trap had grown up mimicking it.

The tracks led around the corner, toward the delivery entrance to the kitchen and the root cellar he'd help enlarge the previous fall. The constricting pair of new shoes lay abandoned beside the worn path.

Trap knelt to study the small print of the girl's bare foot. His open hand almost covered it. Trap's mother often told him to feel the track—*talk to it*, she said. He touched each tiny indentation where toes had dug in lightly to the dark earth, closed his eyes to see what these tracks might tell him.

He heard a sharp yowl, like a bobcat caught in a snare.

Trap's eyes snapped open and he sprinted around the building.

The Van Zandt's Creamery wagon was parked beside the kitchen entrance. Another yowl came from the open door of the root cellar. Moments later a fuming Harry Van Zandt scampered out of the dark opening, the remains of a jar of currant jelly dripping off the top of his head. At seventeen, Harry was nearly six feet tall with menacing features and a permanent scowl on his long face. His younger brother Roth was nowhere to be seen.

Harry cast his eyes back and forth on the ground while he wiped the sticky red goop off his face.

"Watch her, Roth," he yelled into the cellar as he found an oak branch the size of his arm. "She's a scrapper. Them jars hurt, I'm tellin' ya." He tested the club on his open palm and started for the door again.

There was a commotion of breaking bottles and more cries from the cellar.

"Where you aim to go with that?" Trap nodded toward the piece of oak in Harry's hand.

"None of your damned business, runt," the other boy said. "I'm gonna teach that little red whore some manners. She's a looker, but that don't give her no right. . . ."

The stone caught Harry high in the side of the head, glancing off a glob of current jelly. Dark eyes rolled back in his head, lids fluttering life a leaf on the wind. He swayed on his feet, teetered for a moment, then collapsed into the dirt by the back wheel of his delivery wagon.

He was still breathing, but a nasty knot was already rising over his left temple. That was *his* problem.

Trap bent to scooped up the oak club and trotted the two steps to the open root cellar. A jar of tomatoes shattered against the timber door frame.

Once his eyes adjusted to the dim light, he could see Roth Van Zandt holding a wooden barrel lid like a shield as he advanced on the new girl at the far end of the narrow earthen room.

Tomatoes had been a bumper crop the previous summer, and there was an almost endless supply of jars she could use to defend herself.

"Almost there, darlin'," Roth giggled as another jar of tomatoes exploded off the wooden lid. He didn't look up as Trap moved up behind him. "Me and Harry here gonna show you some fun, that's all. . . . We ain't gonna hurt you, are we, Harry?"

Trap moved up so he was within striking distance with the oak club. "No," he said. "We're not."

Roth lowered the barrel lid in time to catch a quart jar on the point of his chin. Glass shattered and Trap stepped back to avoid getting splattered.

"You're brother's outside with a bad headache," Trap said, gesturing with the wood. "Take him on back to town before this girl knocks your head off."

Van Zandt wiped the red juice off his face and chest. His tongue flicked across his lips in disgust.

"Havin' a white pa didn't help you much when it came to brains, O'Shannon." Roth spit. "Just goes to prove it only takes a drop of the heathen blood to ruin a body."

Trap raised the club. "Go ahead and say another word about my mother," he whispered. "I'll finish what the girl started."

Roth talked big, but he had no intention of facing Trap

alone. He backed outside with the barrel lid in hand before helping his half-conscious brother back to the wagon.

"You ain't heard the last of us, O'Shannon." Roth gathered up the reins and clucked to the Cleveland Bay mare to get her moving. "Or you either, Miss Tomato Chucker. You're bound to see us again, that's for damned sure."

Trap threw the oak club at Van Zandt to hurry him along. When the wagon was safely down the gravel drive, he turned to face the new girl. She was even more beautiful up close than from his father's window. He could think of nothing to say, so he just stood and looked.

"You are Indian?" she said at length. His staring didn't seem to bother her.

Trap swallowed hard. "Yes. I mean, sort of. My mother is Chiricahua Apache." He felt as if he was tripping over every word.

"My name is Maggie Sundown of the Nimi'ipuu—the whites call us Wallowa Nez Percé." Her chest still heaved. Her eyes, the color of black coffee, glistened as she calmed herself from her run-in with the Van Zandts.

"I'm Patrick O'Shannon, but everyone calls me Trap."

"Reverend O'Shannon is your father?"

Trap nodded.

Maggie smiled. "So you live here, like I do."

All Trap ever wanted to do again was stand there and watch this girl smile. Then he thought about what she'd just said and the happiness drained out of him.

"Only a few more days." The words tasted bitter as he said them. "We're moving to Arizona."

Maggie brushed a lock of hair away from her full cheek. The smile was gone.

"That is a very sad thing to hear, Patrick Trap O'Shannon of the Chiricahua Apache."

The promise of an interesting week hung heavy on her sigh.

CHAPTER 7

Trap decided early on that whatever he decided to do with his life, it would not involve wearing a necktie. Even if he had shared his father's zeal for the ministry, the way he'd have to dress alone was enough to keep him from following in the man's steps. He considered the infernal things instruments of unbearable torture, and avoided them as he would any other form of slow, strangling death.

Unfortunately, the reverend saw things differently and required a tie for church and all important social events—like dinner with the new superintendent.

The Reverend Tobias Drum had arrived that morning by wagon with a pile of worn carpetbags and a fine Thoroughbred gelding, the color of a roasted chestnut. His coming was like a dark cloud over the school. The students had lined up at the windows in stunned sadness to witness the proof that the O'Shannons were leaving very soon.

Trap tried to keep an open mind, but Drum seemed to him a particularly oily man, both in body and demeanor. He was stout, a half a head taller than Trap's father, who stood nearly six feet. Where the Reverend O'Shannon possessed the gaunt appearance of a hungry boxer, Drum was a blocky brute with the well-fed look and sullen eyes of one more accustomed to barroom brawls. Bushy sideburns covered pink jowls, and a greasy ponytail dusted the collar of his black frock coat with a steady sifting of dandruff.

From the time the man had arrived, Trap's father had become almost subservient to him, yielding the school as if he'd turned over the reins already. What was worse is that Drum appeared to expect such treatment.

The men's voices hummed through the panel door off the dining room while Trap helped his mother fill crystal water glasses and finish setting the table. He tugged at the knot in his silk tie.

A sumptuous meal of roast pork, turnips, string beans, and hot bread spread across the expansive oak table—the table his mother would have to leave behind in two days time when they left for Arizona.

"Why don't you take this fine table and leave me behind?" Trap said before he thought much about it. He would never have spoken so directly to his father.

Hummingbird smiled softly as she always did, reacting to what he meant, not what he said. "The table is only planks and sticks." She smoothed the front of her white apron with a copper hand. Her hair was long, but she kept it coiled and pinned up so Trap hardly ever saw it down. "I'm sure there will be tables in Arizona." She put a hand on Trap's shoulder. "But I do worry for you, my son. There is more to this than you can understand. I have asked your father to tell you, and maybe he will in his time. You are almost grown. . . ."

The Reverend O'Shannon's face was locked in a wooden half frown when he came through the door ahead of Drum.

"We have a job to do," Drum was saying. "It's not always pleasant, but it is, nonetheless, our duty."

Trap's jaw dropped when the new superintendent took the chair at the head of the long table—his father's spot—and flopped down in it before his mother was seated.

Reverend O'Shannon said grace and carved the roast while he listened in stony silence as Drum droned on with his philosophy about running an Indian school.

Drum began eating as soon as his plate was filled. "The

United States Army has made my orders clear," he said
around a fork piled high with roast pork and turnips.

"Chuparosa," O'Shannon said, calling his wife by name
to get her to hold up her plate. He gave her a thick slice of
end-cut. Trap knew the seasoned, outer edge of the roast
was his mother's favorite, and his father always made certain she got this choice morsel, no matter who was eating
with them. The reverend looked up at Drum and moved the
knife to cut Trap's portion. "I was under the impression we
got our orders from a higher authority than the Army," he
said. His voice was tight but controlled.

Drum waved him off with the fork. "Of course we do, but
the Army brings us the students. We have to learn to work
hand in glove. Don't disparage the military, O'Shannon. The
God of the Israelites utilized an army to work miracles."

"True enough," Trap's father said. Everyone served, he
sat down to his own plate.

"I couldn't help but notice you called your wife by an
Indian name. Do you believe that is wise?" Drum continued to eat as he spoke. He appeared to be numb to the fact
that Mrs. O'Shannon sat directly to his right, and spoke of
her more as if she were a valued hunting dog than another
human being.

"Ah, yes." O'Shannon said. "Chuparosa. It's Spanish for
Hummingbird. The Apache often use Spanish appella-
tions—Geronimo, Magnus Colorado—beyond that . . ." He
shrugged. "It was her name before I knew her and it con-
tinues to be so. I see no reason to call her anything else."

Drum grunted through a full mouth of meat and turnips.
"This meal prepared by your lovely Hummingbird is a
perfect example of what I'm talking about." Other than a
backhanded gesture toward Trap's mother, he ignored
her completely. "She has learned to cook as good as any
white woman."

The man's flippant tone made Trap grip his knife tighter
and chased away any thought of an appetite.

"See what the savage Indian is capable of when properly
schooled and trained." Drum pushed ahead, unwavering in
his rude behavior. "Left to her own devices—her natural and

carnal state, if you will—who knows what kind of grubs we'd be eating. Likely a feast stolen horse and potent corn *tiswin.*"

Reverend O'Shannon put his fork and knife on the table and took a deep breath. His fists clenched white beside his plate. Trap had seen his father box many times, and wondered if Drum knew he was about to get a sound whipping.

"You've overstepped your bounds, sir, in speaking this way of my wife."

Drum dabbed at the corner of his mouth with a linen napkin and flicked a thick hand. "I meant no offense, Reverend." It was a halfhearted apology at best, and Trap felt compelled to bash the man's stodgy face against the fine oak table. A look from his mother held him back.

"I did not intend to insult your family. On the contrary. I only mean to point out that you have done exactly that of which I speak. 'Kill everything in them that is Indian,' the Army says. 'Civilize them and teach them solid Christian doctrine.' That's what we are to do with our charges here at White Oak." Drum looked suddenly at Trap from under a bushy brow and pointed at him with a fork.

"How about you, boy? From what I've heard, you've grown up here. Are you a Christian or an Indian?"

"Can't I be both?" Trap said, though his thoughts at the moment were anything but Christian.

"I don't believe you can," Drum said, banging his fist on the table. The dishes rattled and water sloshed out of the glass at his side. "And neither does the Army. This was a tasty meal, Reverend. And now, if you'll excuse me, I've had a long trip and wish to retire early. I'll have a look around the school tomorrow on my own. You'll be on your way the day after?"

"We will," Trap's father said. He pushed back his chair and rose. Trap could not remember him ever looking sadder. "I'll show you to your room."

When the men had gone, Trap noticed his mother hadn't eaten a bite. "Are you all right?" he asked, knowing the answer before it came.

"I am afraid for you," Hummingbird said. "You will find

that some people are like one-eyed mules. No matter how you turn them, they can only see a single point of view." She pushed her plate away and put a hand on top of Trap's. "Hard things await you, my son. I only hope we have prepared you well enough."

CHAPTER 8

Reverend Drum's presence hung over the school like a putrid illness. He lurked around every corner and at the end of every path, always with a sour look of disapproval on his pink face. For the most part, he held his tongue until the O'Shannons left. He didn't have to wait long for that.

The students threw a quiet going-away party at supper on their last night, and took turns giving the O'Shannons small, handmade tokens to remember them by. Trap's normally stoic father was moved to the point of tears by the time the meal was complete. His mother wept openly throughout the entire affair. Drum stood in the corner with his hands behind him, the tiniest hint of a sneer on his carplike lips.

As the party began to wind down, Trap felt a gnawing urgency to spend a few moments alone with Maggie.

It was Maggie who suggested they go for a walk—not with words but with a casual glance toward the door. Trap looked up at his mother, who also spoke much without speaking at all.

Hummingbird nodded gently, then turned to occupy her husband's attention while Trap and Maggie slipped out together. Drum gave the young couple a sidelong eye, but Mrs. Tally swooped in to intercept him like a fluttering mother dove when a fox is too near her nest, as if she were working in concert with Trap's mother to allow the two youngsters a few moments alone together.

Trap had never been much of a talker, finding himself more at home alone in the woods than with any other human being—until Maggie Sundown came along. He talked to her more than he'd talked to anyone, and still much of their time together was spent sitting quietly.

"The Apache value silence," his mother had always told him. From what he could see, the Nez Percé thought a lot of it too. Maggie appeared to enjoy his company, but she was just as content to sit and study the earth as he was. To Trap's way of thinking, more got said between him and Maggie in an hour of near silence than most people accomplished in a whole day of wordy conversation.

The evening was crisp, with a waning half-moon that cast dark shadows along the gravel path beyond the root cellar. Once in a while, Trap could hear the patient, baritone voice of his father drifting out amid the more tentative students' voices through the kitchen door.

Maggie found a spot on the stone wall along the path and sat down among the shadows. She said nothing.

Trap sat beside her, a few inches away, and folded his hands in his lap. A million bees buzzed inside his chest.

After a time, Maggie broke the silence.

"My people, the Nimi'ipuu, are a people of the horse." Her voice was soft and throaty—almost a whisper. She turned to look at him in the scant moonlight. "I haven't seen too many horses around here."

Trap stared down at his feet, afraid he might say something foolish if he met her eye. "I used to have a nice little bay, but we had to sell them all for this move. The school owns the ones that are left—mostly cart horses."

"I miss watching the herds running together. . . ."

"That would be a beautiful sight," Trap whispered. He could only think of leaving the next day. He wanted to say more, but didn't know how. When he looked up, Maggie held a small bracelet in her hand.

"I made this from the hair of my father's finest horses. I braided in some of my own hair as well." She held it out to him. "I wish you to have it . . . to remember me when you are in Arizona." Her voice was barren of emotion, but her eyes shone bright and clear in the moonlight. "Perhaps you will find a beautiful Apache girl and have many children with her. If you do, you should throw the bracelet away so it doesn't haunt your marriage."

He took the gift and slid it over his hand, pulling it snug with the intricately braided button of hair. "Thank you," he said, his voice catching in his throat. "I would never throw anything away I received from you."

Surely this was what his father had meant when he spoke of meeting the person who would mean more to him than anything else. He'd thought about giving something to her as well, but never would have had the courage to be the first to mention it.

He fished in his trouser pocket for a moment.

"It's not much." He held a silver coin out on the palm of his hand.

Maggie took it and held it up in the moonlight to get a good look.

"It's the O'Shannon crest. Three stars over two hunting dogs."

"What does it say around the edge?" Maggie traced the face of the coin gently with her finger.

"It's the family motto in Latin—*Under the Guidance of Valor*."

Maggie held it up next to Trap's face. Her fingers brushed his cheek. He squirmed.

She smiled—it at once calmed him and sent his mind spinning out of control. "I will put this in my medicine bag where I keep things most important to me," she said.

Arizona seemed like an ax ready to chop off his head. Trap had little experience with such things, but felt pretty certain that girls like Maggie Sundown didn't come along more than once in a person's life. He felt like he should give her more than a silver medallion before he left. The idea that he might never see her again was unthinkable.

"Maggie . . ." he whispered.

She took the small leather bag from around her neck and slipped the coin inside. She must have moved closer to him when they exchanged gifts, because he could feel her body move with each breath. Her thigh was warm against him through their clothes. He found it almost impossible to think, let alone speak a coherent thought.

"Maggie, I . . ." he tried again.

Drum's acid voice cut the night like a knife.

"When the lust hath conceived, it bringeth forth sin: and sin, when it is finished, bringeth forth death." Drum stepped out of the shadows beside the low roof of the root cellar.

Trap shot to his feet. Maggie stayed where she was.

"What's going on here, young Master O'Shannon?" Drum was on them in a stride.

"Nothing, sir." Trap said, upset at his own nervousness. He took a deep breath to calm himself. "I was . . . am saying good-bye to Miss Sundown."

"I'm certain you were," Drum said, raising his brow. The way his eyes slid slowly up and down over Maggie's body made Trap want to bury the man then and there. "It's a blessing I happened to need some fresh air when I did. Saved you from your own sinful nature, I believe. You had best get back inside with the party, young man. I believe it would break your father's heart if he found his son out here in near fornication with one of his students."

"Near fornication? You know that's a lie." Trap gritted his teeth and took a half step closer to the much larger man.

"Don't begin something you aren't prepared to finish, little hero." Drum smiled through a crooked sneer as if he'd won a fight already.

"I should say my good-byes to your mother." Maggie's voice came soft and steady from the shadows. "Come with me, Trap. We have nothing to be ashamed of. The Reverend Drum came out here for some air. Let's give it to him."

"Go with her, boy. Say your good-byes," Drum spit.

"Mr. Drum." Trap refused to call him Reverend anymore. "My family and I are leaving tomorrow. I'm only sixteen, but you should remember this: My mother is Apache, which makes me half Apache."

"O'Shannon," Drum sneered. "You and your kind are no more than a boil on my rump. A trivial inconvenience, but tomorrow I'll be shed of you. Your sweet little Miss Sundown will pine away for you to be sure." He winked and shook his head back and forth behind a wry grin. "But don't you worry, son. I'll see that she is well taken care of."

Trap found himself so mad his head throbbed. Fists clenched at his sides, he stood on the balls of his feet. His voice was quiet and sharp, as merciless as a steel blade. Like his father, Trap became stone cold when he was truly angry. He didn't so much lose his temper as focus it in a single beam of white-hot fury.

"Drum," Trap hissed. He doubted Maggie could even hear him, and she was only a few feet away. "I may not be very old, but you have my word on this: If you act anything other than the complete gentleman to Maggie, I'll cut that black heart out of your worthless body and send you straight to Hell where you belong."

"Listen here, boy . . ." Drum tried to interrupt.

Trap held up his hand. His voice remained calm, but it pierced as surely as any arrow. "No, you listen to me. I'm not fooling. I leave tomorrow. If you say another word to me or Maggie, I'll kill you now, if I have to do it with my teeth."

Trap's shoulders heaved. He almost wished the big man would try something.

Instead, Drum shrugged, tossed his head like an insolent horse, and walked into the darkness.

All the anger drained from Trap's body when Maggie came up behind him and touched his arm.

Trap turned and looked at her. He wanted to tell her he would come back for her someday soon, wanted to tell her she meant more to him than anything he'd ever known. But such words didn't come easy to his lips. The notion of leaving her behind was unthinkable, but he was only a boy. What else could he do but respect his father's wishes?

"Thank you for that," Maggie whispered, moving closer to him in the chilly night air. "I don't think people often stand up to him. He looked like he believed you."

Trap let out a deep breath. The aftereffects of the run-in with Drum and the warmth of Maggie's body combined to make him feel dizzy. "I hope he believed me, because I would have killed him."

CHAPTER 9

The O'Shannons' wagon was not yet past the tall oaks that skirted the gravel drive before Drum made his first sweeping edict. The students were still lined up in neat, uniformed rows from saying their good-byes. Maggie saw bad things coming in the smug grin that spread over the new superintendent's face the further the Reverend O'Shannon got from the school.

She had watched in silence as Trap climbed into the wagon behind his parents and sat facing backward on a wooden trunk. His face was stoic, but Maggie could see the pain in his eyes. Neither had spoken a word that morning. They had said their good-byes the evening before.

"Mrs. Tally," Drum barked. Fully in charge now, he set his bottom jaw after each phrase like a jowly bulldog. Two rough men, wearing low hats and leather braces over course work shirts, stepped from the yard behind the kitchen. The taller of the two wore a set of worn Army trousers. The shorter was as stout and wide as he was tall. A thick wad of gray hair sprouted up from the collar of his threadbare woolen shirt.

"These are my associates Pugh and Foster." Drum nodded at the men. "From here forward they will act as orderlies to assure discipline and structure at all times."

"We've never had a problem with order and discipline before, Reverend." Mrs. Tally cocked her head to one side and gave the two new arrivals a quick perusal. "Are you certain the elders would approve such an expense?"

"Don't concern yourself with the elders, Mrs. Tally. That will be my job. Concern yourself with the new rules and see that the students obey them."

"New rules?"

"First," Drum said, clasping his hands behind the small of his back and stalking up and down the line of wide-eyed students. "As of this moment, any utterance of a heathen tongue will not be tolerated. God's own English is the language of learning and that is what I expect to hear."

Frank Tall Horse stood at the end of the line next to Maggie. He smiled softly and nodded his head. He often commented that the constant jabbering of the other students in their assorted languages gave him a headache.

"Washite," he said under his breath. It was one of the few Sioux words he knew. "Fine by me."

Drum spun when he heard the boy speak. "What did you say, young man?" Small stones crunched under his boots as he strode across the yard.

The smile fell from Tall Horse's lips. His brown eyes went wide and he cowered under the scrutiny of the new superintendent. "I said English is fine by me, sir."

"Before that. You said something else before that." Drum's heavy face was inches away from the boy.

"I said *washite.* It means *good.*"

"Did I not just explain the rule to you regarding use of heathen tongues?"

"Yes, sir," Tall Horse whispered. His face was ashen white. "It was. . . . I mean I was. . . ."

"Do you intend to mock me?"

"No, sir." All the joy appeared to flow out of Tall Horse's normally bright face.

"He doesn't even speak Sioux," Maggie said. She could see where this was leading and it made her sick to her stomach.

"Be still," Drum snapped. "He knows well enough to disregard my mandate only moments after I made it." He nodded to Pugh and Foster, who shuffled up on either side of Tall Horse.

"I am a fair man," Drum said, puffing himself up like the self-important adder that he was. "But I must abide by my own rules or there can be no order." He nodded again at the two men.

They each took one of the boy's arms. He did not struggle.

"This is your first offense, so I will limit your punishment to five stripes."

Maggie stepped forward. "I told you, sir. He doesn't even speak Sioux. He is happy to speak English. You don't have to do this." She knew if she spoke what was truly in her heart, Drum would only take it out on Frank.

"I said be still, young lady." Drum turned to a quivering Mrs. Tally. "Fetch me a strong switch from that willow tree yonder."

"Sir?" Mrs. Tally's mouth fell open. "You don't truly intend to . . . ?"

"Dear Lord, forgive me my thoughts about these imbeciles with whom I am forced to work," Drum muttered. "I'll get the blasted switch myself."

Foster and Pugh made Tall Horse take off his shirt, and then took him again by each arm. There was no need; he endured his whipping without a word. When Maggie took a step forward, he only gritted his teeth and shook his head to keep her back. The younger students looked on with blank eyes. This was not the first time many of them had seen cruelty, only the fist time they'd seen it at the school.

Drum could barely contain his smile as he administered the cruel lashes. When he finished, Drum dismissed the group to return to morning classes. He pitched the offending switch unceremoniously on the ground at his feet and turned a snide face to Maggie while he straightened his frock coat and tie.

"I'll see you in my office at three P.M. sharp," he said. The fire in his eyes from the enjoyment of meting out Tall Horse's punishment had turned to a lecherous glow. "I admire your spirit, young lady. I won't put up with it, but I admire it nonetheless."

Maggie knew her own limits. It would take more than

Drum's pitiful orderlies to hold her. There were certain things she would never stand for. But Drum had his limits as well—he'd shown that.

She helped a tight-lipped Frank Tall Horse back inside the school, and wondered if she would be alive by nightfall.

CHAPTER 10

A thin gash of yellow light cut the dark hallway from the door to Reverend Drum's office. Maggie stood outside until she heard the downstairs clock chime three. She steeled herself for what was sure to await her and put her hand on the knob. She was not afraid to die. A month ago, she would have welcomed the thought, but since she'd met Trap O'Shannon and seen there was still something right with the world, she was not ready to rush into death either.

The door creaked when she pushed it open and stepped inside. Drum sat at his desk, a pair of black-rimmed glasses on the end of his nose. He glanced up when he heard her and gave a cursory nod to one of the high-backed chairs in front of him before going back to his reading.

He ignored her for some time. The shuffling of papers and the sound of his heavy, nasal breathing were the only sounds in the room.

When he finished, Drum closed the folder of papers in front of him. An artificial smile flashed across his face. He came around to sit on the edge of the desk, peeling off his wire glasses with thick fingers. His knees hovered only inches away from her.

"I've been reading your file," he said as if to gloat.

Maggie sat motionless, staring at the floor.

"You know that it can only help you to cooperate with me." He licked his lips.

This Maggie understood, but she pretended like she didn't. "I *am* cooperating with you, Reverend. All the students have always cooperated here at the school."

Drum rubbed his face and changed tacks. "Miss Sundown, you haven't been here for two weeks and have been branded as a troublemaker already." He nodded toward the papers on the desk at his side. "Your file has a complete report and affidavit drawn up by the delivery boys from Van Zandt's Creamery."

Maggie didn't know what an affidavit was, but if the wicked boys from Van Zandt's Creamery wrote it, it couldn't be any good.

He continued. "I am not sure what Reverend O'Shannon intended to do about it, but my course appears to be clear. You assaulted local townsfolk. We can't stand for that, can we?"

"They chased me into the cellar," Maggie said, knowing it wouldn't make any difference.

Drum shook his head. "I have to go by the facts, young lady, not your fanciful stories." He inched to the edge of the desk. He was close enough now that she could smell the foul smell of the sausages he'd eaten for lunch on his breath. "I should tell you, the Van Zandts would see you hang."

He studied her face for a reaction. She gave him none so he plowed ahead. "I could help you," he said. "I believe you would find me as powerful as I find you alluring."

"I do not understand what that word means," Maggie lied. She'd never heard *alluring* before, but she understood all too well.

He chuckled, obviously thinking she was falling under his spell. His voice was low and throaty. "It means I am attracted to you. I find you pleasant to look at."

He reached to touch her hair. Maggie's stomach churned, but she sat completely still while his clumsy fingers slid slowly, lecherously down her cheek. When they were near enough to her mouth that she knew she couldn't miss, she turned and sank her teeth deep into the flesh at the base of the reverend's thumb and hung on.

Drum tried to jerk the hand back, erupting in a fearsome

growl. He clubbed Maggie brutally in the temple with his free fist, hitting her at least three times before the skin on his thumb gave way.

Stunned, Maggie slumped to the floor. Her head reeled and the room spun around her. She tasted blood and flesh in her mouth. It took her a moment to realize it was Drum's. She spat out the chunk of meat in disgust and crawled backward across the floor. If she could only make it to the door . . .

The reverend advanced on her. His hungry look had turned to a blaze of pure hatred. Grabbing her by both shoulders with powerful hands, he hauled her up to face him.

"I'll see you do worse than hang, you deceitful little bitch. . . ."

Maggie spit more blood—his blood—in his face and drove a knee hard into his groin.

He groaned, but his grip held firm and he pulled her to him, pinning her arms by her side. He kissed her brutally on the mouth, stifling the scream that hung there with the press of his cold lips.

Mrs. Tally opened the door and stepped inside.

"Reverend, I . . ." Her mouth hung open as she took in the scene in front of her.

Drum released his hold and Maggie fell to the floor, panting. He wiped the blood from his face with his good hand and made a feeble attempt to straighten his clothes.

"I . . . What happened, child? Reverend Drum, you're bleeding. What's the matter with your hand?" Mrs. Tally's face was ashen white.

Maggie took the opportunity to scramble to her feet and stand behind the head matron.

"Mrs. Tally, take this young trollop out of my sight. She still has a long way to go before she is anywhere near civilized," Drum fumed. "We must yet kill everything in her that is Indian. We'll begin with that long mop of unruly hair. See that it's cut to a respectable length at once." He took a length of white cloth from his desk drawer and began to wrap his hand. "Bring them around to God and away from their heathen ways of savagery."

Mrs. Tally bit her lip and turned to go. Maggie could feel the woman's heavy shoulders trembling next to her.

"I'll personally inspect the haircut tomorrow morning," he said through clenched teeth. "And Mrs. Tally . . ."

"Reverend?" She stopped in her tracks but didn't turn around. She swallowed hard.

His voice was acid and venomous. "If you ever enter my office without knocking again, I'll have Pugh and Foster escort you off the grounds so fast your head will spin."

CHAPTER 11

The train out of Lebanon didn't leave until after ten in the morning. It was a great, leaking beast that blew off more steam than it used to turn its massive wheels and lumbered along at a mind-numbing pace that tore a hole in Trap's nerves.

The hole in the boy's gut grew deeper with every slow, excruciating mile the rattling train took him from Maggie Sundown.

By the time they reached Carthage, the engine had about boiled dry and had to stop and take on water. It was early evening and the sun hung low on the western horizon.

A cloud of mosquitoes and biting gnats pestered a gray Brahma bull across the split-oak fence. Trap squatted next to the bottom rail looking alternately at the dusty ground and the long line of trees to the north—back toward the school. He shooed a gnat out of his face. Behind him, the train vented a gasp of steam and covered the crunch of his mother's footsteps until she was almost on top of him.

"I can see you are badly troubled, Denihii." She called him by the Apache nickname she'd given him when he was a small boy. It meant Tracker.

"I am fine, Mother." He knew she didn't believe him.

Hummingbird sighed and knelt on the ground next to her son. Trap would always remember that though his mother was the wife of a reputable Presbyterian minister and wore decent, respectable dresses, she never hesitated to sit on the ground.

"It is a good thing to respect your father," she began, studying a blade of broad grass. "But when your heart tells you something is good, there are times you must follow what it says."

Trap looked up at her. "I understand you want to be with your people."

Hummingbird smiled. "Trap, I left the Chiricahua when I was yet a girl. You and your father are my people. I go to Arizona for the same reason you do—to honor your father."

"But he said you . . ."

She put up her hand. "It will be good to see my relatives. But I was not the one that asked him to go. The church was. He will not admit it, but there are some on the board of directors—as well as in the Army—who do not approve of the way your father ran White Oak. I've heard them say he used too soft a hand." She cast her eyes down at the grass again. "Likely because of you and me."

It had always been her custom to speak frankly with her son, but she'd never spoken so openly to him about his father. "The church asked him to go to Arizona to get him out of the way."

"I didn't know." Trap found it a difficult thing to grow up—to learn that his father had a bit of an ego.

The conductor called for all to board, and the engine vented more steam in preparation to move.

Trap shook his head as if he could shake off his thoughts. "I didn't know," he repeated himself.

"He wouldn't want you to." Hummingbird let Trap help her to her feet. She took his hand and pressed a wad of money into it.

"What is this?" He stood with her beside him.

"In the world of the whites a man should always have at least a small amount of money. You are all grown up now. So much like your father—and yet your own man . . ."

The conductor called again, giving them an impatient glare.

"Walk with me to the train," she said, still holding his

hand. "I have a little more to say. People will tell you that you must choose between your Apache and your white blood. Do not listen to them. Choose only the good from each. My forebears were tenacious and often ferocious people. Though it is not always evident, your father is much the same if he has to be. . . . As you will soon learn, both Indians and whites can be cruel beyond belief."

By the time they reached the train Trap was speechless. He'd never had a need for money, and couldn't understand why he would need any now. He stared down at the wad of bills in his hand.

"It is not much," Hummingbird said. "But if you are careful, you will have enough to buy a good horse and a few other things you may need."

She took a small bundle of red cloth from under the smock she wore to protect her dress and placed it in Trap's hand on top of the money.

"This belonged to my father." She stepped up onto the train so she was looking down at him. A shrill whistle split the air as the huge arms on the steam engine sprang to life and jerked at the metal wheels.

Trap unrolled the cloth to find a gleaming, bone-handled hunting knife.

"It is a hard world, my son. I wish I could give you more, but it has always been my experience that wits are your best weapons—and you have plenty of those."

She stayed in the doorway, blocking Trap's path while the train began to pick up speed. She was kicking him out of the nest. A warm breeze tugged at a stray lock of hair over her high forehead. She smiled softly while she looked at him.

Trap moved along at a fast walk, shaking his head.

The train picked up speed in earnest now. Hummingbird reached out with a slender hand and touched Trap's outstretched fingers. "I'll talk to your father," she said. She had to shout as the train began to move faster than Trap could walk. "I was foolish to let you come this far. Go back and get that girl, Denihii. In the future, when you see that something is right, do not wait this long to do it."

CHAPTER 12

"It's nothing short of dreadful," Mrs. Tally sniffed. "The plight of womanhood in general, I mean to say." She stood behind a stoic Maggie, a pair of shears poised over the girl's head. "Understand, dear, that I am loath to speak out against the superintendent, but I see no reason to cut this beautiful hair except his spite for your rebuff."

Maggie sat quietly, her hands folded in her lap, her eyes shut. She could hear the metal blades whisper as they came together. She felt the gossamer softness of each lock of hair as it fell down her shoulders and gently brushed her arms on the way to the floor.

Mrs. Tally spoke through her tears as she cut. "I mean to say, I know it's the way the Good Lord made us. We are after all the weaker sex—born to a life of servitude, the bearing of babies, and the pleasures of wicked men." She stomped her foot. Maggie could hear her gritting her teeth. "But sometimes, when I meet a man like Drum, I wish I could take these snips and do some quick surgery."

She stepped back and wiped her nose with the back of her sleeve, a sure sign the normally fastidious woman was nearing a complete breakdown. "Still," she sighed. "We have to be reasonable as women and know our own limitations. Sometimes it's better to give in a little rather than suffer. What I mean to say is, if something is inevitable, perhaps one should make the best of it to survive the situation." The poor woman's face was drawn, and looked ten years older than it had the day before.

Maggie said nothing.

Mrs. Tally handed her a small mirror. "There now, I left it over your ears. You are still as lovely as ever. Perhaps he will leave you alone—now he knows I'm on to his game."

"You know that will never happen," Maggie said. "I've made him angry. Cutting my hair is but a small thing compared to what he plans to do with me. This no longer has anything to do with his pleasure; it is about resentment."

Mrs. Tally flashed a sorrowful smile. "It most usually is, my dear. It most usually is."

"I will kill him when he tries to touch me again."

"Oh, I don't doubt it, child. But I am just as certain the people in town will hang you for your trouble. The sad truth is. . . ." Mrs. Tally wrung her hands and stared at the floor, biting on her bottom lip. "What I mean to say is, if you were to let him . . . have his way, he might hurt you some in the process—but if you fight him, he'll kill you for sure." She suddenly looked up, new tears welling in her weary eyes. "I fear your options are but few are far between."

Maggie picked up the small mirror and looked at her new hair. It made her face look bigger, maybe a little older—but not as old as she felt. Fourteen was not so young in the great scheme of things. Back in the Wallowa she would likely have been married very soon.

"Options," she whispered to herself. The sound was so soft it must have sounded like a sigh to Mrs. Tally.

There was another option. She could run.

CHAPTER 13

Maggie Sundown began to plan her escape the day she'd first set foot on the grounds of the White Oak Indian Academy. She'd stashed a water jug and a small carving knife she'd stolen from the kitchen under her bed. Her geography textbooks contained decent maps, and she had spent several evenings gazing at the angled lines that represented the mountains and rivers of her beloved Wallowa Valley. One map in particular showed hash marks representing railroads and a detailed rendition of the entire United States over a two-page spread. She'd torn our both pages, folded them carefully, and put them in the small poke with her food—some dried beef and two small jars of strawberry jam sealed with wax. The jam was sweet, and she reckoned a spoonful would keep her going for some time on the trail.

She decided to leave during the evening meal, fearing that if she waited until after dark, Drum might call her to his study again before she could get away.

The older girls took turns helping in the kitchen. It wasn't Maggie's turn, but she volunteered to trade with a timid Cheyenne girl to give her a little extra time out from under the headmaster's nose.

Drum's eyes burned at her constantly throughout the entire meal. Her stomach knotted at the thought of food, but she knew she would soon need all her strength. When she'd cleaned every last morsel of chicken from her plate, she carried it to the kitchen, retrieved her meager supplies, and walked straight out the back door.

Gray dusk had settled over the grounds by the time she made it down the little path that led to the stables. Cool air pinked Maggie's cheeks. Gut-wrenching tension sent a trickle of sweat down the small of her back, and she looked behind her in spite of her self. The headmaster was nowhere to be seen. Mrs. Tally was in the dining hall with the other students. If she noticed Maggie's absence, she wouldn't be likely to say anything.

Pugh and Foster had disappeared into the root cellar before supper. There was a supply of medicinal liquor in there that would keep them busy for some time.

Maggie knew she'd be easier to track on horseback, but she needed to get as far away from the school as she could in a night's time. Most of the animals in the barn were heavy draft types, meant for pulling one of the school wagons or plows. The choice of which one to take was easy.

Drum's brown Thoroughbred nickered softly when she stepped into the stall. It was a leggy horse with a flowing mane and long head. Built for speed, but unlikely to have the endurance for long days on the trail like the spotted ponies of the Nimi'ipuu, the gelding had the lean look of a racehorse. For the time being at least, a racehorse was just what she wanted.

She decided to saddle in the cramped stall, in case anyone happened to come in. Drum rode a light plantation saddle with no horn, a padded leather seat, and metal stirrups. It was not meant for strenuous cross-county riding, but it looked comfortable enough. Small brass D rings behind the low cantle enabled her to tie on an extra saddle blanket rolled to contain her poke of gear. The Thoroughbred turned its head and sniffed Maggie's arm as she finished tightening the girth strap. She hummed softly, and the big animal released a rumbling sigh.

Once she'd saddled the horse, Maggie slipped out of the blue-gray uniform skirt and picked up the fawn-colored skirt she'd had on the day she'd come to the school. It was lighter, but made with a fuller cut so she could straddle a horse without exposing most of her legs as she rode. She kept the gray kersey uniform blouse, but left the tail out and unbuttoned the top two buttons so it hung open at the collar. She fastened a wide leather belt around her waist and tucked the hunting knife in next to her side. Untucked, the blouse was just long enough to cover the wooden handle.

The thrum of deep voices at the outer door sent Maggie's hand to the handle of her knife. She ducked her head behind the horse and held her breath. Slowly, the voices faded as the speakers moved away.

Maggie swallowed hard. She couldn't stay in the stall much longer without being seen. She reached over the door and moved the metal latch. Her hand trembled and she took a deep breath to calm herself. If she could only make it out to the trees, she knew she could disappear in an instant.

Poking her head around the stall door, she chanced a look up and down the dim alleyway of the barn. She led the gelding out, turned her back to the door, and put a small foot in the stirrup to climb into the saddle.

A heavy crunch of gravel behind her sent a cold chill up Maggie's spine. Her throat tightened. Reins in one hand and the stirrup leather in the other, she made ready to spring aboard the horse and run for it.

"*Washite,*" a soft voice said from the doorway. It was Frank Tall Horse. "I'm glad you're getting away from here."

Maggie gave a sigh of relief and turned to face him, the reins still in her left hand. The gelding seemed to feel her mood change, and hung its head to sniff the ground. Lips gave off loud pops as the horse nibbled at the bits of hay that littered the stable floor.

"You could go too," she said. "You are old enough to make it away from this place." It was a difficult thing, leaving the tenderhearted boy behind.

Frank toed the dirt. "No. I got nowhere else to go. I been at this school nearly my whole life. I'd probably get lost and wander into all kinds of trouble."

Tall Horse stepped closer and rubbed the gelding's long neck. "Thank you for trying to help me this morning."

"You would have done the same for me."

"I'd like to think so," he said. "But I don't know. I believe you are braver than me." He smiled at her with deep brown eyes. "Watch yourself, Maggie Sundown. There are people out there just as bad as the reverend—maybe worse."

Maggie gave a solemn nod. "I know." She took the map from her breast pocket and unfolded it. There was just enough light to make out the lines. "Am I right that we are here?"

The boy studied the map for a moment, then nodded. "This is Lebanon and this is us. It doesn't show you much of what else is out there—only the big rivers and some of the mountains." He pointed to the area south and a little west of them, just north of Texas. "They call this Indian Territory, but from what I hear, it's mostly outlaws and cutthroats. I'd steer well clear of it if it was me."

Maggie shrugged that off. She tapped the map with the tip of her finger. "I am told the Nimi'ipuu, my people, are imprisoned somewhere in Kansas. That is this place?"

Tall Horse smiled. "That's what I have heard. But you can't fool me." He tapped the map on the outline of Arizona. "You are going here."

He clasped both hands and held them at waist level in front of him to give her a step up into the saddle.

"Good-bye, Frank Tall Horse of the Ogallala Sioux. You are a good Indian, do not forget that. Perhaps we will meet again," Maggie whispered, knowing the chances were unlikely.

"Good-bye." Tall Horse patted the horse on the shoulder and handed Maggie the reins. "You are a good human being. Do not forget *that*. Say hello to my friend for me when you see him. I hope I can meet your children someday."

The road away from the Indian school led directly south, and Maggie kept to it for the first hour. Though the moon waned to less than half, the road was bumpy and rife with low branches and sinkholes. She held the powerful horse to a gentle lope for several minutes, fighting the urge to gallop until it was worn completely out or worse.

She calculated she had about nine hours until the sun rose, and she intended to use every minute of it.

Lamplights from small farmhouses flickered every few miles in the trees along the roadway and kept her moving forward. Dogs barked here and there, but none came after her. As long as she was around people, she would be in danger. The further south she got, the less of a problem that would be. According to her map, the city of Springfield lay somewhere to the southwest, but she intended to stay well away from there.

The big gelding proved to be tireless as long as she kept him pulled back in the easy, ground-eating lope. She pointed south until the lamplights were spaced further apart and she felt she was well past town. When she found a stream she took to it, hoping to throw off any would-be pursuers until she could make more distance. Twice, she wasted precious minutes to double back on her own trail, working her way through a fetid swamp, full of dark shadows and hanging vines as big around as her wrist. The terrain was anything but flat, and she made much slower progress than she'd hoped. She could only hope the thick hardwood forests and rocky creeks slowed Drum as well.

Two hours before daylight, Maggie began to look for a place to hide. She hadn't seen a house for some time, but wanted to be well entrenched before daybreak and out of the eyes of any wandering travelers who might be able to help Drum when he did come looking.

Thoughts of the wicked man sent her hand to the knife at her side. She wished for a gun, but consoled herself that it was better to play the rabbit than the wolf for the time being. If she could hide long enough, perhaps Drum would give up and she could make it to this place called Arizona.

CHAPTER 14

Trap figured the train had gone a little over a hundred miles to reach the water stop outside of Carthage. The tracks did a fair amount of snaking back and forth through the hills, so he could cut off a third of that distance if he took a more direct route. A night and a day of hard riding could get him back.

As usual, Trap spent little time planning for the future. He had no idea what he would say when he reached White Oak, but figured his father would be proud of him for letting the Good Lord take care of the morrow. He'd decide what to do when he got there.

To get there at all, he had to buy a horse. Though he was almost seventeen and comfortable enough in the saddle, he'd never had occasion to buy much of anything, let alone something as important as a horse. He knew a good one when he saw it, and hoped the money his mother had given him would be enough.

The livery stable was a located about a block from the water tower across the tracks from Carthage proper. It was a low structure, cobbled together of rough-hewn lumber and rusty tin. A low sun shone through a multitude of old nail holes on the large open door, proving that the forlorn building was little more than a pile of previously used scrap.

Trap stopped halfway there and divided his bankroll into three small stacks. He put one in his vest pocket, a second in his front trouser pocket with his jackknife, and the rest he slipped inside the belly of his shirt. He knew enough to be sure there would be some bargaining involved in any horse trade, and didn't want to be in a position where he played his entire hand at once.

When he started walking again, he saw a boy about his age come out the double doors and dip two wooden buckets in the long water trough out front under the eaves. Trap waved at him. The boy looked up while he pushed the buckets down in the water and let them fill. He spit and turned his head to wipe his mouth on his shoulder. A grimy spot on his pale yellow shirt showed this was a regular habit.

"Help you?" the boy said, hoisting the brimming buckets. He was hatless, blond, and several inches taller than Trap.

"I was hopin' to buy a horse," Trap said. He came up beside the trough. "Want a hand with one of those?"

The boy shook his head. "Nope. I'd lose my balance and keel over if you took one." He stuck out his chin to point toward the doors. "My uncle's inside pouring oats while I do the waterin'. He's the man you'd wanta talk to about a horse."

Inside, the livery was as spotless as a horse barn could be. The wide alleyway was clean and uncluttered. The warm, comfortable smell of fresh hay and saddle soap hung in the cool shadows. Well-groomed animals stuck contented noses out of nearly every stall. The interior was in all ways the opposite of what the outside of the place looked to be.

A row of polished saddles on pegs along the far wall reminded Trap that he'd not only have to buy a horse, but tack as well. He chewed the inside of his jaw and tried to look like he knew what he was doing. The boy went to fetch his uncle from a back stall.

"What can I do for you, lad?" A smiling man strode forward on a wooden leg. He wiped his hands on a towel he had stuck in his belt and reached to shake Trap's hand. "Nathan Bowdecker. I'm the proprietor hereabouts."

"Trap O'Shannon." He shook the offered hand. It seemed honest enough—if a person could tell that sort of thing from a handshake. "I need to buy a horse." He tried to keep his voice from sounding urgent.

Bowdecker rubbed his chin in thought. He looked Trap over with deep-set eyes. "It's awful late," he finally said. "How'd you get here?"

"Train," Trap said simply.

"You James O'Shannon's boy?"

Trap nodded. He wasn't surprised. His father often traveled to do a little preaching. It helped tone down his otherwise restless nature. "Yessir."

"He's a fine man, your pa," Bowdecker said. "I've heard him go to expoundin' a time or two. I'm a Lutheran myself, but I do enjoy hearing the good word of God from you Presbyterians once in a great while." His gaze narrowed. "It don't add up, James O'Shannon's boy running around Missouri this time of an evenin' looking to purchase hisself a horse. You're either running from somethin' or to somethin'. . . ."

Nathan Bowdecker had the forthright look of a man who would see straight through a lie, so Trap told him the whole story, including his observations of Drum.

"Sounds like you're on a mission," Bowdecker said when Trap finished. "I reckon a man oughta follow his gut." He rubbed his face in thought, then tapped his wooden leg. "My gut told me to go to sea on a whalin' ship when I was still a lad. Lost my leg, but I saw things I'd never seen otherwise. I reckon it was worth the price. . . . Let's get our business done then so you can be on your way. I got just the mount for you."

Mr. Bowdecker said he felt duty-bound to supply Trap with a sound animal, capable of making it all the way to Arizona.

"I ain't runnin' any charity ward here." Bowdecker smiled as he led out the short-coupled black. The gelding had a round spot at the point of its croup and a shock of white hair tucked into the thick black tail. "Skunk here will do you a good service, but he won't come cheap."

When he heard the price, Trap sucked in air through the corner of his mouth like he'd seen his father do when negotiating the price of mutton.

"I don't feel right about sellin' you anything less," Bowdecker said. "The Comanche are still hittin' it pretty good down Texas way and the trail between here and Arizona is chockablock full of outlaws and bandits. A man's horse is sometimes the onliest way out of a pickle—particularly a half-Apache Presbyterian who doesn't even appear to pack a pistol."

"Is that your bottom dollar?" Trap's heart sank as he figured out how little money he'd have left over. He'd have to live off the land most of the way to Arizona—and without a rifle, that would be a pretty tall order.

Bowdecker nodded. "Son, take a lesson from the Greeks; never trust a man who is willin' to let you have a horse for less than market value. It's a good bet such a beast has a bowed tendon or some other such malady—or at the very least is ornery as all get-out." He leaned in close to Trap. "Tell you what I'll do. You take ol' Skunk off my hands and I'll throw in all the tack as a gift for the service your pa did for this little part of God's vineyard. Those Greeks never said a word about a gift saddle."

"He handles good?" Trap already had his mind made up to take the deal.

Bowdecker gave him the lead. "Clamber on up and give him a try. You'll find none better in all of Missouri for what you have in mind."

It was nearly dark by the time Trap paid the liveryman his price and finished tacking up. He had nothing in the way of supplies, so it didn't take him long to pack. The kind-hearted liveryman gave him a small coffee sack with some biscuits and a battered canteen full of water. Along with the money, Trap gave Bowdecker his heartfelt thanks.

Skunk had a remarkably smooth gait for such short legs. He seemed to sense the urgency Trap felt to get back to Maggie, and covered the ground with a vengeance. Five minutes away from the livery, the stout little horse settled into a five-beat trot so smooth, Trap took a drink from the canteen and didn't spill a drop.

He was dog-tired, but that didn't matter. Maggie was ahead—at White Oak. He couldn't wait to see her, to see the look on her beautiful face when he rode up and finally told her how he felt.

CHAPTER 15

The Right Reverend Tobias Drum drew back and slapped Mrs. Tally across her round face. He wanted to punch her, but there were too many witnesses. A slap would be easier to explain away. The heavy woman staggered, swayed, and then fell back on her broad rump with a loud *whoompf*. Her face reddened, but it was not as red as Drum's.

"You were fully aware she was going, weren't you?" the headmaster raged. He towered over the pitiful woman, contemplating how good it would feel to give her a swift boot to her heaving belly. "You let her slip away to make me look foolish."

Mrs. Tally gulped for air trying to catch her wind. A river of tears poured down her cheeks. She could only shake her head.

Drum waved her off in disgust. She was too stupid to draw breath. A useless breather, that's what she was, a pure waste of good air. She contributed little to society but snivels and weakness.

He turned his attention to the red-eyed duo of Foster and Pugh. Both reeked like a whiskey keg.

"And look at you two," Drum spit. His voice shook. Dark eyes looked as though they could melt stone. "The one and only reason I hired you two idiots is to keep this sort of thing from happening."

Pugh opened his mouth to speak, but Drum raised his

fist and gave it a vehement shake. "Do yourself a favor and keep quiet while you leave the grounds. I'll not have buffoons in my employ."

The useless breathers taken care of, Drum turned his attention to the problem at hand. He couldn't let the girl escape unpunished. She'd taken his horse, but worse than that, she'd usurped his authority. The Army and the church would surely look down on a man who couldn't even keep fourteen-year-old Indian children in custody.

Drum knew he'd have to follow her, catch her, and teach her a lesson she'd not soon forget—a lesson he'd enjoy teaching very much.

Van Zandt's Creamery wagon chattered up the drive, a sullen Cleveland bay mare in the traces. The boy driving it had an equally sullen look. A yellow bruise healed slowly in front of his left ear. A brindle hound slouched on the wooden seat beside him, lips pulled back in a smiling half snarl.

Drum nodded to himself. This was perfect.

"Does that dog know how to track?" Drum asked when the wagon came closer.

"It do at that," the boy said. "Toot can trail anything livin'."

"How about Indian girls?"

"Injun gals got enough stink to 'em, I reckon just about any old dog could trail one," the boy said with a grin. He knew most of the children surrounding Mrs. Tally could understand everything he said. "Why, you got one that's escaped on you?"

Drum nodded. "I do. What's your name?"

"Harry Van Zandt."

"That's what I thought," Drum said. He walked up to the wagon, ignoring the growling hound. "The girl who's gone missing is the same one who's responsible for the bruise on your face."

Harry rubbed his ear and took a deep breath. His face grew dark and began to resemble his snarling dog. "The O'Shannon runt done this to me, then slipped outta here before I could get even with him."

Drum raised an eyebrow. "O'Shannon may have done it, but he did it for the girl. And now she's run off with my horse. I'll be putting up a hundred-dollar bounty to those who ride with me. . . ."

"And help bring her back?" Van Zandt finished the sentence. His eyes sparkled at the mention of such a large sum of money.

Drum shrugged. "Let's just see how it turns out. She's a fighter—and she has stolen a horse. I'm not sure she'll let us bring her back. Some around here might say hanging's too good for the likes of her."

Harry's scowl blossomed into a full-face grin. Even the dog appeared to glow with added enthusiasm.

"I'll go get my pa. He's the best hunter you ever laid your eyes across. Toot can track with the best of 'em, but Pa's dog, Zip, he's got a mean streak, I'm here to tell you. Pa won't let us bring ol' Zip on our rounds on account of he hates redskins with a purple passion. He'd chew these young nits to pieces in no time." The Van Zandt boy giggled. "When ol' Zip catches the little tart, he'll rip her to bloody red shreds."

Drum heard Mrs. Tally gasp behind him, but she said nothing. The pathetic woman was too weak to make any sort of stand against him. At least the Nez Percé girl was a fighter.

"Very well," he said to Harry Van Zandt. "You go get your father and his mean dog, Zip. We'll leave in two hours time. She's a wily one, this Sundown girl. Be prepared to spend a night on the trail."

A string of drool dripped from the brindle dog's mouth. She growled and licked her lips in anticipation.

CHAPTER 16

Trap had covered more than half the ground he needed to by the time the sun crested the line of green-topped hickory and smaller ash trees on a tumbled line of low hills to the east. Bolstered by the warmth of the rising sun, fatigue settled around him shortly after dawn. Every few steps Skunk's smooth gait rocked Trap to sleep. Dreams of Maggie jerked him awake. Each time, the little gelding pushed on in the direction it was pointed.

Trap followed the train tracks some, cut through a newly planted field of black soil, then moved to a brushy trail along a river he didn't know the name of by the time the sun was full up.

Shaking off the weariness, he thought of Maggie trapped at the school with Reverend Drum. Dread and worry chased away the thought of sleep. He took a biscuit from the coffee sack tied to his saddle horn, eating while he rode to make better time.

Half an hour later, the heat of the day and the food in his belly sent another wave of sleep rolling over him.

It was too powerful to fight and he lolled, relaxed in the saddle, falling forward when the gelding stopped dead in the trail. He grabbed a handful of mane to keep from tumbling into a locust bush. His eyes snapped open and when his vision cleared, he saw a muscular blue roan facing him, sniffing noses with Skunk.

A sleeping boy about Trap's age sat astraddle the new horse, his wide-brimmed hat thrown against a leather stampede string behind broad shoulders. He wore an ivory-handled revolver on his hip. His fancy white shirt was covered with dust. Sweat rendered it almost transparent.

Trap cleared his throat and the boy clutched at the saddle horn, jerking awake.

"Jeez-o'-Pete!" he said, rubbing his eyes. "How long you been sittin' there starin' at me? It ain't polite."

Trap grinned. "Wouldn't know," he said. "I only just woke up myself."

The boy chuckled and settled the hat back on his head. He urged his roan up next to Skunk and reached a big hand across the pommel of his saddle. "In that case, I'm Clay Madsen hailin' from Bastrop, Texas. Glad to meet you."

Trap shook the offered hand. "Trap O'Shannon."

Madsen threw a quick glance over his shoulder before he turned his attention back to Trap. "You don't look Irish."

"O'Shannon is Scots-Irish."

"You don't look Scots either," Madsen said, looking behind him again.

Trap saw no reason to start explaining his heritage to everyone he met on the trail. He didn't have time to sit and jabber the morning away, so he picked up the reins to take his leave.

"Well," he said. "It looks like you're waiting for somebody. Guess I'll just push on."

The other boy shrugged and cocked back his hat with a knuckle. "I ain't waitin' for no one," he said, casting another glance over a muscular shoulder. He brought the blue roan up beside Trap so they faced the same direction. "Mind if I ride along with you for a little spell? I could use a speck of friendly conversation."

"I reckon I'm friendly enough," Trap said. "But I'm not much of a talker."

"Perfect." Madsen gave him a wide grin. "You're just the sort of feller I like to converse with."

Trap picked up the pace and Clay Madsen matched it with ease. With the sun higher in the sky, the day grew warm and sticky. Moisture hung heavy in the hot air, and felt thick enough to drown anyone who took in a full breath.

The talkative Texan had the relaxed yet supremely confident air of a man three times his age. He spoke the miles away as the two picked their way through hardwood forests and loped through knee-high grass along lush floodplains. Even the blue roan, who must surely have heard them all before, cocked an inquisitive ear back to listen to Madsen's stories.

The Texan recounted that he'd left his father's ranch in south central Texas three months earlier to strike out for adventure and fortune on his own. In gritty detail, he described how he'd wiled away the last few weeks with a pretty young whore in St. Joe, who'd befriended him without charging a cent for her time.

Trap never considered himself a prude, but all Clay's talk of drinking, gambling, and half-naked women needled at his conscience. His father would have had him reciting Scripture until his tongue fell off.

The most bothersome fact was that he found Madsen's stories interesting. The way the boy told them made Trap feel as if he was being trusted with a family confidence.

"Her name was Vera," Clay said as their horses lugged up the crest of a red clay embankment. The going was steep, but he spoke on without any concern. He was a superb horseman and rode as an extension of the handsome blue roan. "Course, that was her given name. I called her Popper."

Trap shook his head. He didn't really think he should hear why anyone would give a nickname like Popper to a whore.

Clay gave him no notice and pushed ahead, twirling the end of his reins absentmindedly as he spoke. "Called her that on account of the way she was always a-poppin' her knuckles and what not."

Trap relaxed a notch. That wasn't so bad.

"Sometimes she'd have me give her a big squeeze around the middle, like a bear hug. Her spine would pop like a row of dominoes clinkin' over." Madsen leaned over in the saddle across the gap between the two riders. He raised dark eyebrows under the brim of his hat and spoke in a hushed tone. "Once in a while, she even had me tug on her little ol' toes and give each of them a pop." He grinned at Trap. "You ever hear of such a thing?" He sighed, looking away. "She had danged fine toes too, like peas in a pod. . . ." His voice trailed off.

"Why didn't you stay with her?" Trap heard himself ask. His mouth felt dry and he found himself pondering on Maggie's toes. He could still picture the tiny impressions they made from the first time he'd tracked her to the root cellar. As a student of tracking, if there was one thing Trap noticed, it was feet. Now that he thought of it, Maggie Sundown had some danged pretty toes herself.

Madsen interrupted his thoughts.

"A no-account son-of-a-bitch gambler named Haywood."

"What?" Trap snapped out of his reverie over the details of Maggie's body.

"You asked why I didn't stay with Popper. It was that sorry pimp gambler of hers named Haywood. He reckoned I owed him money even if she decided not to charge a handsome young feller like myself. I may be long on charm when it comes to the womenfolk." Clay winked. "But I don't have two shinplasters to rub together. I coulda taken the bucktoothed bastard in a fair fight, but I knew he'd force my hand. Be a hell of a poor start if I had to go and kill somebody before I was gone from the home place three months."

"That's good thinking," Trap agreed, but his mind was elsewhere.

They topped a hill overlooking a valley choked with tall grass. A swift creek wound its way through groves of pecans and other hardwoods. They were still a good thirty miles away from the school.

A glint of steel and movement a scant half mile to the north caught his eye. It was late afternoon and the sun was behind them, casting long shadows to the fore. Trap figured he and Madsen were all but invisible to the four approaching riders with the sun in their eyes.

Something about the lead rider—something he couldn't put his finger on—made Trap pause.

"I need to get closer," he muttered under his breath. Thoughts of Maggie's toes still lingered, giving the boy a warm knot, low in his belly.

"It ain't Haywood," Madsen said. "Not unless he's lost, comin' from that direction." He took a brass spyglass out of his saddlebag and held it up to his eye. "I don't recognize any of them. But them dogs sure look mean. We best give them a wide berth." He passed the telescope to Trap.

O'Shannon caught his breath when he moved the metal tubes into focus. The only reason Tobias Drum would ride this far south with a group of hard cases like the Van Zandts and their vicious dogs was to hunt someone who'd left without permission. The only person he knew with enough guts to run away from the school was Maggie Sundown.

The two boys backed down the hill and watched Drum and his men move methodically through the groves of nut trees. One of the striped dogs kept his nose to the ground and tracked, the other, the bigger one, sniffed the air. Even from a distance, Trap could see the animal was a mean one, capable of tearing an unarmed man to shreds.

It took an hour for Drum and his group to move far enough away that Trap considered it safe to approach the trail below.

Trap dismounted and looped Skunk's reins around a low limb of scrub oak. Clay remained in the saddle, keeping watch.

"This Indian girl you're looking for," Madsen said. "If she knew you were comin' back for her, why'd she take to the woods like this?"

Trap knelt and touched the ground, studying the tracks left by the Drum and the others. A fifth set of tracks caught his attention. Most of the hoofprints had been walked over by the others, but a few were still visible.

"Drum must have forced her hand after I left." Trap didn't think he'd ever be able to talk about Maggie with the same easy detail Clay used to speak about women. He tapped the loose soil with his fingers. "I'm betting this is her horse. It's dragging its toes like it's getting tired. She'd likely ran it a good ways before she got here. The way it's movin', I'd say it's picked up a stone in the forefoot."

Trap stood and led Skunk toward the shallow stream. "She would have dismounted and gotten the stone out."

"This Maggie girl must know her horses," Madsen said. He threw back his hat and slid a hand over his thick, chocolate hair. "I believe I'd like to meet her someday."

Trap looked up and shielded his eyes from the low sun with the flat of his hand. "Sounds like you got women a-plenty from all the stories you tell. I only got the one. I'd be much obliged if you didn't try to steal her."

Madsen gave him a good-natured grin. "I may not have to try. She's likely to fall into my arms all on her own."

Trap stood and studied the tracks at his feet beside a leaning cottonwood. Two moccasin prints straddled a damp spot in the earth where Maggie had made water. He didn't tell Clay; it seemed too private a thing to talk about out loud.

The thought of Drum and the others chasing her gnawed hard at Trap's gut, but another, more sobering thought filled him with a feeling he'd never quite experienced. It was the same feeling he'd had as he contemplated Maggie's toes earlier, only multiplied until he felt his insides might burst.

She was not only running away from the school. Maggie Sundown was running *to* him.

CHAPTER 17

Maggie used a rock to kill a fat grouse just before sunset. Fearful of being seen if she started a fire, she hung the bird on her saddle string and rode on. She wanted to keep riding throughout the night, but her horse stumbled more often now and groaned for a rest at every step. He was a lanky beast not cut out for this type of labor, and Maggie knew he would lose flesh rapidly if she didn't give him plenty of time to graze.

The trees began to thin out not long after sunset. Here and there a lamp flickered in the window of some farmhouse, but Maggie was careful to steer clear of those. She turned more south to keep to thicker country, and was relieved when the forests began to come back. Guided by the stars and little more than the feeling inside her, she worked her way southwest until midnight. A crescent moon cast black pools of shadow among the trees and bushes.

The weary gelding jerked to a twitchy stop as something crashed through the bushes in the thicket to the right ahead of them and splashed in the water on the other side. Maggie leaned forward in the saddle and patted the horse's neck. A warm wind blew across her face.

The darkness and unseen noises might have frightened a lesser girl, but Maggie had been chased by the Army, shot at, clubbed on the head with a pistol, and assaulted by Reverend Drum. Worse, she'd had to watch while her once-proud people were conquered. Few things in the night were as frightening as that.

Maggie dismounted under the protection of a large cottonwood, loosened the girth, and let the saddle slide to the ground. Her bones ached from the constant pounding of riding over rough terrain. The brown gelding nosed her hand and gave a rattling groan. She blew softly into its nose and hummed a soothing tune her mother used to sing when she worked around horses.

Maggie used her knife to cut a strip off the saddle blanket about three inches wide. She knotted one end, and after cutting a slit like a button hole in the middle and the opposite end, wove the cloth back and forth through itself to make a set of figure-eight hobbles. The horse was sweat-stained and exhausted enough, it would likely stay near her little camp while it grazed, but she had to be sure.

Once the animal was watered, she turned it out, hobbled, and sank down at the base of a tree against the soft fleece pad on her saddle. She still didn't want to risk a fire, but the weather was cool and the grouse would keep a while longer.

A breeze blew across her neck, and she reached up to smooth her hair. She'd forgotten Reverend Drum had ordered it cut. She hated the greasy man as much as she'd ever hated anyone. Her heart told her she'd have the chance to kill him someday. Not for cutting her hair or even what he did in his office—no, when next they met, Drum would surely give her a reason much more vile.

Leaning her head back against the rough bark on the tree, she gazed up at the myriad of stars that speckled white on the night sky, like the blanket on an Appaloosa horse.

She wondered if Trap O'Shannon would be surprised to see her—if she made it to Arizona. She wondered if he might be thinking of her at all since he left.

Drum would follow her, there was no doubt about that. She'd made good time, but he was close; she could feel it. The Thoroughbred needed rest; that was something she couldn't get around. Without the big gelding she'd move so slowly, she was sure to be caught. But the horse also left an easy trail to follow. She had to do something to discourage her pursuers—to slow them down.

Her breathing came deep and steady as drowsiness tugged at her body. Asleep only a few seconds, she was startled awake by a familiar whistling grunt in the bushes beside her. When she figured out what it was she smiled, a plan already forming in her mind.

CHAPTER 18

"I'm not too keen on them dogs hearing us," Clay whispered. Drops of dew covered the grass in front of their faces. A black and yellow spider the size of a twenty-dollar gold piece scuttled up and down the damp stems to repair a glistening web only inches from the Texan's nose. He paid it no mind, concentrating instead on the brindle dogs below. "I got bit by a dog once when I was a boy and I gotta tell you, I'd rather be in a gunfight without a gun than go through that again."

"Wind's wrong," Trap grunted beside him. "We've stayed well away so they won't even cross our trail."

The two boys watched from a thick stand of tall grass and berry brush on a chalk bluff above the river bottom. The sun had been up less than an hour when they saw Drum pick his way though a thin layer of fog that hugged the waterline. The Van Zandts followed, rifles at the ready, as if they were hunting escaped convicts instead of a fourteen-year-old Indian girl. The brindle dogs ranged in front of the group, padding up to this tree or that, pausing to sniff out every possible trail.

The small one took the lead, while the meaner one hung back a little.

"Looks like the monster's waitin' for his little buddy to flush out something for him to rip to pieces," Clay whispered.

Trap nodded slowly. The morning felt so quiet, he didn't dare speak.

Without warning the smaller dog, who sniffed at the base of a large cottonwood, let out a mournful howl and ran yelping back to Harry Van Zandt. The bigger dog broke into a ferocious snarling fit. It faced another tree, not ten feet away from the first along the water's edge.

Trap's heart jumped in his chest. He shot a glance at Clay. "I'm afraid she might be in those bushes. Wish we had a rifle."

"We don't need no rifle to shoot that little piece," Clay scoffed. "I could part their hair with this peashooter at this distance if they try and do the girl any harm."

The big dog suddenly tore up to the tree and pawed at the ground around it. Seconds later, it flipped over backward with a yowling cry, more wildcat than hunting dog. Regaining its feet, the yelping animal retreated to a dismayed master, tail between its legs.

Clay took up the telescope and studied the scene in more detail. He chuckled and passed it to Trap.

"She's a smart one, this girl of yours," Madsen whispered. "She must have got herself a porcupine last night and set some snares with the quills. Both dogs got a snootful. That little one looks to have three or four up around the eyes. Wouldn't be surprised if it's blinded. The kid holding it looks mad as a hornet."

Unable to move without being seen, Trap and Clay lay still in the grass and watched the scene below them. The Van Zandt boys were furious at the injuries to their pets. Their vehement curses and oaths carried on the stiff breeze, but it was impossible to make out more than a few words.

It took an hour to get all the quills out of both dogs. The monster bit Roth in the hand during the process, and they had to use a belt to muzzle the snarling thing. It took more time to doctor the wound.

In the end, the two brothers left with their injured little dog, while Mr. Van Zandt and Drum followed the monster up the trail that ran along the water.

Ten minutes later, Trap and Clay moved down to take a look at the sign. Five minutes of study and Trap began to chuckle. He swung back on his horse, shaking his head.

"They're following the wrong trail," he said. "You're right, she is a smart girl."

Madsen stood dumbfounded, holding the roan's lead in his hand. "How do you know it's the wrong trail?"

Trap smiled. "You ever have a dog mix it up with a porcupine?"

Madsen nodded.

"Could you ever break him of it?"

"I guess not," the Texan admitted. "Seems like they get more quills each time they tangle with one. It's like they hold a grudge or something."

"Exactly. They get all caught up in a blind rage and can't think of anything but revenge," Trap said. "Drum's relying too much on the dog." He nodded back to the northeast. "There are rocks turned over in the water heading upriver. I reckon Maggie will go that way a spell before she turns back south."

"If she headed back upriver, who's the evil reverend followin'?"

"He's following the dog." Trap waited for Clay to make the connection.

A smile slowly spread across Clay's face. "And the dog's followin' the porcupine where Maggie got the quills. . . ."

Chapter 19

1910
Montana

"You were some woman then and you're some woman now, Maggie darlin'," Clay said, bouncing his fist on top of the table. "I still don't see why you didn't take up with me all those years ago. . . ."

"Mr. O'Shannon, I'm amazed you didn't shoot this scoundrel two days after you met," Hanna said.

"He never had the need to." Clay shrugged. "I can't figure it out, but she picked him over big, strappin' me."

Hanna leaned forward on the table. "Clay was telling me you all rode from St. Louis to Arizona, dodging Comanche troubles, whiskey peddlers, and outlaws all the way. I suppose there were still buffalo back then."

Trap nodded. "Some. Hide hunters had already made a good mark against them, but we ran across several sizable herds." It was funny, but looking back, he'd been so focused on finding Maggie, he'd likely let half the country slip by him without really taking the time to notice it.

A blast of cold air tore through the narrow dining car when the conductor poked his head inside. His face was flushed, his hat dusted with snow.

"Sorry to bother you folks," he panted as if he'd just run

the length of the train. "But Mrs. Cobb, have you by chance seen that man you said looked ill earlier?"

Hanna shook her head. "It's just us," she said. "I'm hearing an awfully good story, though. You should take a rest and join us."

"Wish I could," the conductor said, setting his jaw. "But I need to find that fellow. I've had a bucketful of complaints on him, but he keeps giving me the slip." The door shut as he withdrew his head to continue his search.

"Brrrr." Hanna leaned across the table to take Clay's hands. "It's freezing in here. Come now, I still don't know how you three got together and came to know your good Captain Roman. Finish telling me about how you got to Arizona. I wish I could have been there."

"So does Clay." Maggie grinned.

CHAPTER 20

1878
Arizona

"You ever notice how that gal of yours has a knack for pickin' the routes with the best grass for her horse?" Clay let his boot swing free of the stirrups as if there weren't a dozen rattlesnakes per square yard that might spook his horse and dump him on his hind parts. "You sure she hadn't been this way before?"

Trap grunted. Over the past few weeks he'd grown accustomed to having Clay Madsen along, even come to count on him when they spotted signs of a Comanche raiding party or any of the dozen other dangers they faced on the trail. For the most part, the brash Texan was an easy keeper, content to yammer on about whatever might be running though his mind at the moment, happy to hear himself talk as long as Trap gave him an occasional grunt or nod to show he hadn't gone to sleep.

Maggie had stayed south when she left Missouri, just nicking the northwest corner of Arkansas before she turned due west into Indian Territory.

Trap felt certain they would be able to catch her in the wide-open country of the Texas Panhandle, but she always stayed a step or two ahead. By the time they crossed into the high country in northern Arizona, Trap felt like they were getting close.

For weeks, there had been no sign of Drum or the remaining Van Zandt and his dog.

"You certain we're still on her trail?" Clay asked the same question about every three days. Trap assumed it was when the boy's mind ran dry and he needed time to reload new ammo for his dissertations. On these occasions Madsen required more than a grunt.

"Pretty certain," Trap said. "She's a sly one. I'm able to follow her, but I have to go slow. She's an expert at blending in with game trails or old Indian roads." He was on the ground now, looking at a spot where a set of new tracks joined Maggie's in the red earth.

"Looks like a wagon," Madsen said, nodding down from the back of his horse.

Trap nodded. "Stagecoach maybe. Whoever it is, there are three riders following it." He ran his hand over the parallel lines in the ground.

"Maybe outriders," Clay shrugged. "Guarding a payroll or something."

"Maybe," Trap said. He took off his hat and squinted at the blazing sun overhead. It beat down like an unrelenting forge. "Stage throws up a lot of dust. Look how it's settled here in the wheel tracks and all of these hoofprints." He toed another set of tracks off to the side. "Not as much dust in these. I'm thinking they came along sometime later. . . ."

A low whine echoed across the barren earth, barely audible behind a long jumble of red sandstone and cactus ahead on the trail. Clay and Trap looked at each other.

"What was that?" Trap said. He shaded his eyes with his hand and stared toward the rocks.

Clay gathered up the reins and speared both boots into the stirrups. "I ain't certain," he said. "But I think it was a gunshot." His hand drifted toward the pistol at his belt.

So far, the boys had eluded contact with much of anyone but a stray cowboy or two. Following the gunshot was sure to change that.

Trap climbed back into the saddle. "Whatever it was, it

came from the direction Maggie's headed. Might as well check it out, we're going that way anyway."

The boys nearly stumbled onto the robbery before they knew what was going on. Trap drew his gelding to a skittering stop. Clay's blue roan plowed into him from behind.

" . . . when we find an innocent girl out here all by her lonesome like this, we got to do somethin' about it." A raspy voice came from around the red rock outcrop in front of them.

"Yeah, yeah, that's it, our hands are tied," another, higher voice cackled. "We got to do somethin' about it. It's almost a law out here."

"I am Pilar de la Cruz," a fiery female voice spit. "My father is Colonel Hernan de la Cruz of the Mexican cavalry. He will surely hunt you all down for this outrage. Poor Gerardo did nothing to deserve being shot."

"Pilar de la-la-ti-da Cruz," the cackling voice said again. "Ain't that somethin'? We done captured the daughter of a real live Mexican cavalry colonel."

"You boys shut up and drag her outta the coach," another voice said. This one was calm and in complete control.

Trap looked at Clay and held up three fingers.

The Texan already had his pistol out. "It was four months last week since I left home. I guess I been good as long as can be expected. I'm sure wishin' you had a gun about now," he whispered.

Trap drew the bone-handled knife and took a better grip on the reins. "Me too," he said. "What do you think? Can you shoot all three without hitting the girl?"

Clay shrugged. "I won't know until we ride around the rock and take a look. For all we know, there could be another ten of them who haven't said anything."

"Stop it!" Pilar de la Cruz screamed. "Take your filty hands off me."

"Careful, Buster, she'll cut you," the raspy voice snapped. There was a yowl from Buster and a laugh from the other men.

Trap set his teeth. Attacking at least three bandits with

nothing but a knife in his hand was a foolish endeavor and he knew it, but he couldn't very well let Clay do all the work by himself.

"That's enough," the calm voice said. "You listen to me, your little highness; I don't give a mule's dirty ass if your daddy's the potentate of your stinkin' greaser country, you got no choice in the matter. My compadres are in need of a little company." The voice grew in volume and timbre as he spoke. "Now get out of the damned coach or I'll shoot you in the gut. It won't bother the boys a speck if you got a little hole in your belly."

Clay settled his hat firmly. "I do believe I'll shoot that one first," he whispered.

As the two boys gathered their reins to charge, a blood-curdling scream rent the air high in the sandstone above them. Trap shivered in spite of himself. The cry came again, echoing like a banshee scream from one of his father's stories, through the cactus and sheer cliffs above them. Trap fully expected to see either the devil himself or a whole party of Apache warriors swoop down at any moment.

The black gelding bolted around the rock in the excitement and Madsen's roan followed.

Three men stood by the coach. One of them went for the pistol at his belt and Madsen sent a bullet through his chest. The pistol slipped out of his hand and he tumbled out of the saddle as his wild-eyed horse squirted out from under him. Trap grabbed the animal's reins as it went past.

The remaining two men stood with their hands above their heads, frozen in time on the ground beside the coach and their intended victim. Dressed like gamblers, they looked out of place in clothes too fancy for desert travel. Closer inspection showed their dirty faces and hands didn't quite match up with the rest of the outfits they'd likely stolen from unsuspecting travelers on the trail.

When the men saw they were being faced by two boys, they both relaxed a notch. The one nearest Clay grinned.

"What do you aim to do now, kid? You think you can take both of us before one of us gets you?" He tipped his head toward Trap, then shot a nervous glance at the rock above. Beads of sweat dotted his grizzled upper lip. "Your partner there don't even have a gun. And even if you do kill us, you'll still have them Apache to deal with."

Clay kept the pistol pointed at the pair. Trap slid a Winchester out of the dead outlaw's saddle scabbard, worked the lever, and leveled it at the rough talker.

Clay sighed. "We just can't let you boys bother a poor innocent girl out here all by her lonesome like this." He mimicked the man's gravel voice. "Our hands are tied, you no-account bastards." Clay dipped his head. "Señorita de la Cruz, I apologize for my harsh choice of words there."

The Mexican girl smiled. "Think nothing of it, kind sir."

Trap heard a skittering of rocks from above and chanced a look. In the low sun, he could just make out a shadowed form working its way down a narrow trail. When the lone form dropped below the rim and into the shadows, he could see it was no Apache war party.

It was Maggie.

"Don't look now, boys," the outlaw with the cackling voice whispered. "But the Injuns are sending a squaw down to cut our cojones off. Shoot me if you have to, but I aim to kill me at least one more redskin before I die." He grabbed for the pistol at his belt.

The man's head exploded like a ripe melon and Trap levered another shell in the Winchester. The second outlaw got his gun out and ran for the safety of the coach. Both boys cut him down and he pitched headlong into the sand.

When the smoke cleared, one horse was down and bleeding in the traces while another wild-eyed beast stood blowing and shaking beside its fallen companion. Three outlaws lay dead on the ground. An ashen-faced Pilar de la Cruz trembled as badly as the surviving horse.

Clay saw to comforting the young woman while Trap spurred his gelding over the rocks and dismounted. Maggie slid down the mountain and into his arms.

The shock of finally seeing her mingled with the feeling in his gut. He'd never killed anyone before, and it made him go hollow inside at the thought of it. Then he looked at Maggie and the hollowness filled up to overflowing.

CHAPTER 21

"Your hair," Trap said. He couldn't bring himself to let go of Maggie's hand.

She gave him a self-conscious smile and ran her fingers through her short locks. "Drum decided I needed to look like more like a white woman." The smile faded and she set her jaw. Her eyes narrowed. "I'll not cut it again. Not for Drum, not for anyone. I'd die first."

"Oh, Maggie darlin'," Clay said from the coach where he'd sidled up to a dazed Pilar de la Cruz. "You say that now, but poor ol' Trap would rather have you plumb bald-headed as not to have you at all."

Trap nodded toward Madsen. "He says pretty much whatever pops into his mind."

"Well, it's the damned truth and you know it." Clay pretended to sulk for a moment, but couldn't keep it up with Pilar at his arm. "Your little friend is not near as talkative as I am, but believe me, he's easy to read when it comes to you. We been trackin' you for so long now I feel like I know you already."

Maggie's dark eyes glistened. "You were tracking me?" She looked back and forth from Clay to Trap.

"Doggone right he was tracking you," Clay said. "This boy's like a danged hound when it comes to findin' you."

A party of six Mexicans in civilian dress clattered over the sandstone with rifles drawn and wary looks on their faces.

They rode with the tight formality of soldiers. Pilar put her arm around Clay to show he was friendly and waved at a young man in the lead. He had a thin mustache and brooding black eyes. A wide sombrero fell back on a leather string around his shoulders. He kept his gun trained on Clay and appeared to want to shoot him on general principles.

"Norman," Pilar cried. She spoke to him in rapid Spanish.

Norman reined his bald-faced sorrel to a clattering stop. He lowered his rifle grudgingly after Pilar repeated herself.

"I told him you saved my life," she said out of the corner of her beautiful mouth. "May I present Captain Norman Francisco Garza of my father's cavalry command. They are my escorts on my trip to the United States."

Garza dipped his head slightly and spoke to Pilar in Spanish. His tone was polite, but strained.

Trap's mother spoke Spanish and he'd learned a little as a child. From what he could pick out of the conversation, Pilar had slipped away from the rest of the group to do some exploring on her own. The captain could barely contain his anger and embarrassment that his charge had gotten away from him and almost gotten herself killed.

Trap wondered if Clay could see this man harbored strong feelings for the commander's daughter. If he did, it didn't slow him down.

Madsen stuck out his hand. "Clay Madsen out of Bastrop, Texas," he said. "Pleasure to meet you, Captain Garza. I assume you will be escorting the young lady back to safety. I'd be happy to accompany you and assist if . . ."

"That will be most unnecessary, Señor." Captain Garza turned to Pilar. "Señorita de la Cruz, we must be going. Your father expects us back in three days time. I do not wish to disappoint him." He broke into clipped Spanish again and Pilar nodded her head.

"Might I see you again, Señor Madsen?" she said while Garza's men tended to the body of the fallen driver, cut the dead horse from the traces, and hitched one of the saddle horses to the coach.

"I'll be in Arizona for some time, I believe," Clay said. He took her hand in his and gently kissed the back of it.

Trap marveled at the simple act and wondered how Madsen knew to do such a thing. "I would say you can count on seeing me again, ma'am. Wild horses or a whole unit of Mexican cavalry couldn't keep me away."

Pilar smiled and handed him a slip of paper. *"Perfecto."* The words clicked off her tongue. "You may find me at this address. Please consider this a formal invitation to come call on my father and me at any time you find convenient."

Garza spurred his horse up and opened the coach door from the saddle. "Pilar," he said curtly, holding the door ajar. The stern look he gave Clay Madsen was as much a challenge as Pilar's little scrap of paper had been an invitation.

Clay fell into a blue depression as soon as Pilar and her entourage rumbled out of sight. He vowed to hunt her as hard as Trap had hunted Maggie—a feat that shouldn't prove too difficult since he had her address.

Only the sight of the dead outlaws' firearms helped bring the young cowboy out of his love-struck stupor. He stood beside a dusky, jug-headed horse and picked through the saddle kit. He whistled under his breath when he slid a rifle out of its sheepskin scabbard.

"I do believe this is the most handsome rifle I've ever set my eyes on." Madsen ran a hand over the rich wooden stock. "A .45-90 buffalo Sharps. You can shoot .45-70s out of these too." He threw the gun up to his shoulder and sighted down the thirty-two-inch barrel. "I feel like we just saved her from a life of crime." He cocked his head to one side, like he was trying to drain something out of his ear.

Trap looked at Maggie. "He does that sometimes when he's thinking on something important." Through all the talk, he'd not moved an inch from her side.

"Seems like a good man." Maggie giggled at the funny faces Clay made while he pondered. "How long has he been with you?"

"I've got it." Madsen slapped his leg and let his head bob back to a more natural angle. "I'll call her Clarice." He held the rifle up to Trap and Maggie. "She weighs as much as a small pony, but I always did like my lady friends on the beefy side."

Clay lowered the gun slowly and stared into the pink glow in the west. The drawn look of melancholy washed over his face again. There was a catch in his voice. "You ever feel like you're riding off from your one true love?"

Trap looked at Maggie and smiled.

"I guess I have," he said.

CHAPTER 22

Van Zandt squatted next to his brindle dog and let a handful of sand sift through his fingers. "She ain't far now," he said, spitting a slurry of tobacco juice onto the ground. Remnants of the brown goo dribbled down his chin.

"That's the same song you've been singing for the past three weeks." Drum took off his hat and mopped his brow with a dirty rag from his back pocket. His oily look had taken on a wilted appearance, like a piece of fatty bacon left too long in grease not quite hot enough to cook it.

Van Zandt rubbed his dog behind the ears. "Ol' Zip knows we're close. Tracks don't stay too long in this wind and sand. If we don't get ourselves kilt by Apaches, we should have her by tomorrow night." He squinted up at Drum. "How do you aim to get her back to Missouri once we catch her?"

Drum patted the thick leather reins against his thigh and thought about his answer. Take her back after all this? That was a funny notion. He'd be lucky if the church would let him return at all after he left without giving any notice. Of course, that idiot Mrs. Tally had surely given a full report of what she'd seen, no doubt blowing everything out of proportion as if Maggie Sundown was a white girl.

The sun throbbed against Drum's head with a vengeance and threatened to boil his brain. He squinted through the endless waves of sand and stone and heat and tried to keep his eyes from crossing. He'd sweated through his clothes many times over, and his rump was chaffed raw from weeks in the saddle on a gimpy horse.

This little Indian tramp had not only run off with his favorite horse. She'd stolen his career, his comfortable life, and his reputation. No, she'd not be going back to the school. Neither of them would.

Drum had seen the fight in the girl's eyes before, when she'd bitten him. It warmed him inside to think of it. He hoped she fought again this time. It would make what he planned to do all the sweeter. And, in the end, it would make it easier to kill her.

CHAPTER 23

A day south of old Fort Defiance, Trap decided he wanted to buy Maggie a new dress. A passing stranger, likely a deserting soldier, had told them there was a town a few hours ahead. They were still a few days out of Camp Apache, but Trap didn't know how many opportunities he'd have to buy anything like that. From what he'd seen of the frontier, new clothes and shops to buy them in were seriously lacking.

Maggie insisted her faded skirt only needed time with a needle and thread to render it good as new, but Trap showed he'd inherited his father's Scots-Irish resolution and insisted right back that she was getting a new dress. If she wanted to mend the old one, then she'd have two.

Of course, he had no idea how much such a thing might cost. He had a few dollars of the money his mother had given him, and figured he could get a little more for the extra pistols he and Clay had taken from the dead outlaws.

Buying Maggie a dress seemed like a good idea, but leaving her to do it, even for a minute, was like pulling out a perfectly good tooth. Trap held her hand from the back of his horse, looking down at her eyes.

"Jeez-o'-Pete," Clay said from atop his own gelding, stirrup-to-stirrup with Trap. "You two beat all I ever seen. She's made it by herself across half the country. I reckon she'll survive one afternoon without us."

Trap let his fingers slide away.

"We should be back before dark," he said. "You keep the Winchester with you."

"Clay is right," Maggie said. "Everything will be fine. There is a nice pool down at the river. I'll have a cool bath while you are gone."

"Well, then." Madsen winked. "That changes things. I reckon I oughta stay around and see to your safety after all."

Trap took off his hat and slapped Clay's horse on the rump. The startled roan jumped forward and broke into a fast walk toward town. "She needs protection from you. Let's get gone so we can get back."

Trap looked over his shoulder as he urged his horse into a trot. He wondered if it would always make him so sick when he rode away from this woman.

Maggie watched the boys ride into the swaying waves of desert heat. It didn't take them long to disappear among the Joshua trees and barrel cactus. She rubbed the sweat out of her eyes and sighed. Her memories of the cool mountain air of the Wallowa Valley tugged at her heart—but her future lay with Trap O'Shannon. If he was to go to Arizona, that's where she would go as well.

A new dress seemed a silly extravagance, but she supposed it would be nice to look her best when next she met the Reverend and Mrs. O'Shannon alongside their son.

It felt strange to be alone again after days with the two boys. Trap was quiet for the most part, but Clay Madsen spoke enough for all three of them. Maggie walked toward the line of shimmering acacia trees that lined the riverbank. The catclaw thorns on just such trees were responsible for most of the rips on her shredded skirt.

She smiled to herself at the thought of the fun-loving Texan. As quiet as Trap was, it was easy to tell he possessed strong feelings for her. Clay flirted constantly, but it was obvious he loved all womankind—the one he was with at the moment just a little more than all the rest.

Black streaks lined the red sandstone cliffs that towered

over the slow-moving river like a castle wall and provided
a comfortable shade from the midday sun. Long strands of
lime-green moss swayed like hair in the lazy current where
the river widened into an emerald pool in the mountain's
shadow.

Maggie took a quick look around and leaned the Winchester against a low bush of salt cedar at the water's edge
so she could get to it in a hurry if she had to. She hung her
medicine bag beside the rifle before slipping nimbly out
of her skirt and pulling her loose blouse over her head. Her
knee-high moccasins came off last, and she hung them
across a low branch. It was a tactic she'd learned the hard
way to discourage scorpions and other stinging crawlers
from making a home in the dark recesses of her tattered
footgear.

Naked on the bank, she let the hot breeze blow across
her skin while she inspected the ragged clothes. Miles in
the saddle and countless nights sleeping on the ground had
taken their toll. Cactus and acacia brush had ripped the
threadbare garments in countless spots. Maybe the new
dress wasn't such a bad idea. She carried her old clothes
into the water with her. Hopefully, they would stand up to
one more good washing.

The water was warm, a refreshing contrast to the blazing air, the rock bed slick with moss. Gradually, she waded
deeper into the stream until she had to hop to keep her
head above water. Letting her legs come up, she floated on
her back and gazed at the perfect blue sky while she kicked
slowly across the deep pool. She was happy to be alone with
her thoughts until Trap returned—happy to make herself
feel and smell clean for him.

With her ears underwater she couldn't hear the rocks
skitter down the red sandstone bluff above.

Two ravens circle overhead, cawing and playing with one
another like the tricksters they were. Suddenly, one of the
birds dipped its wings and plummeted straight for her.
Inches above the water, the raven pulled out of its dive and
flew to the acacia tree beside her rifle.

Startled, Maggie sat up to tread water. She brushed a lock

of wet hair out of her eyes. The bird cawed again, then turned its head sideways and blinked a shining black eye.

A hot wind rippled the water in front of her, sending a wave of goose flesh over her body. Something was wrong.

Two strong kicks took her to the shore. Dripping wet, she picked up the Winchester and scanned the shadows among the bushes and rocks before she wriggled into her wet clothes one arm at a time.

The raven flew to a nearby mesquite and began to preen while its mate soared among the cliffs above.

Water dripped from Maggie's hair and ran down her spine beneath her shirt. A familiar feeling tugged at her chest, as if she had walked through a spiderweb. She nodded her thanks to the bird for its warning and backed slowly into the trees.

Someone was out there, watching her.

CHAPTER 24

Trap had the skinny Mexican girl at the mercantile wrap the new dress in brown paper and string. He figured Maggie hadn't been able to open too many presents in her life, and thought she might enjoy it. It took a few minutes to pry Clay away from his flirting, but after a quick trip to the dry-goods store for a few supplies, the boys were on their way back to camp.

Trap was anxious to get back, and kept his horse to a trot. He would have galloped if he hadn't been afraid the heat would kill his horse.

Skunk's ears perked up a half mile away from the river. Trap felt the little gelding tighten its gait, and scanned the area ahead. If he'd learned anything in his short life away from civilization, it was to trust his mount's instincts. He shot a glance at Clay, who was neck-deep in a convoluted story about his plans to ride to Mexico and marry Pilar de la Cruz.

Madsen stopped in mid-sentence. "What's wrong, partner? Looks like you just swallowed a bug."

"Can't tell." Trap gave the gelding its head.

Both horses slid to a stop in the trees beside the remains of Maggie's small fire. The pungent smell of cedar smoke hung heavy in the still air. Trap swung a leg over the saddle horn and hopped to the ground. His voice was tight as a skin drum.

"I shouldn't have left her."

"Aw, she's likely just enjoying her little bath," Clay said from the back of his roan. He raised his dark eyebrows up and down. "I'd be happy to go check on her."

Trap squatted and studied the petite moccasin tracks that led through the dark portal of acacias along the river. "We been gone a good while. I can't see her taking a bath that . . ."

The sharp crack of a Winchester creased the hot evening air. It came from the river.

Trap was back in the saddle in a flash. Clay drew his pistol and the boys spurred their horses into the trees.

A dead man lay facedown in the water, legs bobbing in the current, his hands clawed at the bunchgrass along the rocky bank. Blood oozed from a wound underneath him and mingled with the green moss. A brindle dog lay a few feet away. A shotgun blast had torn the animal in half. Blood streaked the rock and grass where the mortally wounded animal had tried in vain to drag itself to the dead man in the water. A swarm of flies buzzed around the dog's shining entrails and the man's open eyes. Neither had been dead very long.

"Van Zandt," Trap said in a tight whisper.

Clay scanned the waterline, his eyes following his pistol. "Yeah, I recognize that mean critter layin' dead beside him. Glad I don't have to fret over him anymore. I reckon that means Drum's lurkin' around here somewhere."

Trap nodded, walking along the river's edge in search of tracks. "Van Zandt got it with a shotgun. Maggie only had the Winchester."

"Drum killed his own man?"

"Here." Trap found the cloudy boot prints in the slow-moving water where Drum had crossed. He swung back on his horse and splashed across, keeping his eyes on the water. "Clay," he said without looking up. "I'd be much obliged if you'd keep your eyes peeled and see that I don't get shot while I figure out where Maggie went."

Madsen gave a curt nod. "I'm hurt you thought I'd do

anything else. Be happy to kill that son of a bitch Drum for you too."

"If he's harmed Maggie, there won't be anything of him left for you to kill."

Two hundred yards downriver, past the swimming hole, they heard voices coming through the trees. Trap dismounted and motioned silently for Clay to follow suit. The boys tied their horses and crept forward on foot.

The evening was already warm, but Trap's mind burned at the thought of any harm coming to Maggie. All he'd wanted to do over the last few months, all he'd thought about was to find and protect her. Now, he was afraid he'd failed.

Dwarf willows and salt cedar grew thick along the sandy bank. Drum's deep voice filtered through the course foliage.

" . . . you really believed you could get away from me, you filthy little whore? Well, let me tell you something. When a woman makes eyes at me the way you did, I know what she wants. . . ." His voice was strained and breathy.

Maggie screamed.

"Go on and yell your fool head off." Drum laughed manically. "There's nobody out here to save you."

Trap had heard enough. He crashed through the trees with Clay tight on his heels. What he saw was like a kick to his stomach.

Maggie's shirt hung from her shoulders. Drum knelt on top of her, pinning both arms up above her head with a powerful left hand. His right gripped cruelly at her face, pinching her cheeks into a pitiful grimace.

Her screams came out in a muffled groan and she arched her back, trying to throw him off. He was a big man and as feisty as she was, Maggie was no match for him in strength. Blood oozed from a jagged bite wound on her neck. The ground was plowed around them. Her bare feet bled from her kicks and struggles.

Trap felt Clay bring up the pistol on his left. He raised a hand to stop him. "Don't want you to have to live with this one," he heard himself say.

Trap's bone-handled knife hissed from the sheath and he flew at Drum with a fury he'd never known. A brutal kick to the big man's ribs sent him flying off Maggie with a *whoof* as the air left his lungs. Trap heard bones crack, but Drum lashed out with a powerful hand and swiped him off his feet. Buoyed by rage, the boy rolled quickly and was on his feet in an instant.

Maggie ripped away the remainder of her torn blouse and moved in with him, shoulder-to-shoulder. Blood from her nose and the wound at her neck covered her heaving chest. A blade gleamed in her hand.

"Good Lord," Clay gasped.

Drum lay on his side, panting and clutching his injured ribs. His eyes grew wide when he saw the knives. He shot a glance at the shotgun ten feet away, then raised a hand to ward off the attack, trying to push himself to his knees.

It was too late.

Trap and Maggie fell on him as one, a flash of steel, blood, and teeth—a flurry of black hair, bronze skin, and righteous indignation.

It was over as fast as it had begun.

"Van Zandt wanted him to share me. Drum didn't feel like sharing." Maggie stooped to clean her knife and hands in the river. "I guess I need another bath."

Trap stood beside her. They were both covered in blood. "Are you all right?" he asked. His voice was distant in his head, as if it were coming from someone else's mouth.

Maggie used a bit of her torn shirt to dab some blood out of his eye. It didn't appear to bother her that she was naked from the waist up. "He never got to do anything but bite me." She touched the same piece of cloth to the crescent-shaped wound below her ear. "I hid in the trees as long as I could. I knew you would make it back in time." Her eyes sparkled in the low light. Her bare shoulders trembled, but she didn't cry.

Clay Madsen, who talked about naked women more than any single thing in the world, took off his own shirt and held it out to Maggie. "You need this more than I do, Maggie darlin'," he whispered gently. For all his talk, he kept his eyes pointed at the ground. He shook his head, his face a little on the pale side. "You two beat all. I seen of some strange ways of consummatin' a relationship in my short years, but I ain't never even heard of anything quite so unifyin' as two lovebirds fighting side by side to hack a common enemy to pieces."

CHAPTER 25

1910
Idaho

The train chugged over Lookout Pass a little before noon, belching thick clouds of smoke and steam, a long black snake against a white backdrop. It lumbered slowly through the deep snow, and the engineer made frequent stops to clear downed trees or heavy drifts in the narrow canyons.

The passengers were used to such stops and starts, so when gears ground and wheels squealed against wet tracks and they began to slow, hardly anyone gave it a second thought.

"We oughta be getting into Mullan anytime," Clay said. His eyes sparkled with the memories of their conversation. "I could use a little stretch. How about . . ."

The throaty boom outside the train cut him short. Trap shot a worried look at Clay, then at his wife.

"Was that what I think I was?" Hanna's green eyes went wide.

Trap stood, his hand on Maggie's shoulder. "Let's move away from the window until we figure out what's going on out there." He took a black pistol from under his coat and gave it to Maggie. "We'll be right back."

Clay gave Hanna a peck on the nose. "Stay with Maggie."

* * *

They met the red-faced conductor stepping back inside the door.

"What's the news?" Clay put a hand up to stop the blustering man. "Somebody get shot?"

"Not as of yet." The beefy conductor's face glowed red, more from a brush with death than the cold. His chin quivered a little as if he might start to sob at any moment. "There's a mob of men out there threatening to shoot anyone who gets off the train." He took his hat off and ran a hand over a sweating scalp. "This has been one hell of a day: a phantom passenger, that high-toned Baker woman, and now I almost get my head blown off. I don't get paid enough for all this."

"Did they give you a reason?" Trap needed answers, not a bunch of talk about the conductor's bad day at work.

The man scoffed. "Said they had orders to keep us on the train to protect the good citizens of Idaho." He scuttled past in the narrow hallway, eager to get the train moving again.

Clay put his hand on the door handle and shot a grin at Trap. "I was lookin' forward to wettin' my whistle in Mullan. Shall we see what's eatin' these folks?"

"Move slow so they don't get antsy with that scattergun," Trap said. "I don't like the idea of buryin' two friends on one trip."

"You always were the brains of this outfit," Clay said as he pushed open the door.

A cold blast of air hit them full in the face. A bellowing order followed.

"We mean business," a gruff voice shouted from the tree line. "I'll cut down the first man who steps off that train."

Clay held both hands out the door. "We're not armed."

"I don't give a ding-dong damn."

Clay turned to Trap and shrugged. "Never heard that one before." He shouted back out the door. "You want to tell us what's got into you folks? Mullan used to be a right hospitable place."

"We got orders from the United States marshal to keep all of you on that train. Deputized me over the phone, he did." The voice was pinched, as if the speaker had a hand caught in a vise.

"The marshal?" Trap began to chew the inside of his cheek, wondering how Blake might fit into all this.

"That's right. So you best stay on that train just like I tell you and nobody'll get hurt."

"You allowed to tell us why?" Clay always sounded like he was in charge—mainly because he believed he always was.

A buzzing silence followed while the men at the tree line conferred with each other. Finally, the leader spoke up again. "We're supposed to keep you on this train until a deputy gets here from Montana this evenin'. Somebody on your train has the smallpox."

"Smallpox?" Clay pushed the door open and put his foot on the top step. "Do I look like I have smallpox?"

The roar of a shotgun split the cold air. A splattering of snow kicked up on the ground twenty feet away.

Clay moved back in the doorway beside Trap. "Whoa, whoa, whoa, I'm not gettin' off the train."

He slammed the door shut behind him.

"Good thing he fired another warning shot." Trap smirked and let out a tense sigh.

"I don't believe it was a warnin'." Clay winked. "I reckon that ol' boy just didn't know the shotgun would shoot so low at that distance. You think Blake is the one comin'?"

"A deputy from Montana . . ." Trap mused. "The chances are good. I guess we'll have to wait and see. I want to get back to Maggie as quick as we can." Waiting was something Trap was never good at.

"Know what you mean," Clay whispered, digesting the news. "I should check on Hanna."

"A word with you, sir!" a low voice said from the wood-paneled aisle behind them.

"Me?" Trap said, turning. He relaxed his shoulders, ready to block a punch.

A broad man with wire glasses and a thick neck stood square in the middle of their path. The sleeves on his white shirt were rolled up to reveal thick forearms and huge hands. "No, not you. I'll deal with your issue later. I'm looking to settle with this man here." He nodded his balding head at Madsen.

"Are you Mr. Baker, the postmaster of Dillon, Montana?" Clay moved up beside Trap, shouldering in front of him slightly.

"I am."

"Well, sir, that's impressive, a real live, honest-to-goodness postmaster." Clay fawned, bringing both hands up to his face as if he was smitten with a bad case of puppy love. "Now . . ." Madsen's face grew dark. He let his hands fall to his side. "We have business elsewhere and you're in our way. I'll ask you once to step aside. I hope you heard me because I said once."

Baker's eyes flamed. He wasn't going anywhere. "You, sir, were extremely ungentlemanly toward my . . ."

Clay's right hand shot out and connected with Baker's nose. The man's glasses shattered, then swung from one ear. Blood covered his lips and chin. He swayed for a moment, blinking, then pitched across the back of a padded bench.

"Now, that's what I wanted to do to his wife." Clay smirked. He rubbed the back of his hand, grimacing when he touched his knuckle. "Damn, those postmasters sure have hard faces in Dillon, Montana."

Sidney, the waiter brought four coffees and set them on the table. Jittery about the prospect of smallpox, but resigned to a long wait, the passengers were circumspect. Every seat in the dining car was full, but conversations were hushed and tense. Birdie was nowhere to be seen.

"Don't you think Mr. Baker will come for you again?" Hanna said. She was sitting beside Clay now and Trap was next to Maggie.

"I hope so." Clay grinned. "Hate to leave anything unfinished. Trap and I were in a hurry to get back to you beautiful womenfolk so I didn't have time to do things proper."

Trap lifted his coffee, eager to change the subject.

"Here's to Hezekiah Roman, the best captain a man could have."

Clay clinked his cup against Trap's. "You got that right, partner."

"So you joined the Army and got assigned to Roman's Scout Trackers after you made it to Arizona?"

"Not exactly." Clay shot a knowing glance at Trap. "We didn't meet up with him for sometime—and the Scout Trackers didn't even exist before us. We were the first."

Hanna peered across her cup at Maggie as she took a sip. "But you and Trap got married as soon as you got to Fort Apache?"

"Not for a while," Maggie said. "And Camp Apache wasn't even a fort yet. It was still just a pile of buildings and squad huts."

"This is all so fascinating. Here you are taking your captain—your dear friend—back to his wife in Arizona to be buried—that's an extraordinary friendship."

"Ky Roman was an extraordinary man," Maggie sighed. "When Trap went out under his command, I knew things would be all right."

"I should write down all those stories you told me." Hanna leaned her head against Clay's shoulder and sighed. "A half-Apache tracker, his beautiful Nez Percé wife, a stalwart Mormon captain, and a handsome Texan who flirts with everything in petticoats . . ."

Clay let the comment about his past indiscretions slide. "It was a moment in time, Hanna, darlin'. When the Scout Trackers were up and runnin', we were a force to be reckoned with . . . and the force behind us was Captain Hezekiah Roman."

"Tell me more," Hanna said.

Trap shrugged. "I'll leave the storytellin' to Clay. He's got a way of making tales considerably more interesting than they really were."

Hanna snuggled down in her shawl, like a child getting tucked in for her nightly bedtime story. "I've read my last good book," she said. "What else is there to do on such a chilly afternoon?"

Clay grinned down at her through narrow, wolfish eyes. "I can think of a thing of two."

"You hush," she said. "Now, go ahead and start telling. I'm waiting. . . ."

PART TWO

CHAPTER 26

October 1878
Camp Apache, Arizona

When they reached the camp, the three adventurers decided it would be better to leave out any mention of Tobias Drum. They spoke only vaguely about Pilar de la Cruz and the bandits, but Trap could tell his mother viewed him differently. She seemed to know he'd moved to another level in his life, to sense that he'd spilled blood.

The fact that he'd survived months on the trail, tracking Maggie all the way to Arizona, wasn't quite enough to prove to the O'Shannons that their only son was old enough to get married. Though it was not uncommon for girls Maggie's age to tie the knot, the reverend insisted the two lovebirds wait a year at the very least.

Unwilling to throw Maggie to the mercy of the Army, the reverend and Hummingbird informally adopted the girl and let her live in the other half of their dog-run cabin beside the crude log school. He'd clasped his hands behind his back as he made the pronouncement.

Trap and Clay were able to secure jobs working as packers and mule handlers for the Army's campaign against renegade Apache. Clay was a talker, but he was a hard worker as well. The two were well liked by their superiors, and life around the Camp Apache, though full of sweat and long hours, was better than bearable.

"I've got to draw a new pair of gloves," Madsen allowed one evening on the way to check on a string of new shave-tail mules. "These old ones are about rotted through with sweat." As junior teamsters on the mule crew, Clay and Trap invariably drew the short straw when it came to work details. Breaking a rank mule was smack at the bottom of everybody's list of enjoyable things to do.

In keeping with post orders, both boys led their horses rather than riding them through the dusty parade ground. It was a sore spot with Clay, who considered it demeaning to have to walk anywhere he could ride. He squinted at the low orange sun and used a sweaty bandanna to wipe the grime and dust off the back of his neck. "King James is likely still puttering around in his shack. I bet he'd let me have a new pair gloves if I took him some whiskey. We have to go by there anyway to get to the mules."

Sergeant Riley James, King James to those who dealt with him, was the quartermaster in Camp Apache. A grizzled and bent man in his early fifties, he appeared as old as dirt to the sixteen-year-old boys. In charge of uniform and equipment issue, King James held the ultimate power of comfort over men in employ of the Army. Uniforms only came in three sizes: small, medium, and large—and the large sizes went quickly. Though cavalry soldiers were normally chosen for their small build, there were plenty of hefty troopers. If offered a tot of whiskey, the king could usually be counted on to turn up at least one pair of large trousers. For a little more, he'd search until he found a large tunic hiding among his stores.

His power alone was enough for the men to dub him King, but the real reason everyone, including his old friend General Crook, called him King James was because of the way he spoke. A whack on the noggin from an Apache war club had addled his brain, and though he still had a head for numbers, everything he said came out of his whiskered mouth like a verse from the Good Book. He did his job, but everyone knew Crook had asked his subsequent replacements in Arizona to look after him as an act of kindness for his previous loyalty in battle.

A huge padlock hung open on the hasp at the front door to King James's adobe storehouse. Both boys removed their hats—a covered head could bring forth an entire barn-load of damnation and wrath—and stepped into the dim interior. The smell of oiled paper and mothballs hung heavy in the musty air. A wooden counter ran the length of the place, separating the bulk of the stores from the narrow lobby area out front. On busy days the king opened both front doors so troopers could come in one entry for issue and go out the other. Today, only one door stood open.

Trap waited just inside while Clay stood at the counter and cleared his throat. Wax-paper bundles, piled almost to the rafters, lined the back walls. Wooden crates of varying sizes marked "U.S." in bold black lettering were stacked to the ceiling. For a soldier, it was like a candy store. Many of the items would bring a tidy sum if sold on the civilian market, and thus were kept under lock and key. The quartermaster was nowhere to be found.

"Odd he left and didn't lock up," Clay muttered. "Sergeant James is particular about his kingdom."

There was a bundle of leather gloves tied with twine at the far end of the counter, but it didn't occur to either boy to take anything without the king there to issue it. The wrath of King James would only bring the wrath of the iron-fisted Colonel Branchflower—and no man in his right mind wanted to risk that.

"Maybe somebody already brought him some whiskey and he went to enjoy it while he watched the sunset.

It was common knowledge that James often drank a little on the job, but he waited until sundown to get really drunk. Trap suspected the man lived with a powerful headache from his injuries and used the whiskey to dull the pain.

"I reckon my poor old paws can get by another day with the rags I got now," Clay muttered. "Expect we better lock up as we go, in case he don't come back tonight."

Trap gave a grunting nod.

Two of the new shavetail mules were branded as incorrigible the day after they jogged grudgingly into Camp Apache. The big red animals had nearly kicked a young private's head off when he got too close during Call to Feed. Had the mules been of lesser quality, the chief packer, Jose Morales, said he would have run the lot of them over the rim of the canyon to drown in the White River. As it was, the two culprits, along with three other white-eyed beasts, had been quarantined from the gentler stock and placed in a stout cedar corral out behind the quartermaster's shack for Clay to work in the cool of the evening.

Trap could tell the animals were gone as soon as he rounded the corner of the long adobe building. There's a forlorn and lonely look about an empty corral, even from a hundred yards away. No guards were in sight and the double corral gates yawned open toward the far-off hills.

A brooding line of gray-black thunderheads boiled on the horizon. The warm, earthy aroma of a distant rain mixed with the ever-present odor of cavalry horses and hung on the stiffening breeze.

A jumble of tracks scratched the dust around the corral. Trap counted two distinct pair of flat-toed moccasin prints and an equal number of horses. He was easily able to pick out the slimmer, more U-shaped tracks of the Army mules, all of which were yet unshod because of their foul tempers and snakelike speed when it came to dealing with shoers.

"Renegades," Clay hissed under his breath. The young Texan's attempt at a mustache finally had a good crop of brown whiskers cultivated on his upper lip. He'd taken to toying with the end of his new accessory when he was deep in thought. "They must have snuck in here while the sentry was off on some kind of frolic. There'll be hell to pay when Colonel Branchflower finds out about this. Makes me glad I'm just a lowly civilian."

"The Army hangs civilians too," Trap said under his breath.

Clay shuddered. "You always do come up with words to comfort me."

Trap studied the rocky line of tree-topped mesas in the

direction of the tracks. Dark clouds loomed closer by the moment. In a short time, all sign would be as gone as the mules, washed away in the rain.

A voice from behind the loafing shed snapped him out of his thoughts and sent Madsen's hand to his pistol.

"Verily," the wobbly voice proclaimed. "The wrath of the Lord will surely come upon one Private Penny for abandoning his post to chase strong drink and all manner of abominations."

Clay let his gun hand relax and grinned. "I can't believe they didn't finish off the old fool."

"I hear your words, my sons," King James called from around the shed. "Come hither while I bear witness of what terrible deeds have come to pass."

Trap sighed. "Most Indians look at crazy folks like they got a little better chance at communing with the spirits."

"Lucky for Sergeant James he's as numb in the head as they get."

King James leaned against the stack-pole wall of the loafing shed. He was bound hand and foot with frayed bits of hay twine. Flecks of straw mingled with his gray beard. Dirt covered his normally impeccable uniform. In ornate Biblical detail he explained that he'd heard a commotion coming from the mule pen. Worrying that Private Penny, the sentry on duty, had gotten too close to one of the rank mules, he'd gone to check on him and received a club to the head for his troubles.

"Lo, they have fled with the wretched beasts, fled I say." His voice rose in pitch and timbre. "Sound the trump and shout from the rooftops, heathens are among the tents."

Trap unfolded his jackknife and bent to cut the old man free. "Sergeant," he said. "Begging your pardon, but can you walk?"

"Yea, I say, verily I say, it would be easier for a camel to pass through the eye of a needle than for any damned Apache to rob me of my power to ambulate."

Trap shot an entertained looked at Clay, then turned back to Sergeant James. "Would you be so kind as to go back and sound the general alarm? That storm is coming in fast.

If we don't take up the trail now, we'll lose the stock for certain. Clay and me will get right on it. You send reinforcements out as soon as you can."

"Yea, ask and ye shall receive, knock and the very same shall come to pass," King James decreed with a wobbly head.

"Does that mean you'll get us some help?" Clay raised a wary eyebrow. He was losing patience fast.

"Yea." The man groaned up on bent knees. He grabbed Trap's hand with gnarled fingers and pulled himself the rest of the way to his feet. "It doth."

At first, the tracks were easy to follow—down the brushy slope, along the White River, and then back south down a narrow canyon. The spot where the renegades forded was plainly visible, and Trap was able to keep the speed up for almost two hours while Clay kept his eyes on the surrounding trees and rocks, watching for signs of the mule thieves with weapons.

The air crackled with the excitement of hot pursuit. Long hours on the trail together had taught them to anticipate each other's movements. Both had learned enough of life to know that what they were doing was extremely dangerous. But neither considered turning back. The trail was before them, so they took it.

The advancing storm pushed columns of wind before it, sending twirling dust devils through the piñons and scrub juniper.

Evergreen trees gave way to sandstone and cactus about the time the first large drops of rain plopped against the brim of Trap's hat.

"Ashamed we don't have a bugle with us so we could blow Call to Feed. I bet them mules would come runnin' back to their oats no matter how mean they are." Clay slumped in the saddle, both hands resting across the horn,

"I don't know how to play the bugle," Trap said. He studied a pinched draw almost choked closed by a tumbled pile of gray rock. "And unless you been practicin' while I wasn't looking, you don't know how either."

Clay smiled. "That's the trouble with you, O'Shannon. You're too damned practical." He followed Trap's gaze to a tower of sandstone, sculpted over time by wind and water. "You think they went up there?"

"I do," Trap said over a rising wind. He had to squint against the blowing dust and ducked his head to keep his hat from blowing off. "Those mules are mean as snakes, right?"

Clay nodded. "I guess I seen meaner down home."

To Clay's way of thinking everything was meaner, prettier, or hotter in Texas. "Well, if they gave us trouble, they're sure to do likewise to these Apaches. I only count two sets of tracks. Five vicious mules can make a handful of trouble for two of anybody—even renegade Indians. The tracks go every which way here, like the mules pitched a huge fit. I'm betting the thieves won't go much further before they hide the stock and go for help—particularly with this storm coming in."

It was a long speech for Trap.

"Well, sir." Clay nodded at the rocks while he held his hat on against a howling wind. "If I was going to hide a passel of sorry mules, I guess that's as good a place as any." The Texan snugged his hat down over his head and pulled the Sharps out of its scabbard. "We best keep a sharp eye peeled. If the mules didn't kill 'em, them boogers are likely to be holed up in there. Best I let Clarice out to play."

Trap grinned. "That's why I brought you along."

CHAPTER 27

Madsen hung his head in mock disappointment when they found the mules bunched in a piled-brush corral and no Apaches around to fight. He returned Clarice to her rifle boot and untied his lariat to build a catch loop for the brawny red boss mule.

Rain pelted the rock with a fury now, splattering off every surface. It seemed to come just as hard from the ground as it did from above. Lightning periodically forked across the gray sky. Thunder cracked, echoing through the sandstone hills, dark red now from the sudden rain.

The mules, still tied together with short lengths of rope between halter and tail, milled and bunched against the rock face at the far end of the thorny enclosure. Steam rose from their wet backs and disappeared in the chilling rain. The whites of their eyes rolled back and they stomped their feet nervously at each clap of thunder. Trap had watched one of these mules nearly bite the head off a stable hand. He'd narrowly missed getting his own skull kicked in on more than one occasion. It was a marvel that anyone, even an Apache warrior, had been able to even get near them, much less tie anything to their tails.

Clay's lariat settled over the neck of a snorting beast as Al Seiber, chief of scouts, splashed up the little canyon on a copper sorrel. A squad of mounted troopers from C company followed a hundred yards to the rear, flankers out as far as they could get in the narrow confines of the canyon.

Clay took a dally around his saddle horn and came as close to attention as Trap ever saw him. The strong-jawed chief of scouts was one of the few people who caused Madsen to go quiet. Trap didn't ever mention it, but he was pretty certain Clay hadn't even considered growing a mustache until his met his new mentor.

Seiber was an affable man, with a direct manner that made him either feared or admired. His Apache scouts followed him faithfully and trusted him as they did one another. "I always tell 'em the truth," he would often say. "When I tell an Apache, 'If you do thus and such, I'll kill you,' and he does it, well, then, he knows I'll keep my word, because he's seen me do it before. If I promise one I'll help him, he knows he can count on that too, just as sure as the other."

The capable frontiersman lived an honest life out in the open and his motives lived out there too for everyone to see. Seiber reined his Roman-nosed gelding to a sliding stop and pulled his oilskin tighter around his neck to ward off the pelting rain.

"Good work, boys," he shouted above the squall. He eyed the brooding herd of mules with a jaundiced gaze. "Don't know whether you saved the Army some money by recovering stolen stock or cost it in the way of medical bills for the damage these cursed animals are bound to inflict." The rain began to ease as quickly as it started. Seiber took a kerchief from the crown of his wide-brimmed hat and wiped rainwater off his face and high forehead. He took great care to smooth his thick mustache before he replaced the hat.

"Still," he continued. "We can't have the hostiles stealin' our animals, no matter how wicked the beasts are. Did you boys catch sight of the renegades? It took some cojones for sure—you almost have to admire 'em."

"No, sir," Trap said.

Seiber rubbed a strong jaw in thought. "I got me a little problem, boys."

Trap watched as the ramrod-straight lieutenant in charge of C Company broke away from his men and picked his way through the rocks toward them.

"My problem is thus," the chief of scouts continued. "Victorio and that spooky sister of his are causin' quite a stir since they slipped away. I'm to guide a company of troops east to join forces with men from Grant and see if we can't catch the wily son of a bitch."

The tall lieutenant dismounted and checked his cinch while Seiber continued with his explanation. The rain had stopped, but a bitter wind blew down the mountain like an omen of things to come.

"To be honest," Seiber said, "I didn't have a lot of faith that you boys would be able to hold the trail with the rain and all. I should have brought a couple of the White Mountain scouts with me."

The lieutenant removed a gauntlet and stepped forward to shake Trap's hand and then Clay's hand in turn. Gray eyes peered over a slightly hooked nose. There was a hint of honest weariness about his angular face, as if he carried the burden of the world on his shoulders.

"Hezekiah Roman," he said, leaving off his rank since he was speaking to civilians. It didn't matter. Though he was no more than five or six years older than Trap, Roman had a dignified air about him that left no doubt about who was in charge. Even Seiber took note of the young officer's quiet, yet piercing voice.

"I wonder if you men would feel comfortable tracking for my column while we go after these renegades." He scanned the surrounding mesas with a gaze so flint-hard, it looked as though he might set fire to every tree. "It was a bold move to come right onto the compound like that— a move that can't go unpunished."

Trap shot a glance at Clay, who looked at him and shrugged.

Seiber cleared his throat. "They're young, sir—young but capable. I've been watching them and I've not seen many of my Apache scouts that can track as good as young O'Shannon here. Both know their way around a horse. And if you can get past his constant jabbering, Madsen is as stalwart a hand on the trail as any man in the Army. He's got an eye like a hawk and can use that fancy long gun of his to shoot the heads off turkeys for the camp pot at two hundred paces."

Trap hated to admit it, but the prospect of tracking the mule thieves appealed to him. He could see by the glint in Clay's eyes he felt the same way. The adventure would be a welcome change to the drudgery of garrison life even if it did mean time away from Maggie. Under the watchful eye of the Reverend O'Shannon, the two hardly got to spend any time alone together anyway.

"We'll do our best for you, Lieutenant Roman." Trap held out his hand to shake again. It seemed to be the proper thing to do since an agreement had been reached.

"Excellent," Roman said. He remounted immediately and nodded up the canyon. It was apparent that he was not the sort to sit around and contemplate things once a decision was made. He turned and spoke over his shoulder to a gaunt sergeant who'd ridden up behind him. "Sergeant Martini, have a detail of two men fall out and take that string of mules from Mr. Madsen and see them back to the camp. The rest of us will take up the trail."

"Aye, sir," the sallow sergeant said in a clipped Italian accent. "Fitzsimmons, Wallace, fall out for detail!" His barked orders belied his slender build.

"You'll need supplies, men," Roman said, turning matter-of-factly back to Trap and Clay. "I took the liberty of packing you each a kit when Sergeant James came in with the news. Mr. Webber." Roman didn't so much raise his voice as he put more energy into it. A redheaded trooper riding a massive bay gelding trotted up from the ranks.

The lieutenant dipped his head at the trooper. "Private Webber will see that you have your gear. From this point on, I'd suggest neither of you leave the camp without at least enough supplies to spend the night. It's been my experience that things seldom go as planned."

* * *

Trap O'Shannon knew how to track, but the idea of having a column of twenty armed soldiers behind him was a big responsibility and it put him a little on edge.

The steady rain had washed away almost all sign of the renegades. For the first two hours, Trap went on little more than instinct and the fact that there were very few directions meant anyone could take a horse in the jagged confines of the red rock canyon. As the sandstone walls began to fan out, the options for travel increased and the tension mounted inside the young tracker.

He moved slowly, leading his little black gelding, stooping now and then to study a bit of compressed gravel or crushed vegetation. Often, he had little more to go on than a flake of earth that looked out of place for its surroundings or the telltale scuff a hoof might leave behind on wet rock. Always, he was aware of the soldiers behind him, pressing him. The rattle of bits and groan of horses added to his stress.

Luckily, the rain had not come as hard on the far side of the mountains. Trap was relieved to find the faint tracks of unshod horses weaving in and out between the pungent creosote bushes and chaparral. The ground softened and the trail became easier to follow just before sundown.

"We'll stop up there by that little creek and rest the horses," Roman said, pointing with his gauntlet at a line of scrubby salt cedars.

"Beggin' your pardon, Lieutenant," Clay said, drawing rein beside the officer. "But these animals look mighty near worn out and we haven't been gone more than a few hours."

Trap had been so focused on the trail he hadn't noticed how poor and stumble-footed most of the Army mounts were. Roman's was in good flesh, as was Private Webber's bay and a handful of others, but by and large the horses were winded and hollow-eyed.

Lieutenant Roman rested both hands on the smooth pommel of his McClellan saddle. "Yes, Mr. Madsen, I'm afraid they are. All the best stock went out after Victorio, along with Mr. Seiber and Captain Rollins' company. I'm afraid bringing in a couple of renegade mule thieves didn't rate high on the colonel's priorities when it came to doling out supplies and horseflesh."

Fifty yards from the creek, Trap pulled up short and scanned the darkening horizon. He slid off his horse and studied the mass of tracks before him in the dust. At least ten new riders had joined the two renegades, maybe as many as fifteen.

It was getting too dark to see well, but Trap could tell the new horses were shod, so if they were Indians they were riding stolen ponies.

Still, something nagged at Trap as he studied the tracks in the long shadows of waning light. He nodded his head slowly when he'd figured it out.

Trap looked up at Roman as the young officer rode up along side him.

"Sir." Trap gazed into the gathering darkness and shivered in spite of himself. "Someone else is chasing the Apaches. Somebody besides us."

"Chasing, you say?" Roman raised an eyebrow.

"Yes, sir. The two that took our mules have picked up their pace some. They spin every now and again to catch a look behind them. The new tracks never look back, and they're moving at a pretty good clip."

"Another cavalry unit?" Clay smoothed his fledgling mustache.

"Could be," Roman said.

Trap put a hand flat on the ground, feeling the tracks. "I don't think so, sir. No rank and file to this group. Whoever it is, they ride as a bunch, not a disciplined column."

A drawn look spread over Roman's weary face. "That's what I was afraid of," he whispered. His breath clouded in front of him in the cold night air. "This is troublesome," he said, as much to himself as anyone else. "Extremely troublesome."

He didn't say why.

Lieutenant Roman chose the only seven men with fit horses to ride before dawn, Private Webber and Sergeant

Martini among them. "We need to make good speed, men," he said as the group mounted up in the gray darkness. He was not a man to explain himself any more than that.

The remaining horses appeared unable to follow at any speed, and though he was loath to split his forces, Roman left thirteen men behind to pick their way back to Camp Apache as their mounts were able.

The trail was a bold one, with at least a dozen shod horses producing a considerable amount of sign. Trap had no trouble following it even in the scant light of false dawn.

When the sun was still a faint orange wafer on the knife edge of the eastern horizon, Trap reined in his horse and motioned for the others to stop. Crows circled above a distant pueblo, whirling black dots against a gunmetal sky. Their grating caws added to the chill on morning air and sent a shiver up the young tracker's spine.

"Can you smell it, Lieutenant?" Private Webber stood in the stirrups and inclined his read head toward the handful of drab adobe buildings and rough goat pens.

"Keep to your column, Mr. Webber," Roman said without looking back.

"Yessir." The private lifted his reins and moved his gelding back two steps into the ranks.

"Smell what?" Clay turned in the saddle from his spot beside Trap. "I don't smell anything but dirt and wind."

Roman rode forward and motioned for the column to follow with a flick of his hand. "Death, Mr. Madsen," he said over his shoulder. "That smell on the wind is the smell of death."

CHAPTER 28

Huge flies crowded around the exposed white skull of a butchered Mexican goatherd at the outskirts of the little town. A shotgun blast to the chest had torn half of his slight body away.

The tracks showed how a group of mounted men had swept through the village like a bad storm. A dozen other bodies littered the street, each mutilated and scalped like the goatherd. Three women lay clumped together in the threshold of a tiny pink church. Bullet holes riddled the adobe walls like pockmarks where the women had been cut down, seeking refuge in the only sanctuary they knew.

The troopers dismounted and led their skittish mounts through the grizzly scene, checking for survivors. Trap knew there wouldn't be any.

"Those two Apaches we're after didn't do all this," Trap said in a husky voice, full of disgust.

Lieutenant Roman took a deep breath and looked south toward the Black River. "No, Mr. O'Shannon" he whispered. "This is the work of scalp hunters. The Apache kills his share of Mexicans, mind you—and in some awful ways. . . ." Roman closed his gray eyes, remembering. When he opened them again, he moved off to survey the rest of the scene.

"The Mexican government still pays quite a few pesos for Apache scalps," Johannes Webber said. His voice was quiet but stoic, as if he was reading all this from a book and not living in the middle of it. He flipped his gelding's reins around a broken fence rail. "It was big business back in the forties and fifties. Lots of folks came down to collect a quick fortune. Now, only Mexican citizens can collect the bounty, but that doesn't stop the determined ones. Hard to tell the difference between an Apache scalp and a peon goatherd's."

The red-haired trooper toed at the body of an elderly woman. "They took both her ears. That's the only way the Mexican government can be sure the scalp hunters aren't cheating them—you know, trying to get two for one."

"Oh, no, no, no . . ." Clay Madsen's voice drifted soft and piteous from a slumped adobe shack on the sad little street. He appeared a moment later, framed in the black backdrop of an open doorway. The lifeless body of a girl in her teens was draped across his arms. Slender arms and legs hung in the air. Her face and bare chest were covered with blood. A modest peasant dress was ripped to tattered rags. Her scalp, along with both of her ears, had been peeled away.

Flecks of vomit dripped from Madsen's chin. He shook his head solemnly and held the dead girl up to Roman. "Who would do such a thing, Lieutenant? She ain't no older than I am."

Fire burned in the back of Trap's throat and he thought of Maggie. Whenever he worried, his thoughts always turned to her.

"Sergeant Martini," Roman said. His voice was clipped and quiet.

"Aye, sir." Martini stepped forward leading his mount.

"Get the men to move these bodies into the pueblos where the birds and coyotes can't get them."

"Yes, Lieutenant." Martini turned to carry out his orders.

"Sergeant," Roman said, removing his hat. "One more thing; you're Catholic, I believe."

Martini turned back on his heels. "I am at that, sir."

"Very good." Roman's voice was little more than a whisper. "I imagine most of these people were as well. Please see to whatever it is good Catholics need at times like this. We'll come back and bury them after we tend to our more pressing matters." He returned the hat to his head and stepped forward to put a hand on Madsen's shoulder.

Tears streamed down the boy's cheeks. "I'm sorry to be such a bawl-baby, Lieutenant Roman." Clay set the dead girl gently at his feet. He sniffed and wiped his face with the back of his sleeve. "I won't let it happen again."

"You're a strong one, Mr. Madsen, chock-full of wit and humor. I know, I've watched you." Roman looked wistfully at the ground. "This world is full of wicked men—and what these wicked men chiefly lack is heart. I've seen a bundle of evil men who were chock-full of bravery, but I've never seen one of them cry for anyone but himself. In my book, a man who'll weep for the soul of another is a man indeed."

Roman turned and started for the edge of town. "You two come with me," he said over his shoulder. "Mr. O'Shannon, can you find us the trail?"

Trap took off his hat and rubbed a hand through his hair. "The scalp hunters are all riding shod horses. There's fourteen or fifteen of them. Should be a simple trail to follow."

"Good," Roman said. "Our Apaches are most certainly heading back to their own people. The time to punish them for their thievery will have to wait. Our primary mission now is to save their lives."

CHAPTER 29

No matter how the O'Shannons saw it, Maggie already thought of Hummingbird as her mother-in-law and gave her all the respect and deference a daughter should. For the first time in two years, she found herself truly happy—even with Trap gone on frequent little forays with the Army. Just knowing he shared her feelings was enough to make her glow.

Though not as beautiful as the Wallowa, the mountains around Camp Apache held their own quiet splendor and enjoyed a pleasantly cool fall. A nice breeze blew through the canyon along the White River, and the hot-natured girl would often go sit on a rock below a twisted pine to think and feel the wind. While others layered on cloaks and woolen wraps of assorted sizes, Maggie stalked about the camp with nothing more than a light shawl and her feelings for Trap to keep her warm.

Maggie drew plenty of looks and smiles from the enlisted men when they were in garrison. Not so much because she was an Indian. Most of the Apache had been moved to San Carlos, but there were plenty around camp. Some worked as domestic help for the married soldiers. Most of the others were little more than beggars, dressed in rags and begging for their rations. Some of the Apache women were pretty, or would have been if given their freedom, but reservation life had taken its toll.

Star, a young woman only a few years Maggie's senior, worked as a housekeeper for the colonel's wife. She seemed happy enough, and often joked with Maggie when they bumped into one another around camp. Star stood out as one of the true beauties among her people, until her husband, a sullen, filthy man, accused her of infidelity and cut off the fleshy part of her nose. She disappeared from the camp shortly afterward and forced the colonel's wife to find a new maid.

After that, Maggie resolved to keep to herself and save her friendships for Trap.

Maggie's hair had always grown fast, and by October hung well below her shoulders. Sometimes, the way the soldiers looked at her made her smile. Other times, it put her on edge and she longed for Trap's quick return.

Apart from working around the modest school, Maggie had little to do but help Mrs. O'Shannon when she could. Trap's mother was a quiet woman, pensive and slow to speak, when she said anything at all, but she had a kind look in her deep brown eyes. There was no judgment in her words, as one might expect from a mother-in-law, and Maggie enjoyed their time together.

She especially liked shopping. Even the modest sutler's store at a remote post like Camp Apache had so many things to choose from, a girl like Maggie, who was used to a frugal life, could spend hours browsing at the buttons and fabric and letting her imagination run wild. The only trouble was, the Reverend O'Shannon enjoyed shopping with his wife as well, and Maggie couldn't quite tell how he felt about her.

Rather than acceptance from the man she considered her father-in-law, she felt a sort of quiet resignation to the fact that Trap had chosen to spend the rest of his life with her. He was always kind, but distant in all his communications. Hummingbird smiled and looked at her whenever he spoke, but never made any apology for his cool behavior. The poor man appeared to be exhausted by the mere act of living since he'd had to leave White Oak.

"I must speak to Mr. Sorenson about some socks," the

reverend said as they entered the long adobe-and-log store, one end of which sold spirits to the troops. His wife and Maggie both knew the talk about socks would be preceded and followed by a whiskey toddy to warm his bones. The store was not so large as to hide the fact that he was drinking, and he did not try. He just saw no reason to mention it out loud.

Hummingbird gave her husband a soft look and motioned Maggie toward the bolts of cloth. They'd spoken of making some new winter dresses. "I'll fill my list while you talk to him," Hummingbird said to the reverend, touching him on the hand as she always did when they parted ways. "Tell me if you think of anything else you need me to buy."

A copper cowbell clanked on the door behind them and a familiar voice cut the close air inside the building. Maggie had her back to the entrance and couldn't place it for a moment. When she did, her blood ran cold.

"Peter Grant!" James O'Shannon's face brightened and he took the new arrival by both shoulders. "What brings you to Arizona?"

The baby-faced lieutenant removed his hat and nodded politely to Mrs. O'Shannon. He smiled at Maggie and blushed. His entire face fluttered with nervous energy.

She tried to keep her eyes from darting back and forth, looking for a way to escape. His countenance held the same missionary zeal as when she'd seen him last. Except for the fact that his hands were not blackened with gunpowder from shooting her people, he looked exactly as he had the day they'd met almost a year before south of the Canadian border.

"How is your uncle these days?" Reverend O'Shannon clapped his hands together, genuinely pleased to see a familiar face in such a lonely place as Camp Apache, Arizona.

"He's well, thank you," Grant said. "He sends his regards and hopes you don't think ill of the council for sending you to this duty." The boy's words were guarded, as if he knew more than he said.

"We were pleased for the opportunity to come and

minister among my people," Hummingbird said, her interjection a little out of character.

James O'Shannon nodded in hearty agreement as if he was still attempting to convince himself. "That's right, that's right," he said. "This is a wonderful opportunity for Chuparosa and me both. And the Lord knows her people need help."

Lieutenant Grant had stopped listening to either O'Shannon and stared intently at Maggie. "The truth is, I went to White Oak a few weeks ago, hoping to look in on Miss Sundown."

Maggie swallowed and bit her bottom lip, trying to keep her face passive. Her head spun, her breath came in shallow gasps.

Cocking his head to one side like a disapproving father, Grant raised his eyebrows. "I found things in a shambles. A young Sioux boy named Big Horse or something or another was virtually running the school. Tall Horse, that's it. He was doing a fair job of it too.

"Mrs. Tally has undergone a complete nervous collapse. She can do little but cry, the poor old girl. She told me between sobs that you and Reverend Drum had both disappeared." He studied Maggie's reaction. "I'm relieved to find you safe, but left wondering what brought you all the way to Arizona. Have you got any notion of what happened to Reverend Drum?"

Maggie shot a glance at Mrs. O'Shannon in spite of herself. Her jaw felt loose, as it did before she got sick to her stomach. "I do not know what became of him," she whispered. She assumed what was left of his butchered body had been torn apart and devoured by coyotes, but she kept that thought to herself.

"Peter." James O'Shannon stepped in. "With all its other endeavors, surely the Army isn't going to concern itself about which Indian school Maggie attends. I can assure you, she won't run away from here."

Grant clenched his freckled jaw, unconvinced. "Reverend, I can assure *you*, the Army takes escape very seriously.

The last thing I want to see is for Maggie to be sent to a reservation or, worse yet, a prison."

"Prison?" Hummingbird scoffed and touched Grant lightly on the shoulder, as if he'd just told a joke. "That is funny. She's under the nose of the Army all day long here at Camp Apache. She's done nothing wrong but run away from a tyrant who, from the sound of things, has disappeared himself." Mrs. O'Shannon could be as protective as a mother bear when provoked. Her eyes suddenly blazed. She pulled Maggie closer with both hands.

Maggie knew no one at Camp Apache, not even Trap's parents, could really protect her if the Army—or more particularly Lieutenant Grant—decided she needed to be somewhere else. She was truly a prisoner of war. Her heart began to flutter in her chest. Her breath came in short gasps and she struggled to remain in control. She would have to run again.

"I've seen it before." The young lieutenant looked defiant. "There's a women's prison in New York with girls in it every bit as young as her. As long as she is a single girl with no one to claim her, she's too vulnerable to be wandering around the frontier."

"We've as good as adopted her," Hummingbird said. "I think of her as a daughter."

Grant stood resolute. It was apparent that he'd given this a lot of thought.

"If you wish to adopt an Indian child, you need to go through proper channels, Mrs. O'Shannon. I'm afraid I have no choice but to take her back."

Maggie moved back a step. She looked for a window, a door—a weapon to defend herself. If she couldn't find a weapon she'd use her teeth and nails.

"Peter." James O'Shannon took Grant by the arm and led him aside. "I can see that you harbor strong feelings for our sweet Maggie. She is a beautiful young woman and I admire your judgment. But now, I must tell you some things that will only break your tender heart. . . ." The two men stepped down the aisle beside a stack of wooden buckets until they were out of earshot.

Maggie steeled herself and made ready to flee out the front door. Hummingbird's calm, summer-breeze voice stopped her.

"He must truly love you, my child," she said.

Maggie gave a frustrated sigh. "I am not sure if what he feels could be called love."

Hummingbird chuckled and shook her head. "No, no, not Peter. I speak of Trap's father. James loves you more than he lets on—to do what he is doing now."

Maggie stopped in her tracks. "What do you mean? What is he doing?"

"Something I have only known him to do twice in all the years I've been with him." A proud smile crossed Hummingbird's face. "He is going to lie."

CHAPTER 30

"Their position is defensible, but they'll run out of water sooner or later," Lieutenant Roman said grimly, and passed a pair of binoculars to Trap.

Roman and his men lay on their bellies surveying the scene before them. A red sandstone monolith rose up from the desert floor. Boulders lined a lip a third of the way down from the top, and a few gnarled trees found purchase in the meager soil among the cliffs. The cutback area in the rock was well fortified and looked big enough to hide a sizable band of Apache if they had enough supplies.

From what Trap could tell, the scalp hunters had surprised the little band, mainly women and children, judging from the tracks, and sent them fleeing for the nearest refuge. Two boys in their teens, who'd stayed behind to give their little group time to escape, had been cut down like summer hay, scalped, and left to rot in the sun. Cedar campfires still smoldered in the sand, and much of their meager equipment lay strewn along the trail.

They couldn't have taken much with them. Trap doubted the whole group had more than a few gourds of water. Some barrel cactus grew up in the cracked rocks. They'd be able to squeeze some moisture out of them, but it wouldn't be much.

The scalp hunters had tied their horses out of rifle range and taken up positions in a sickle-shaped crescent at the lip of a shallow arroyo a hundred yards from the base of the mountain stronghold. Others ghosted in and out of the trees along a narrow creek. A scattering of boulders gave them plenty of cover.

One of the hunters must have gotten bold and underestimated the Apache marksmen. His body pitched forward in the sand. Through the binoculars, Trap could see blood running from a wound in his contorted face. After seeing what he'd seen at the little pueblo, Trap found it impossible to feel anything close to sorrow for the filthy man.

Potshots rang out intermittently from below. Their echoes whined across the desert on the cool evening breeze. In the rocks above, the Apache conserved their ammunition, waiting for someone else to get careless.

Another storm boiled gray-green to the north and threatened to bring snow or hail. If it rained, the Indians could gather water and hold out a day or two more, but as long as the scalp hunters held their positions, it was only a matter of time.

A curving line of trees at the western edge of the mountain base signified the presence of a small spring. The Apache might make a try for it in the dark of night, but Trap was certain it was guarded.

"Beggin' your pardon, Lieutenant." Private Webber took a turn with the glasses. His voice was muffled against his own fists. "But neither one of those little groups has any love lost for the United States Cavalry. We're liable to charge in there and get ourselves killed saving the day."

Trap shot a glance at Clay. He'd spent enough time around the military to know low-ranking enlisted men did not often speak so freely with an officer—even a young lieutenant. There was talk that Roman put up with it because Webber was a genius and could speak six or seven languages, including Apache and Spanish, as well as his native tongue.

Roman demanded respect from the ranks, but he seemed to give Webber a little more leeway than normal. Martini said it was because the lieutenant knew about the man's rough upbringing and wanted to give him an extra chance to make something of himself. Whatever the reason, Roman treated the young redhead like a wayward son who showed promise, if not forethought, in his actions.

"Surely you have heard the old adage," Roman patiently explained so everyone on the line could hear. "The enemy of my enemy must be my friend."

The troopers nodded in agreement up and down the line. Webber grinned and gave a little shrug before handing the binoculars back to his commanding officer.

Roman scooted back a few feet behind the cover of Joshua trees before pushing himself to a kneeling position. He used a dried stick to scratch a rough map of his plan in the alkali dirt. "Mr. Martini, we'll loop around from the west there and hit the main body of the scalp hunters from the arroyo in which they sit. Mr. Madsen, see that lone rock there above the scalp hunters and behind them?"

Clay nodded. "Yes, sir."

"Think you can take your fancy rifle up there and pick off the ones hiding in the trees, give us a little more of an edge until the Apaches join the fight?"

"Nothing would easier," Madsen said with a grim stare at the ruthless outlaws in the distance. Trap could see in the flash of his eyes he was remembering the mutilated girl back at the pueblo. "Or more of a pleasure."

"Very well," Roman said. There was a fire in his eyes. He was pleased to enter into battle against such evil men. "Mr. O'Shannon, you go with Madsen and watch his back. When we take the butchers at their flank, the Apache will see we've given them an advantage and join the attack. That's Juan Caesar's band up there—not a coward in the group, I assure you." The lieutenant looked over his small command. "We're not great in number, but we have surprise and right thinking on our side. When the course is clear, gentlemen, never pause—proceed. Mr. Madsen, give the men ten minutes to get into position, then take the first shot that presents itself. Your gunfire will be our signal to attack."

"An enemy of my enemy is my friend," Clay repeated as the group made their way, bent at the waist, through the

cactus and back to their horses. "That's an Apache sayin'
I've never heard of."

Roman chuckled, then whispered so only Trap and Clay
could hear him. "That's because it's not an Apache saying,
Mr. Madsen. It's a custom of the Arabian sheiks." The
lieutenant speared a dusty boot through a stirrup and
pulled himself up in the saddle. "But I can only assume the
Apache feel the same way in that regard. I know I would."

The two boys worked their way along a rocky incline
across the arroyo toward a jutting stone tower. They were
in full view of the besieged Apaches the entire time, but well
out of rifle range.

"Those scalp hunters are focused on the Apache and
don't know hell's about to rain down on 'em from behind,"
Clay panted as they took up a position behind a lump of
orange sandstone the size of a large ox.

He dampened the bead on his front sight with the tip
of his finger so it would catch the light better, and looked
down his barrel at the dark form of one of the outlaws hun-
kering beneath a lip of cactus and rock, out of sight of the
Apache.

"How far away you think we are?" Trap asked, taking up
a position with his own rifle.

Clay picked up a bit of sand and let it stream out between
his thumb and forefinger to check the wind. He sighted
down the barrel of his Sharps and adjusted the ladder on
his Vernier sights. "I don't know, two hundred yards, give
or take—not far enough to fret over. You know what's
funny about this group?" Madsen looked up at Trap. "They
all still got blood on 'em."

Over the last few months, Trap had learned that
Madsen's eyesight was impeccable. He squinted at the
men squatting or kneeling here and there among the
rocks below the mountain, then grunted. "Sure enough,"
he said. At two hundred yards, the Texan could see as
good as most people could at fifty.

"It's like they don't even care if decent folks know they're bald-faced killers." Clay sighted down the barrel again and settled the long rifle firmly against his shoulder. "Well, sir, I'm proud to do my part to send a few of the buggers straight to Hell."

Clarice barked once. The big rifle bucked against Madsen's shoulder, but her twelve-pound heft helped dampen the recoil some. A low whine flattened out against the desert sand culminating in a faint thwack an instant after one of the killers slumped to the ground. His stone hiding place was now his tomb.

Smoke curled out of the breech as Madsen slid another round into the chamber and closed the block. He swung the Sharps to search for another target.

There was no bugle call to signal Roman's attack, only a wilting volley of gunfire as eight troopers swept down the arroyo at the gallop, engaging everything in their path.

"There's another one in the rocks over there with a gun pretty near like this one." Madsen's voice was tight and he spoke into the cheek-piece of his rifle. "If he gets above the lieutenant, it'll be a cinch for him to cut 'em all down one by one."

"Can you take him?" Trap asked, looking down the barrel of the Winchester and wondering if he should even try a shot at such a distance.

"It's better than three hundred yards," Clay whispered. "Almost four. That's a hell of a long shot, even for me. I think I got. . . ."

Instead of shooting, Clay yelped and rolled to his left. "Damned scorpion!" he hissed, clutching at his right leg.

When the boys looked between them, they saw not a scorpion, but the feather fletching of an arrow sticking up from the sand next to Clay's leg. They made it behind the safety of a boulder, just as another arrow whistled in, zinged off a stone and careened into the canyon below.

"Well, this mucks things up considerably," Clay snorted. He checked the wound at his leg and found the arrow had only nicked him. "They likely dipped the damned thing in dog crap or some other such nasty thing. You think it's Apache?"

"Could be." Trap lay on his back, staring up at the sky. He clutched the Winchester to his chest. The weapon felt useless against an opponent he couldn't even see. "Webber told me there's a big Comanche who rides with the scalp hunters. He's called Slow Killer because he likes to scalp his victims before they're dead. I caught a glimpse of a big boy. I think it's him out there."

"Well, that's dandy." Madsen gritted his teeth. "I need to take care of that other shooter across the canyon before he starts takin' out troopers, and here we are penned in by a big Comanche who wants to torture us a little before he kills us."

Trap glanced across the arroyo. He could just make out a lone figure picking its way through the high rocks. Gunfire in the valley said the fighting there was intense. "I see him," Trap said. "Can you make the shot from here?"

"I think so," Clay muttered. "If you'll keep Slow Killer from raisin' my hair while I work."

"Do my best." Trap gave his friend a pat on the shoulder. "You do yours."

When Trap chanced a look around the boulder, Slow Killer jumped him. Webber had been right; this Comanche was one huge Indian. He hit Trap full force, swinging an ironwood war club that missed the boy's skull by mere inches. Trap felt the wind of it on his cheek. He brought the Winchester up to ward off a second blow just in time, and felt the gun give way in his hands like splintering stove wood.

On his back again, he rolled to one side as the heavy club pounded the ground where his head had been. He lashed out with the rifle barrel and connected with the Comanche's leg, but the force of the blow tore the weapon from Trap's grasp.

Slow Killer grinned, pulling up his long nose like a snarling wolf, and fell on top of him. The Comanche screamed like a wild man and drove a knee into the boy's belly. Trap brought a leg up to defend himself, but felt all the wind gush from his lungs. His head reeled and he struggled to stay conscious. If he passed out for even a moment, he knew he would die.

The Comanche wore leather leggings but no shirt. He was smeared with some kind of rancid grease, and though Trap clawed and grabbed with all his might, he found it difficult to find anything to hang on to.

The two combatants rolled in the dirt, locked in mortal combat only feet from Clay Madsen.

"He's settin' up to shoot," Clay shouted above the fray. "Hold on one more second, Trapper, and I'll be over there to help you. I might not get another chance at this."

Trap knew he didn't have much more than a second left. Slow Killer was a powerful man and though Trap was holding his own, none of his blows or kicks appeared to have any effect of the huge Comanche.

Summoning all his strength, Trap pushed off with both legs and rolled toward a low rock ledge. It was just high enough off the ground that both men wedged underneath it, scraping their shoulders on the top. They'd likely be sharing it with a snake or two, but that was the least of Trap's worries. He tried to pull away and go for his knife, but the Comanche caught him in a bear hug and pulled him back, baring his teeth.

"You stay with me, little man," Slow Killer grunted, bashing his forehead into Trap's nose. "You're Apache, I can smell it."

Trap tried to push away, but found his strength was failing. The big Indian had him in a death grip now, pulling and threatening to break him in two. Trap struck out with his free hand, bloodying his fists as he hit sandstone as often as he connected with Slow Killer's greased face.

Then, Trap's thumb slid across the Comanche's eye. The Indian tried to jerk away, but the back of his head was tight against the rock overhang. Trap pushed hard, gouging as deeply as he could, aiming for the back of the Indian's skull. He felt muscles separate, then tear as Slow Killer yowled and flailed wildly under the rock. There was nowhere for him to go. The Comanche vomited when his eye tore free and hung on its stem, mingling with the blood and grease on the side of his cheek.

The crushing grip around Trap's ribs relaxed. He gulped

in air, the sound of his own wheezing loud in his ears. As soon as he could work his hands again, he drew his knife and finished the big Comanche quickly.

Slow Killer ceased his struggles just as Clay made his shot and drew his pistol to help.

"Damn, boy." Clay blinked and stared, mouth agape at the gruesome scene in front of him. All the color had drained from his normally robust face. "Can't you get in a fight without gettin' covered in blood and guts and who knows what else?"

Trap tried to straighten his stiff neck. His nose was completely plugged with blood from the head butt Slow Killer had given him. He panted through an open mouth.

"Did you get him?" His vision was too cloudy to see the rocks across the valley.

Clay grinned. "I got him. You sit down so you don't fall down while me and Clarice give the lieutenant a little more help." Clay picked up the Sharps again and spoke out of the corner of his mouth. "If I ever decide to fight you, remind me to shoot you from a distance. You're too damn mean to go toe-to-toe with."

True to the lieutenant's presumption, Juan Caesar and his band poured from their hiding places among the rocks to join the battle. There were no more than a half-dozen fighting men among the Apache, but their addition demoralized the surviving scalp hunters.

Five of the bloodstained killers attempted surrender. The Apache shot at them in any case and Private Webber, at full gallop with his saber drawn, took the head and one hand off one of the outlaws just as he was raising his arms. Only two were left alive by the time Roman called for a ceasefire and gained control of the Apaches.

Trap and Clay stood when they saw things were well in hand below them, and half-slid, half-ran down the arroyo. By the time they arrived, Martini had the two prisoners bound with their hands behind their backs. Webber was acting as translator between Roman and a dark, pockmarked man. He was taller than the others, with a round chest that was set on somewhat gangly legs. A feather and grass hat haloed deep-set eyes that looked as though they had the capacity to melt stone. A splash of blood dripped from his right arm and the side of his ragged face where he'd killed one of the scalp hunters at close range.

The Apache demanded control of the prisoners. Roman said the men were the Army's problem and they would be dealt with fairly and justly for what they had done. Webber spoke excellent Apache. Better than Trap, and his rapid-fire words shot back and forth between the two leaders.

At length, Juan Caesar tired of using a go-between and fell into halting English.

"Will the Army use the same fairness the lying Indian Agent Brandywine uses to weigh our beef? Will it give them the same justice it gives the white settlers that fool with our women?" Juan Caesar spit vehemently on the ground, then looked directly into Roman's face. Trap wondered how he'd fare if this man ever looked at him so directly. "I believe the words, Lieutenant-with-the-crooked-nose, but I know enough to know you cannot speak for all white eyes. You are not all places at once. Bad things happen, no matter what you say."

"Juan Caesar," Roman said. "You know I am a man of my word. These men will stand trial in a military court and I myself will bear witness of the evil they have done. I will look into Mr. Brandywine and make certain he treats you with fairness. But you and your people must return with me to Camp Apache."

The two leaders looked at each other for a time, their eyes locked in a silent battle of wills. A dozen men, Apache and soldier alike, stood tense and ready to fight again. It was quiet enough to hear flies buzzing around the freshly fallen bodies. No one breathed.

Juan Caesar let out a great sigh as his eyes darted from a ragged group of Apache women and children to the approaching storm clouds. His proud shoulders slumped and he appeared to deflate to half his former size.

"We will go with you, Lieutenant Roman." The Apache

stared, blank-faced and focused on nothing. "What other choice do I have but to fight and die? Someday it will come to that, I think—but not this day."

A baby whimpered until a short woman with a scarred face hushed it with a rough hand over its mouth. Trap shuddered to think of what the ruthless scalp hunters would have done to the child.

The Indians traveled light and were ready to go from the moment the battle was over. Trap could tell Lieutenant Roman wanted to get back to garrison with all due speed while the Apache were being agreeable. But the coordinated movement of troops was an easy thing compared to keeping fourteen tired, hungry Indians on the trail, no matter how stoic they were.

Roman studied the storm clouds for a moment, then turned to Sergeant Martini and spoke so Juan Caesar could hear. "We'll ride back north for a few hours and get to the cliffs by Black Mesa. That will give us some shelter in case this weather doesn't pass us by. Bring that sorrel gelding we saw tied in the thicket back there. We'll butcher him when we get to camp. It looks as though these poor people haven't had a good meal in some time."

The soldiers had all eaten their share of horse during hard campaigns, but none of them relished the idea of killing a perfectly good animal to feed Apache renegades. The Indians, on the other hand, lengthened their stride at the thought of fresh meat, and the party began to make good time. Two of the younger children climbed into the saddle with Clay. The Texan's genuine smile was enough to calm the fears of the Apache mothers.

Trap kept to the rear of the column now that his services as a tracker were not needed. He wanted to listen to the Apaches as much as he could, study the way they walked, and bone up on the language. The women and children grew more animated at the thought of food, and chattered enough for Trap to pick up a word or two.

Juan Caesar, who had secured a piebald buckskin from the scalp hunters' horses, trotted up next to him.

"You are Denehii—the tracker," the Indian grunted. He rode with his legs out of the stirrups.

"That's the name my mother calls me," Trap answered.

"Your mother, she is Chuparosa, an Apache?" There was a wildness about this man that set Trap's nerves on edge, as if he was on always on the brink of losing his temper and lashing out with bullet or blade.

"She is Chiricahua."

Juan Caesar rode for a while before speaking again. "The holy men have spoken of you and your woman."

"My mother?"

The Apache scoffed. "Your woman—the Nez Percé."

Trap smiled at the thought of Maggie being identified as his woman.

"The holy men say this girl from the north has power," the Apache continued. "They say she is like Lozan, the sister of Victorio. Some are afraid."

"Is that so," Trap said, suddenly worried about what else Apache holy men might be saying about Maggie.

Juan Caesar urged his horse faster, bolting ahead, then wheeling to block Trap's path. Skunk pulled up short, nose-to-nose with the crazy-eyed buckskin. The Apache leaned forward in the saddle and glared with his molten eyes. He jerked a thumb back toward his chest.

His voice was low, but strained, like a whispered shout. "I am not afraid. I see the truth about you and your woman."

With that, he spun the beleaguered horse again on its haunches and trotted off toward his men without looking back.

CHAPTER 31

There was a fair amount of backslapping and congratulations from the garrison soldiers as Roman's troop returned to Camp Apache.

Juan Caesar and his band were confined to the camp until a detail could be formed to take them on to San Carlos.

Ever mindful of the dangers that faced their husbands in the field, the troopers' wives lined the dusty parade ground as soon as they received word their men were returning from patrol. Officers' and enlisted men's wives mingled together at a time like this when no one knew for certain if their husbands would be part of the patrol trotting back through the gate, or slung over the back of a horse, a casualty of the mission. When Roman led his entire troop back alive, with the band of renegades, he was a hero in the eyes of the military, and more especially the military women.

A tall blond beauty, with robin's-egg eyes to match her smock and a smile powerful enough to knock a man off a horse, looked wistfully at Lieutenant Roman as he brought his horse to a stop and dismissed his troop to see to their mounts. An officer's wife to the very core, she kept her distance while Roman handed his reins to a young man wearing a tan stable smock and farrier's leather apron. He gave the man some last-minute instructions about the horse's feet. When his business was done, he removed his gloves and hat just in time to receive a proper welcome-home kiss.

Trap was thrilled to see his beautiful Maggie waiting for him at the far end of the parade ground, a few yards apart from the wives. His mother and father stood behind her. The looks they bore didn't add up.

Maggie's round face was passive, but she bounced on her feet while she waited for him to dismount, as if she was standing on a bed of hot coals. His mother carried an expression of fatigued happiness, the way he'd seen her look after an exhausting walk in the woods. A stray lock of black hair hung across her face and fluttered with the breeze.

The reverend looked as if he'd just taken a mouthful of sour milk and didn't quite know where to spit it.

Hairs stood on the back of Trap's neck. Something was very wrong.

Clay noticed it too. "Here you go, little buddy," he said, drawing his face back in a mock grimace. "I'll take Skunk for you and give him his oats and a good brush-down." He tipped his head to Maggie and the O'Shannons, but kept his voice low, speaking from the corner of his mouth. "I'd rather face a firin' squad than face whatever slow death they got lined up for you."

All instincts told Trap he should go with Clay, but the thought of being with Maggie after the long absence drew him forward. "Much obliged," he croaked through a rapidly tightening throat.

"You look as though you've taken quite a beating, son," the reverend said as Trap approached the tight-lipped group. He could tell his father had worried about him—was glad to see him home. The poor man winced slightly at every word he spoke.

Trap looked more like a raccoon than a man with his two black eyes and swollen nose, all courtesy of Slow Killer.

"I am fine, thank you," he said. "Just took a little punch in the nose." Trap shook the reverend's hand, kissed his mother on the cheek, and put an arm around Maggie's shoulders to give her a squeeze. "Is everything all right here?"

The three looked at each other. Maggie leaned into

Trap, nuzzling her head against his shoulder, hiding from the rest of the world. Her whole body trembled. She appeared more vulnerable than Trap had ever seen her.

The reverend chewed on the inside of his cheek and released a tortured breath.

Hummingbird used both hands to smooth the front of her white smock before clasping them together in front of her. It was she who broke the awkward silence.

"Things have happened while you were away," she began. It reminded him of the way she'd spoken to him when he was a small child and his favorite puppy had died. "A soldier has come to call on Maggie—the very same soldier who captured her from her people and sent her to us at White Oak. It seems he has always thought to return and take her as a wife."

A shot through the heart would have pained Trap less. He pulled Maggie even closer and shook his head violently. "No! He can't. I'll fight him—we'll run; I don't care what I have to do." He turned to his father. "Whatever it takes, sir, I'll not give her up again."

"I know." Tears rolled down James O'Shannon's red cheeks.

Hummingbird put a hand on her son's shoulder. Her eyes wandered across the parade ground to a group of soldiers while she spoke. "Your father had to tell a little lie in order to keep Maggie from having to return to Missouri before you got back. The young man, Lieutenant Peter Grant is his name, wants to meet you."

The reverend suddenly took Trap by the shoulders and spun him around. His lips pursed until they were almost white and he glanced heavenward. "Forgive me, Lord," he whispered. He shook Trap's shoulders. "Now, son, listen to me carefully. Lieutenant Grant is crossing the parade ground as we speak. In bearing false witness to him, I have become something I despise. I don't wish to turn my son into a liar as well."

Trap looked to Maggie, then his mother for some clue about what was happening. Maggie sighed. Hummingbird's nose turned up and her eyelids fluttered with a hint of quiet amusement.

"What is he talking about?" Trap asked.

James O'Shannon pushed his son's hat off his head so it fell back behind him against the stampede string. He straightened the boy's hair as he'd done so many times before, when they had prepared for church on Sunday mornings. He then took a step back and gazed through moist, resigned eyes.

"Patrick 'Trap' O'Shannon, I ask you, what is the chief end of man?" he said.

Trap answered out of rote habit from years of reciting the Scripture. "The chief end of man is to glorify God and enjoy him forever. . . ."

"Will you be able to accomplish that as the husband of Mary Margaret Sundown, otherwise known as Maggie?" The reverend's face grew somber.

"Yes, I would, but . . ."

"Hush, Trap," the elder O'Shannon snapped, looking across the parade ground. "Grant is less than a stone's throw away.

"Maggie," the reverend said. He took her hand and placed it on top of Trap's, cupping them both between his own trembling fingers. "Would you be able to do the same as the wife of young Patrick?"

"Yes, I could, my father." Her voice was soft as a feather. "And I will."

Hummingbird dabbed a tear out of her eye and sniffed.

Trap looked up and saw a cavalry officer twenty steps away, approaching them at a fast walk, fists clenched at his sides, a determined look on his freckled face.

"Very well then, in the name of Jesus Christ, Our Lord . . ." James O'Shannon gave an exhausted sigh and resumed his sour-milk expression. "When Grant asks you, you may tell him honestly that you are married to Maggie Sundown O'Shannon."

Trap's head spun. He glanced down at Maggie, at his parents, then back to Maggie again. She was the most beautiful thing he'd ever seen in his life. He wanted to speak, but some unseen force worked to bind his tongue. He swallowed hard, trying to keep standing on wobbly legs that felt like they were made of fresh-cut hay instead of bone and muscle.

Grant walked up behind them and cleared his throat. Maggie must have sensed Trap's predicament because she turned and stepped forward. "Lieutenant," she said with an air of staunch formality. "I want you to meet my husband, Trap O'Shannon."

Chapter 32

Lieutenant Grant slinked away, hat crumpled in his hand after a few moments' polite conversation. The poor man was heartbroken at having lost all chance with the beautiful Indian girl who'd no doubt haunted his dreams for the past year.

Trap's knees still felt too weak to operate. He sank on the steps of the modest white house that served as the adjutant's office and attempted to gather his thoughts. Maggie and his parents had had a little time to chew on all this; he was forced to digest it all in one sitting.

"We've moved your things across the dog-run with Maggie," Hummingbird said. "I've been making you a new quilt."

"She stayed up half the night to finish it," Reverend O'Shannon said. Only the hint of a smile perked the corners of his stern lips.

Trap gave a weak grin. He felt like he should say something to Maggie, some words that she might remember on her wedding day, but his brain and tongue conspired against him. When he looked at her and opened his mouth, nothing came out but stutters.

Maggie sat beside him, moving close. He could feel the warmth of her thigh next to him. She sensed his tongue-tied predicament, and rescued him with kind words and the gentlest smile he'd ever seen.

"I remember the missionaries in the Wallowa reading to us from the Bible when I was a little girl. I had a favorite verse: 'Entreat me not to leave thee, or to refrain from following after thee . . . thy people shall be my people and thy God, my God. . . .'" Maggie took his hand in hers and held it on her lap. Her breath came fast and she trembled like a small bird. "I don't remember much of the Bible, but I remember that."

James O'Shannon beamed at the quotation of Scripture from his new daughter-in-law. "I suppose I have only been putting off the inevitable." He gave Trap's hand a hearty shake and patted him on the back. "Remember our talks, son. Her happiness is paramount now."

"It has been for some time, sir."

"Well, then . . . your mother and Mag . . . your wife has been hard at work preparing something of a feast once the word came you were returning today," the reverend said.

"Yes, we have." Hummingbird sighed. "Papa, I suppose you and I should go make the final arrangements while Trap and Maggie sort a few things out and he gets cleaned up."

"I suppose so." The reverend stood his ground, unwilling to leave the newlyweds alone right away. He shook Trap's hand again. Maggie stood and kissed him lightly on the cheek. In all the years he'd known his father, Trap had never seen the man blush before. "Yes, well . . . yes, I suppose we should go and . . ." He turned to his wife. "After you, Chuparosa."

Before the O'Shannons could take their leave, Clay Madsen came striding across the parade ground like a man with a mission. He took off his hat when he neared Maggie and Trap's mother and acknowledged the reverend with a polite nod. He twisted the hat in his hands as he stood.

"What's the matter, Clay?" Hummingbird asked. "You look a little out of sorts."

"I'm fine, ma'am," Clay said. His dark brow was knotted in a strained arch. "Thank you for asking." He looked at Trap and shrugged. "Sorry to drag you away from your sweetheart so soon . . ."

"My wife," Trap corrected. It felt good to say the words.

"Your wife?" Clay's jaw fell. "You hauled off and got married in the last ten minutes?"

"As a matter of fact I did." Trap filled him in about the recent events with Lieutenant Grant.

Maggie eyed Clay like she might carve off a piece of him. "What did you mean drag him away?"

Clay took a defensive step back and raised his hand. "Sorry, Maggie darlin', but the colonel wants to see me and your new husband in his office within the hour—and with the colonel, 'within the hour' means as soon as we can get our behinds over there."

"I'm sure it won't take long," Trap said. He groaned to his feet. Fatigue suddenly overwhelmed his body, and he found himself wondering if getting married was supposed to make a person feel so much older than their natural years. One thing he did know. He thought leaving Maggie had been difficult before. Now, stepping away from her, even for a minute, was nigh to unbearable.

Colonel Branchflower's aide-de-camp was a weasely little lieutenant named Ford Fargo. He had big ears and a shining forehead that reached the uppermost point of his sloping scalp. Fargo's wooden desk was known to be immaculate and polished to a sheen that competed with his gleaming head. He was fastidious in his clerical skills and bordered on maniacal in his grooming.

When Trap and Clay arrived at the office, he was sitting in a wooden chair on the porch cleaning his toenails with a jackknife. His uniform coat was folded neatly across a matching chair at his side.

"Hope you don't peel apples with that thing." Clay curled up his nose at the sight of the other man's feet. "We're here to see the colonel."

"Go right on in." Lieutenant Fargo flicked his knife toward the whitewashed door behind him. "The others are already here."

Trap and Clay exchanged glances. "The others?" Trap said what they were both thinking.

"Umm," Fargo grunted through a nod that flattened his chin to his chest while he concentrated on his ghost-pale foot. "Lieutenant Roman and Private Webber are in there waiting " Fargo wiped his jackknife on a scrap of paper and returned it to his pocket. He took his socks from the chair beside him and began to pull them back on. "Go on inside with them, but don't go past the rail until I come in and announce you."

Both boys stepped onto the small covered porch and hurried through the door. Neither liked spending any more time than necessary around the odd little man.

Thanks to Lieutenant Fargo's compulsions, the front office was spotless. His desk was situated in front of long oaken rails that separated a cramped, but tidy waiting area and telegraph station from the colonel's office proper. Even the trash in the lieutenant's wastebasket appeared to have been arranged with a particular order. A single painting of a matronly redhead in a green dress with eyes remarkably like Fargo's hung on the wall behind a padded chair.

"I bet she digs at her toenails too." Clay smirked.

Roman put a finger to his lips at the comment.

Webber wore a cat-ate-the-canary grin.

The door to Branchflower's office suddenly swung open and the colonel's voice bellowed out like a Biblical whirlwind.

"Fargo!" The shout rattled the painting on the wall.

Roman snapped to attention. "He's not out here, sir."

"I'll be go to hell," the colonel muttered. His chair clattered back from a desk. Heavy footfalls approached the doorway. Branchflower waved the men inside with a hand the size of a shovel blade, his muttonchopped jowls set in annoyance. His bright green eyes narrowed. "He's out cleaning his damned toenails again, isn't he?"

Roman nodded, shooting a wry grin at the others. "He is, sir."

Branchflower moved his massive head back and forth. It reminded Trap of a buffalo bull standing up from a wallow to shake off the dust.

"You know," Branchflower said, his nose turning up in

disgust. "A soldier's feet are important, I'll give Fargo that much. But if a man keeps them clean and changes his socks on a regular basis, his damned toenails ought to take care of themselves." The colonel sank back in a huge leather chair behind an expansive desk, which was far more cluttered than Lieutenant Fargo's. He leaned forward to rest his chin on huge fists. "That peculiar little bastard spends far too much time picking his hooves if you ask me."

The other four men in the room remained on their feet, Roman and Webber at attention, their knuckles planted firmly against the stripe on their uniform britches. Trap was learning early that men in power often took their time to get to the point when they had a captive audience.

"At ease, gentlemen." Branchflower nodded curtly. "I appreciate the speed with which . . ."

Lieutenant Fargo poked his head in the door and smiled under his pencil-thin mustache. "I'm right outside at my desk if you need me, sir."

"You're dismissed for the remainder of the day, Lieutenant," the colonel said without looking at him.

Fargo's face wilted. "But sir, I don't mind staying. It's not yet two P.M."

Branchflower waved him off. "Go get a haircut, then. A visit to the tonsorial parlor will do you some good. You can catch up on the local gossip and give me a full report tomorrow."

"Aye, sir." Fargo's voice was despondent. He seemed to sense something was about to happen and hated to miss out on it. He started to shut the door, but Branchflower stopped him.

"Leave it open. I want to know if anyone is out there spying on us. If someone comes in—or doesn't leave—I'll hear it."

Once his aide was gone, the colonel closed the wooden shutters over the single window in his office. "Every commander needs at least one sycophant—but the need is just as strong to be rid of them once in a while." He lowered his voice to a conspiratorial whisper when he got to the matter at hand.

"Gentlemen, you all know that Victorio has jumped the reservation with his Membreno band of hostiles. We believe he's headed for somewhere in Mexico." The colonel slid a stack of papers to one side and unrolled a parchment map on his desk. He used his ivory pipe and a clay ashtray to hold down the curling edges.

"Lieutenant Gatewood is in pursuit with one company along with Al Seiber and seventeen Chiricahua scouts." Captain Hotchkiss has Company F over here"—he tapped a range of mountains to the southeast—"just in case the hostiles move this way. Troops from Fort Grant are also engaged in the search. We're hoping to catch the wily bastard in a pincer."

Trap and the others studied the map. There were thousands of places the Apache could hide—too many for the cavalry to find Victorio if he didn't want to be found.

"Are we to join in this campaign then, Colonel?" Lieutenant Roman looked up from the map.

"You are not," Branchflower said, surprising them all. "All my men, including the Apache scouts, are either on patrol or needed here in garrison. That said, a delicate issue has arisen that requires our immediate action." Branchflower leaned back in his chair and folded his hands over a ponderous belly. He kept his voice low. "A prominent Mexican colonel named Hernan de la Cruz reported his daughter missing three days ago. She and one of her male escorts were taken while on their way to Phoenix."

"Pilar!" The word came softly under Clay's breath.

The colonel cocked his head to one side. "You know this girl?"

Trap stepped forward. "We do, sir. Mr. Madsen and I helped her out of a little trouble on our way to Arizona last summer."

"I see," Branchflower mused. "That makes things a touch more . . ." The colonel stopped in mid-sentence and shrugged his massive shoulders. He seemed to think better of what he was about to say. "We received a ransom demand, shortly after the girl went missing. It asked for a hundred thousand U.S. dollars."

Webber whistled under his breath, bringing a stare of disapproval from Roman.

"Sorry, sir," the private said without looking a bit sorry. "But that's a lot of money for one girl."

"Yes, it is," Branchflower muttered, almost to himself. "It's as if . . ." He stopped himself again.

He looked up at Roman without elaborating on his last utterance. "The girl's escorts were American. The one who was taken has already been killed. They left his head with the note." Branchflower pulled on his reading glasses again and glanced at some notes on his desk. "Men, the issue is forthright. Relations between Mexico and the United States are strained at best. There's still some fighting going on over on the Nueces Strip. A lot of old grudges have yet to be settled. This Apache issue isn't helping matters at all.

"To make things worse, the girl was under escort by the United States Army. It appears that a member of the military may have been involved in the kidnapping."

The colonel rested his elbows on the table and steepled his fingers, tips together, in front of his face. "General Sheridan has authorized me to assemble a special unit for missions exactly like this one—a group of unconventional fighters—somewhat like Rogers' Rangers during the French and Indian War.

"This mission is more important than you can possibly imagine. Unfortunately, I'm not at liberty to share everything with you at this moment." The colonel's gaze shifted back and forth among the men for a time before it came to rest on Clay. "Mr. Madsen," he said, rubbing his great chin. "Al Seiber tells me you're one of the best horsemen he's ever seen. He also informs me that you have a gift of gab that could ingratiate you to Geronimo himself."

The colonel left Clay to glow from the compliments and shifted his attention to Trap, letting his eyes slide up and down as if he was perusing a horse. He raised a bushy eyebrow. "And you, Mr. O'Shannon. Seiber says you track as well as any Apache he knows—maybe even better. Hell, I guess you are Apache. Is that right?"

"My mother is Chiricahua. My father is Scots-Irish." Trap stood perfectly still and endured the scrutiny. He never tried to hide the fact that he had Apache blood, but he didn't go around wearing the fact on his sleeve either.

"I'm told by many that both of you youngsters would fit the bill nicely for what I have in mind." He sighed and turned to Johannes. "And that brings me to you, Private Webber. From what I hear, you possess a remarkable gift for languages and learning. I need a man with such skills, but I have to be honest with you and say that I am left to wonder why you're not an officer."

Webber didn't answer, and Branchflower didn't pursue the issue. It was obvious any decision about Johannes had already been made or he wouldn't have been present at the meeting.

"Lieutenant Roman," Branchflower continued. "You have the integrity and perseverance I need in a commander. No offense to the good men on Victorio's trail, but if your record was not so stellar, you'd be out with them right now. As it is, I need you here.

"Hear me good, now; this special unit of Scout Trackers will answer only to me." The colonel thumbed his chest. "Me, and no one else; am I clear?"

"Understood," Roman said.

"No staff officers to get in the way and muck things up. I need fresh men, men in the Army but not yet jaded by its politics. Understood?"

Roman nodded. "Yes, Colonel."

"Begging your pardon, sir." Clay cleared his throat.

"Go ahead, Mr. Madsen," Branchflower said.

"Well, sir, it's like this. . . ." Clay stumbled a little, unaccustomed to speaking to the commanding officer of the camp. "Trap, I mean . . . Mr. O'Shannon and me . . . I mean, we ain't exactly in the Army."

Colonel Branchflower gave a knowing smile and produced two parchment documents from the lap drawer of his desk. He'd thought all this through already.

"That is next on my list of problems to address. Lieutenant

Fargo is an odd little bird, but he's a damned good penman, don't you think?"

He pushed the papers across the desk. "Sign on the line at the bottom, gentlemen, and this last issue will be solved. It's a formality really. What with one out of every three men deserting on me, the thing I truly need is your word more than any scrap of paper."

Trap scratched out his name without thinking. From the moment he'd arrived at Camp Apache he'd known, down deep, that it would come to this. He handed the pen to Clay, who paused for a moment. The quill hung over the paper while he thought, rising and falling with each breath.

"It's awful funny, the twists and turns of life," Clay whispered loud enough for all to hear. "I'm about to sign away the next five years of my life, all because I fell asleep on a horse and ran into you, O'Shannon."

"It's voluntary, Mr. Madsen," the colonel said. "No one will force your hand, but we could use your talents." His voice held the closest thing to a plea Clay—or anyone else—would ever get from the proud man.

"The truth is"—the young Texan grinned—"I don't know anything else I'd enjoy doin' more now that I got a taste of this." He gave a resigned sigh and leaned over the desk to scrawl out his name.

"Excellent." Branchflower picked up the enlistment papers and blew on the ink to dry it before slipping them back in his lap drawer.

"Now," the colonel continued. "Webber, Madsen, and O'Shannon, the assignments I have in mind for this unit, hereafter known as the Scout Trackers, will certainly be extremely dangerous and more or less secret in nature. Because of this, I'm promoting each of you to the rank of sergeant with all attendant pay and privileges. Roman, it's a little trickier to promote an officer, what with all the competitive eligibility lists and such, but I did receive permission to brevet you to the rank of captain. I imagine many of your missions will put in you all civilian dress, but if anyone has a problem with your new ranks, direct them to me."

He took a leather dispatch pouch from his desk and slid

it across to Roman. "Here's the formal brief describing Señorita de la Cruz's abduction, along with descriptions of her abductors and full accounts from the sole survivor of the ambush. Review it, and then destroy it. I'm not sure who we can trust with this information."

Branchflower stood and shook each man's hand in turn. "Gentlemen, you will come to realize that five dollars a month extra is small compensation for the harsh and dangerous duties I will assign you. But rest assured, a great deal of thought went into this decision. I have all confidence that you are the right men for the job. I urge you to make all haste in this rescue."

The colonel's tone suddenly became curt and formal. "Sergeants, you are dismissed for the present. Captain Roman, if you would be so kind as to remain behind for a moment. I have another matter I need to discuss with you."

"Yes, sir." Roman fished a gold watch from his trouser pocket. "Men, it's twenty minutes to three. Go and bid your sweethearts good-bye. But don't tell them where you're heading. Meet me in front of King James' at four for gear issue."

"My noggin aches like it's been filled to the brim," Clay muttered after they walked outside.

Webber rolled his eyes and gave Madsen a good-natured slap on the back. "That's not such an accomplishment for our good colonel."

"I mean it," Clay said. "Why so much secrecy over a kidnapped girl? Even if Pilar is a colonel's daughter. Let's just ride in there and take care of it like we took care of those scalp hunters."

"If it were always that easy, we'd let the girls in town do it," Webber scoffed.

Trap touched his sore nose. He didn't remember it being all that simple.

"Whatever you say." Clay went on with his thought, unperturbed by Johannes. "He gave us a heck of a lot of information without telling us much of anything—except that our job would be dangerous."

"Welcome to the Army." Webber gave him a slap on the back.

Clay narrowed his eyes. "That Colonel Branchflower reminds me of a tight silk nightie on a curvy woman—everything gets covered, just not very well."

"I hate to leave her so soon," Trap confided to Clay a few minutes later, after Johannes excused himself to say his good-byes to a Mexican girl he'd been seeing. "An hour isn't gonna be much time for a honeymoon."

"No offense intended, partner." Madsen took off his hat. He grinned wide enough to show all his teeth. "But I seen the look in your child bride's eyes when you walked away from her a little bit ago. Maybe you didn't recognize it, but I sure enough did. I reckon an hour will be more than enough time . . ."

Trap nodded slowly, thinking about what he'd seen in Maggie's eyes. It was what had made his legs go so weak—a hungry look that bored into his very soul. "Well, then," he said. His mouth was dry. Thoughts of Maggie's toes, her face, her smells all flooded in around him like a warm and comforting breeze. "Reckon I should hurry along . . . I guess . . ."

"Go ahead and go then." Clay smirked. "Your damned feet ain't nailed to the ground. Get a move on, she's waitin' for you."

Trap snugged his hat around his ears and took off at a run.

CHAPTER 33

"Yeah, verily." King James wagged his finger at Clay. "If the United States Army sayeth thou shalt be issued a Smith & Wesson Schofield, then that is exactly what thou shalt receive."

Madsen grimaced and shot a pleading look at Roman.

"It's a free pistol," Webber whispered. "He's not saying you have to throw your Colt down the crapper. Just accept the damned thing so we can be on our way."

It took a little over half an hour for Sergeant James to finish gear issue for all four men. Although Clay accepted the Army's new sidearm, a Schofield break-top revolver chambered in .45 Smith & Wesson, he tucked it away in his saddlebag with a snide look and a few choice words. He was comfortable with his Colt Peacemaker, and made it clear that although he enjoyed fine new rifles, as far as pistols were concerned, his old friend with ivory grips and a comfortable feel would remain by his side for as long as he drew breath.

The other three men each took the new-issue sidearm as well as a Winchester 1876 chambered in the new .45-75, a necked-down but still powerful cartridge similar to the .45-70. While not as accurate as Clay's Sharps .45-90, the Winchesters were capable of throwing big chunks of lead downrange at a high rate of speed—a quality that was sure to come in handy in the sort of mission Colonel Branchflower had promised the Scout Trackers.

With no pack mule, each man had to carry all his own gear. Rations consisted of hardtack and salt beef, some of which Webber insisted was left over from the War Between the States. Each man drew two canteens and a new blanket roll.

"He's a straight shooter, that Lieutenant . . . I mean *Captain* Roman," Clay said outside the quartermaster's store. The captain was still inside taking care of a few last-minute details with King James. "I'm sure proud he let me keep Clarice. Reckon he'll do to ride with on this kind of engagement."

"He's more than capable," Webber agreed. He struck a match with his thumbnail and touched it to the end of a short cigar clenched between his teeth. "I'm thinking this will be good duty." He puffed the smoke until the end glowed orange and lit his ruddy face. "Anything is better than the drudgery of garrison duty. Give me the trail any day of the week."

Trap thought about that for a minute. As long as he had Maggie, life at Camp Apache would be a lot of things, but dull wasn't one of them.

Johannes puffed happily at his cigar and smirked at Trap. "Maggie get upset about you leaving so soon when we just got home?"

"She knows I have a job," Trap said. "She wants me to do the right thing. Honor means a lot to her."

"*I tan i epi tas,*" Webber said, nodding his head. "So, our Maggie's a warrior too."

Clay turned around from tying a canvas nose bag full of oats to his saddle and balled up his fists. He had *fight* written all over his face. "*I tan . . .* what the hell did you just call Maggie?"

Webber tapped the ash of his cigar and gave Madsen a patronizing smile. "Hold on there, righter of all wrongs to womanhood. I didn't say anything bad. It's Greek."

"It damn sure is," Clay snorted.

"It's what the Spartan mothers used to tell their sons when they left for battle: *Return with your shield or on it.* Like

Maggie, those women were warriors. They believed in honor."

"I heard my father talk about the Spartans." Trap nodded. "Good fighters, lots of honor, but an awful rough life."

Webber gave Trap an approving look. His brow rose as if he was a bit surprised. "You, or at least your father, knows his Plutarch."

Clay shook his head. "We may not all be as learned as you, Mr. Webber, but even I heard of Plutarch."

"Is that so?"

"I told you I was pretty near raised by my pa's string of whores." Madsen grinned. His ire faded immediately once he found Johannes wasn't saying anything derogatory about Maggie. "Them poor old girls gotta have somethin' to do during the day. Most of 'em develop a powerful appetite for books. When I was a sprout, I just hung around and listened; some of it must have sunk in accidentally."

"Well, I am a happy man," Webber said. "I've not only been made part of an elite team of adventurers, they happen to be semi-learned adventurers as well. I thought I was going to have to do all my philosophizing to Captain Roman. He'll break into a good erudition once in a great while, but most of the time, he likes to keep quiet."

"He strikes me as being very well educated," Trap said, meaning it as a high compliment.

"I heard he's a Mormon." Clay turned to tighten the cinch on his roan. The horse was prone to take in air and snugging the girth was a chore best done in steps. "I don't reckon I ever met a real live Mormon before."

"Hell." Webber picked a bit of tobacco leaf off the tip of his tongue. "You'll meet plenty of 'em out here. They're thick as thieves in some parts of this godforsaken desert. For some reason, the Mormons flock to these desolate places." Webber lowered his voice to make certain Roman, who was still inside, didn't hear him. "I figure they identify with the ancient Children of Israel, running after the Promised Land all the time. The ones I've met are right and honest enough, if a little quirky. Some of them even marry more than one woman at a time."

The way Webber shifted his eyes put a sinking feeling in Trap's gut. He never did like talking about someone when they weren't around.

"I've seen the captain's wife." Clay grinned. "I don't think he'd need another one. I do believe she's the only one he's got."

"She is at that, Mr. Madsen." Roman's voice poured from the dark interior of the adobe building. He followed it out into the flat evening light. The air and the conversation were just cool enough to pink his cheeks. "Her name is Irene and you may address her as such. She is the light of my life."

The captain looked around at the three members of his little group. His face was impassive, a blank page, impossible to read. "She is the only wife I have, or ever will have for that matter."

He took a deep breath, held it a moment while he pondered, then slowly exhaled. "Gentlemen, I should clear the air regarding my religion from the outset. You're welcome to speak to me about it at any time, but I won't push it on you. I attend church with my dear wife when in garrison, but I am not your preachy brand of Mormon. It is my sincere belief that the Good Lord made us each with a purpose: some to be preachers and some to be warriors—each a righteous instrument in His hands. I assume I am riding with warriors.

"Please do me the service of asking if you have a question. I don't want there to be anything unanswered from those who may have to die beside me. Here are a few things to get you acquainted with me. I don't use tobacco, I never consort with lewd women, and I won't partake of beer or hard liquor. The funny thing is, I didn't do these things before I converted, so it hasn't been much of a switch for me. Additionally, I don't happen to drink coffee or tea, though I don't look down on those who do."

The men all stood, still as glass, by their horses. Webber's cigar hung limply in his lips, Trap stared at the ground and Clay wrung his hat in his hands.

A wry smile started slowly at Roman's eyes, spread over his high cheekbones, and down to the corners of his mouth.

"And one more thing. I rarely ever curse, but take heed when I do, for then you can be sure I'm damned good and mad. Now, carry on, men. I'd like to be on the trail inside the hour."

By five o'clock other soldiers began to drift past the quartermaster's store on their way to supper or evening duties. Webber and Madsen were already in the saddle. Their horses seemed to sense their eagerness to regain the trail and pawed the ground, snorting with impatience. Clay let his roan step out a little to work off some of the tension. Webber followed, still talking on about Plutarch, the warriors of Sparta, and their hard-hearted mothers.

Trap thought about leaving Maggie while he put the finishing touches on his gear and checked his cinch one last time. In a way, he supposed, coming back for a short time, then leaving again so soon made it more difficult than if he'd just stayed away. It was like picking off a scab—no, that wasn't it, because riding away from Maggie produced a wound that didn't quite heal.

He resigned himself to the fact that he had to make a living. He hadn't chosen a life on the trail; it had chosen him—or at least Colonel Branchflower had—and Trap had to admit he enjoyed the challenge.

He'd just picked up Skunk's front foot when he caught a hint of something different on the wind. When he looked up, Maggie stood in front of him, smiling softly in her own understated way.

She wore one of his mother's dresses with blue and white checks and a matching ribbon around her loose hair.

"I got you a little something for the trail, husband." She handed him a small parcel, no bigger than a cartridge box. The dress had buttons that went up the front, all the way to the neckline, but Maggie had left the top four undone. The soft skin at her collarbone was flushed and pink. "I wanted to give you this before, but I . . ." Her voice was low and breathy. A mischievous gleam sparkled in her eye. "But my mind was on other things."

Trap blushed. He didn't dare say what he was thinking. Sometimes he wished he had Clay's quick wit so he could make Maggie laugh. He was vaguely aware of Madsen and Webber working their horses a few yards off, and of the creak of saddle leather as the captain climbed aboard his tall bay. Everyone else was mounted and Roman wasn't one to dawdle horseback. Trap knew he didn't have much time. Instead of speaking, he opened the package.

"It's a compass." Maggie lifted the small brass instrument out of the box in Trap's hands and held it up in front of him. "You are a man on the move, Trap O'Shannon. You have been leaving me since the day I met you. This will help you always find your way home."

"Where, I mean how . . . ?"

"Your father paid me a little for helping at the school. I wanted to give you something as a wedding present."

"But I didn't. . . ."

She put a finger to his lips. "Yes, you did. You are my husband. That is all that matters."

A blond corporal leaned on gangly legs against a cedar support post in front of the quartermaster's store and smirked behind a mouth full of crooked teeth. "Well, ain't that just the most precious thing you ever heard, Costello. 'My husband'?" He elbowed a swarthy Italian trooper next to him in the ribs. "We're beddin' down with the enemy now?"

Costello gave a nervous chuckle. "Come on, Fannin. Watch what you do now."

Trap's neck burned. He knew a fight between two soldiers generally saw them both in the stockade—no matter who started it. But some things could not be tolerated. He took a deep breath. Maggie shook her head.

"Don't." She mouthed the word. "If you fight him, you will lose all you have gained today."

Corporal Fannin spit into the sand, then sucked air in through a large gap in his top teeth. "I wonder what it's like to bed a red woman."

Trap gave Maggie the reins to his horse and gave her a

pat on the shoulder, moving her gently out of the way of what was sure to be an all-out brawl. He spun, both fists doubled, to face his loudmouthed adversary.

"I bet they're all hot like a fire coal," the instigator rolled on, raising his eyebrows and rolling his shoulders like he had a chill. "That's the only reason I could see to be with one of the little . . ."

Hezekiah Roman backed his muscular bay straight into the gabby corporal, pinning the surprised man against the cedar post.

Unaccustomed to having anything but a tail occupying the crack of his backside, the molested gelding flattened its ears and pitched, sending the offending man into the air and catching him with both well-shod feet on his way back down.

Corporal Fannin hit the ground with a sickening thud, clutching his groin with both hands. What little color he'd had drained from his pallid face. His Italian friend wisely stepped out of the way as if they'd never met.

"Mr. Fannin," Roman snapped, giving his snorting horse a pat on the neck. "You'd think a man such as yourself, employed in the United States Cavalry, would have the brains to stay out from behind the rear end of a mount. You will assign yourself to stable duty for the next month so you may learn proper horse-handling procedures and protocol." The captain spun his bay, and then side-passed over to the moaning soldier. He was an artist on the back of a horse. Madsen's jaw hung open in pure, unabashed hero worship.

The huge gelding stretched its neck out and nibbled at Corporal Fannin's uniform trousers.

Roman leaned down, his voice a firm stage whisper from which all around could listen and learn. "Cavalry troops of old utilized that move in battle to kill any enemy foolish enough to try and attack them from the rear. This horse could easily jump up flat-footed and kick your fool head off. All I have to do is give the command. Mister, you speak to one of my men or their women like that again, and I'll give that command. Are we clear?"

"Yes, sir," the corporal blubbered, his voice considerably higher than it had been.

As when garrison women lined up to welcome home the troops when they came in, they lined up to say good-bye when their men left. In this case, only Roman and Trap had wives there to see them off, but Clay and Webber both had pretty young things to send them off with a kiss.

"Good-bye, my son of Mars," Irene Roman shouted as the little group trotted out into the piñons outside Camp Apache. "You are my hero!" The captain blew her a kiss and tipped his hat.

Maggie's good-bye was more subtle. She stood watching as the group left, fingering the leather pouch around her soft neck. A smile Trap could feel on the back of his neck blazed like a flame in her black coffee eyes.

Trap turned back to look at her until the trees blocked her from his view.

"I only been in the Army two hours and I hate it already." Clay twirled the reins absentmindedly in his hands and looked up at the darkening sky as he spoke. "I only joined this escapade to get a chance to see that little darlin' Pilar again. Women," he sighed. "What's a man supposed to do?"

Trap kept his eyes forward, studying his horse's twitching ears. He thought about Maggie's tender good-bye to him back at their little dog-run cabin only an hour before. The last thing he wanted to do was talk to Clay about something so private and intimate. He'd surely rib him for the rest of the mission.

Afraid his face was still flushed at the thought of it, Trap kept his eyes focused on the rock-strewn terrain ahead.

"Females can sure enough cause a body a considerable amount of grief." Clay shook his head and sighed again, too caught up in his own thoughts to notice Trap's discomfort. "Ain't that right, partner?"

"I reckon they can," Trap said.

Roman reined up so all four men traveled abreast.

"Leaving is always difficult," he said. "I hate to leave my loved ones as much as the next man. When I am home, I dread the thought of a lonely expedition. I must confess that I truly despise the thought of leaving a hot bed and a hot woman for the cold and bitter trail. But . . ." He stopped his horse and looked his men each in the eye in turn. "Once I'm on the trail, I realize this is where I can be the most use to society. What good am I if I sit at home and tickle my wife? What good are any of us? I know you all want to get home, except maybe for Webber." He grinned, showing he was almost human. "Well, mark my word on this. I'll see that each of you gets back or die trying.

"Remember, though we are few in number, a small but persistent cadre of disciplined men often has an advantage over a much larger force." With that he trotted back into the lead.

Clay turned to Trap and grimaced. "I don't like them odds, partner," he whispered. "I ain't had a disciplined day in my life."

"Today is as good a day as any to begin, Sergeant Madsen," Roman said over his shoulder, proving his hearing was truly beyond human.

"*Sanguis frigitis,*" Webber mused, under his breath.

Now Clay lowered his voice. "Hell's bells! More Greek already? You're making my head hurt."

"Not Greek, oh, wise student of learned whores. Latin. *Sanguis frigitis* literally means *cold blood*—more figuratively, it means *steady under pressure*—calm in the face of danger. Suits the captain right to the core."

Trap stood in the stirrups to stretch his back. "Can't argue there."

"Hell," Clay snorted. "After what I've seen in the last three days, I guess it suits you two as much as him. Gougin' folks' eyes out and loppin' their heads off at the gallop . . . I reckon I'm the only one that gets shook up over anything anymore."

"I don't know about that," Trap said. "You seemed mighty calm making a three-hundred-yard shot to save the captain and his men from that scalp-hunter rifleman."

"Four hundred and thirty," Clay corrected with a wink. "I stepped it off."

"Well, there you go then." Webber raised his fist high in the air, as if in a toast. "I hereby declare the motto of the Scout Trackers to be *Sanguis Frigitis*."

"*Sanguis Frigitis*," Trap and Clay repeated, nodding their heads.

"Has a nice ring to it," Roman said without turning around. The other men jumped when they realized he'd been listening. "*Cold Blood*. I'm afraid we'll need it."

CHAPTER 34

When she moved, she threw up, and throwing up made her move. Beads of sweat covered her forehead, pasting ringlets of black hair against pallid skin. Her body burned with fever, shivers sending bolts of pain down her shoulder and through her right arm. A normally petite hand throbbed purple and yellow at twice its normal size.

The filthy, merciless men had dragged her from her bed in the dead of night and thrown her to the ground in her nightgown. Horses squealed and stomped amid acrid smoke and the clap of gunfire. Riders cursed and shouted at each other in the darkness. She'd tried to crawl away in the confusion, but a horse had stepped on her hand.

The pain had been unbearable. She heard the bones crunch between hoof and rock. Nausea overwhelmed her before unconsciousness silenced her choking screams.

Three days in this sandstone hell had pressed every tear out of her bloodshot eyes. Grit and grime covered every inch of her body, grating and inflaming her pink skin until even a light breeze brought on dizzying waves of agony.

Red sand caked her face where it had pressed against the ground without benefit of a blanket or pillow. Her lavender gown, once a sight to behold, made in Mexico City from the finest cotton, was now reduced to filthy rags. It did little to protect her from the bone-numbing chill at night, and even less to cover her bruised nakedness.

Vile men who cared nothing for her survival squatted and knelt in tiny groups around a crackling cedar fire under the deep rock overhang. The sight of them racked her slight body with sickening panic that made her teeth ache. The things they'd said, the things they'd done to poor Charlie before they finally cut off his head—his pitiful wails still tore at her ears and haunted her fitful dreams. Their gruff voices echoed inside the rock tomb, bouncing around in her head until she thought it might explode.

The flames cast huge shadows along the back of the shallow cave, dancing and crackling with the night wind. Orange sparks rose and swirled like ghostly spirits on the air, stark against the blackness beyond the rocks.

Locked in a game of dice, the men drank and cursed and sometimes hit each other, but they seldom wasted a glance on the pitiful Mexican girl in the corner.

A half-cooked joint of antelope meat lay covered with flies on a greasy rock beside her. She'd eaten a few bites out of desperation earlier that day, but vomited them back up again a few moments later.

She knew she should eat something to keep her strength up, but her stomach churned and boiled every time she looked at the foul thing. Her lips were dry and split from lack of water and purple from slaps and rough taunts.

"Damn every last one of you, you lousy sons of bitches," the man called Jack Straw shouted as he rose from the main game of dice across the flickering chamber. He shook a bottle of liquor at the others. "I ain't gonna hunker here and get cheated by your sorry hides." His stooped shoulders heaved with anger. His craggy face appeared to twitch in the orange firelight. The big Indian slid a huge knife half out of the beaded sheath stuck in his belt. He glared through cruel eyes that shut Straw up as surely as a cold slap in the face.

The girl held her breath. They fought like this all the time, especially in the evening. She'd never seen people argue and scream at each other so violently. Someone would certainly die before long. In the beginning, she was afraid it would be her. Very soon, she knew, she would welcome the thought of it.

Straw skulked to the rear of the cave with a bottle in his hand. Back to the wall, he slid to the sandy floor, shoulders slouched in defeat. His dirty blond head hung between his knees.

When he sat up to take a drink, he caught her looking at him. She held her breath and turned away, but it was too late.

"What the hell are you gawkin' at, Miss Purebred?" Whiskey ran around the mouth of the bottle as he took a pull and dribbled down on his torn shirt. "You ain't never seen a man drunk before?"

She clenched her eyes shut. It did no good to talk to these men. She pressed her face against the sand, hoping against hope that Straw would keep drinking and leave her alone.

She smelled the fetid stench of his body and the sour odor of cheap whiskey before she opened her eyes. The coarse weave of his homespun shirt brushed against her bare shoulder. She flinched, wishing herself deeper into the sand.

"Here you go, Little Highness," Straw slurred, shaking the bottle in her face. His knee bumped her broken hand, and she bit her lip to keep from crying out. Her stomach roiled from the pain and the man's awful smell.

"Have a little drink, Honey Pot. It'll loosen you up."

Clenching her eyes shut, she shook her head and turned away. Her shoulders trembled with fright.

Straw clawed at her shoulder and gave it a brutal yank. "I said have a drink, damn you." He hauled her up by her arm. She moved with him to keep from causing any more pain to her broken hand. His face was only inches from hers. Yellow teeth gleamed dully in the shadows. She winced at his rancid breath, dumb and frozen with fear.

He grabbed her by the face and squeezed until tears poured from her eyes. He slurred through clenched teeth, "Just because them bastards cheat me don't give you the right to give me no sass." He rubbed his greasy forehead against hers as he spoke. "I don't give a damn about the money anymore. I can't spend another minute in this cave with your sweetness a-waftin' up to my old nose just a few feet away. I reckon I'll take my cut of you now."

The other men laughed at their new game of dice. Someone was losing badly, and now that Straw was gone, the group had homed in on him.

Straw was oblivious. He shoved her head tight against the rock wall, pressing her jaw with his thumb and forefinger until he forced her mouth open. She tried to scream, but could only manage a moaning gurgle.

"Come on, take a little swig." Straw leered. "You're gonna need it."

He forced the heavy whiskey bottle through dry, cracked lips. She tasted the saltiness of her own blood an instant before glass hit her teeth with a sickening thud. She gagged as the searing liquid poured against her throat and spewed down her chest.

The pain was excruciating, but she summoned enough strength to struggle, flailing against her attacker with both hands. She felt one of her front teeth snap, and retched as he jammed the bottle deeper against the back of her throat.

Suddenly, Straw stopped. The whiskey bottle fell away and splashed harmlessly to the sand. The panting girl shielded her face with her good hand and braced herself for another attack. When none came, she opened her eyes.

Straw knelt above her, his back arched in agony, his mouth open in a noiseless cry. The big Indian stood behind him, one hand on the hilt of the huge knife that was buried in Straw's spine, the other gripping a fistful of greasy hair.

Straw dropped the bottle and reached over his shoulder with both hands, clawing in vain at his back. His shoulders twitched when the Indian jerked out the knife and stabbed him again and again.

The girl collapsed against the ground and watched in detached silence as Straw's glowing red eyes rolled back in his head. Blood poured out of him, drenching the sand. He lay at her feet, twitching and taking a long time to die.

CHAPTER 35

"Something's been eatin' at me, Webber," Clay confided as the group rode along three abreast. Roman was well in the lead. It was early afternoon on the second day out of Camp Apache. The first night had been chilly, but the sun now hung in a cloudless sky and the weather had warmed considerably.

Trap and Webber rode on without speaking. Both knew they didn't need to say anything to prod Clay into explaining what he meant.

"It's something the colonel said back there." The Texan looked at Johannes. "Webber, don't take this the wrong way, but you're one of the smartest men I ever met when it comes to book learnin'. If you don't mind my asking, how come you never did apply to be an officer?"

The three rode on in silence for quite some time with no sound but the heavy thud of hooves on rock and the lumbering groan of the horses.

"Plato," Webber said, looking ahead. "Among others."

Clay gave a swaggering laugh. "I figured you'd say something about the Greeks. Plato told you not to be an officer?"

Johannes shrugged, not upset from the question, but deadly serious. "Plato believed philosophers should be kings and all kings should be philosophers. He also said a man should do what he was born to do—stay in his own class."

"Well," Clay said. "I ain't sayin' you should be a king, but your philosophizin' ought to at least qualify you for lieutenant."

"Kings," Johannes pointed out, "and other powerful men tend to use their power to further their own selfish goals. They have a way of becoming corrupted."

Clay chewed on that for a while. Trap watched the captain riding out ahead of them. Now there was a man with philosophy and power—and he seemed virtually incorruptible.

"I think you'd make a good enough officer, even with the power it brings." Clay gave a sincere nod as if he was passing judgment.

"My friend," Johannes said, "that just proves how little you know about me."

The wind shifted and sent Clay's mind drifting another direction before he could think of a comeback. He stood in the saddle and sniffed the air. "Reminds me of a pig roast." He turned to Trap, who rode beside him, eyes on the ground looking for sign. "A pig roast and burnt rope. Do you smell what I'm smellin'?"

Trap looked up, took a moment to inhale the dry desert air, and nodded. The smell of cooked meat did hang on the faint wind. He chided himself for not noticing it before Madsen. His mother had often warned him about depending too much on one sense and forgetting the others. Humans had a way of relying only on their eyes while their ears and nose went virtually unused. The little tracker reined in his horse and drew another lungful of air. Something else mixed with the familiar smell—just a whiff. It wasn't rope—it was hair.

Roman and his men saw the buzzards ten minutes later. Some circled lazily overhead, while dark specks against a blinding blue; others perched on the gnarled branches of a dead mesquite in the wavy, heated light of midday. The raucous coughing of crows grated the air shortly after. A sprawling stand of prickly pear cactus hid whatever produced the smell from view, but it was causing quite a fight among the scavenger community.

A heavy sense of doom permeated the air as the men neared the cactus. The smell grew stronger and pinched at Trap's nose. He knew what it was. They all did.

Five turkey buzzards tried to lift off from the nearest of two bodies as the riders approached on snorting horses. Two of the birds found they couldn't fly with their bellies full of rancid meat, and regurgitated it up in a splattering slurry as they winged away. Trap shot a glance at Clay, who was highly likely to throw up at the sight of such a thing. For all his braggadocio, the Texan had a tendency toward a weak stomach. Luckily, he was busy scanning the horizon for trouble and missed the buzzards' display.

"My Lord," Clay said when he finally let his eyes come to rest on the bloated bodies. His voice was shallow. "My poor eyes keep seein' things they don't want to see."

Roman dismounted and looped the bay's reins around the dead mesquite. The buzzards, crows, and a handful of magpies winged off to wait their respective turns after the interloping men moved on. There was a hierarchy among the birds, and they ate in ascending order of their looks.

"O'Shannon," the captain whispered. Trap would come to know that Roman generally spoke quietly around the dead. "Take a look around the bodies and see if you can get an idea of what happened here." He turned to Webber and Madsen, who both stood wide-eyed, entranced at the two naked bodies staked to the ground in front of them. "Men! Snap out of it and secure your horses. Get your rifles and keep a weather eye on those hills. I wouldn't put it past an Apache to use a massacre like this as bait to catch us unawares."

That bit of information was enough to jog Clay out of his stupor. He had Clarice out glinting in the sun in a matter of moments. Webber stood with his Winchester, facing the hills in the opposite direction.

Trap surveyed the grisly scene. Two men, it was impossible to tell how old they were, lay spread-eagle, feet pointing in opposite directions on the rocky ground. Stout leather cord and wooden pegs kept them there. The remains of a fire blacked the earth between what was left of their swollen heads.

Death had not come quickly for the poor souls. Trap could make out the square-toed tracks of Apache moccasins where they had fed the fire a bit at a time, keeping it just large enough to cause excruciating pain without bringing an end to the doomed men's suffering. Trap wondered how long they'd screamed while the flames singed their hair, blistered the tender skin, and finally boiled their brains.

He had to look at them like tracks to keep from getting sick. If he considered them as human beings, his stomach began to rebel. He thought of them as nothing more than sign with a story to tell, and quelled his unruly gut.

The buzzards had started with the cooked parts, and the men stared up at nothing with swollen, eyeless skulls. The sun had taken its toll on the lower half of the bodies, and though the fire had not cooked them, they were bloated and dark.

After he studied the area around the bodies, Trap worked out in ever-growing circles, checking behind every rock and shrub within a fifty-yard circle.

"They been here a while," he said when he was satisfied he had the complete story and came back to the group. "A day or two at least." He stuck his hand in the coals. There was no heat left, even a few inches down. They were as dead as the men they had killed.

"Apache?" Webber shouted from his position a few yards away.

"Looks that way." Roman nodded, slapping his leather gloves against an open hand.

"Victorio's band?" Webber scanned the hills to the east. There was no fear in his voice. He was merely thinking out loud.

Trap stood and walked toward his horse to put some distance between himself and the mutilated bodies. "There are too many hoofprints to count, Captain. Most are unshod. The whole place is covered with moccasin tracks. One set is smaller like those of a woman. It could be Victorio and his sister, Lozan. She relieved herself behind that square stone there." He pointed with an open hand.

Webber took a break from his vigil and cast a sidelong glance over his shoulder. "You can tell it was a woman by looking at where she . . ."

Trap shrugged. His mother had been blunt and open about such things as part of his tracking education. Talk of sex bothered him, but this was different; bodily functions were sign and deserved study. Trap was finding himself a teacher more and more each day.

"A female is generally wary of being discovered in such a delicate position," he pointed out calmly, as if he was instructing a class. "They will look over their shoulder, this way, then that way, back and forth several times during the process." O'Shannon mimicked the motion himself, letting his entire body sway with the movement. "Whatever they leave behind, liquid or solid, is usually in a little crescent shape instead of a circle."

Webber smirked. "Well, sir, that's about as much as I need to know about that." He resumed his guard duties, shaking his head.

Clay giggled, then nodded slowly to himself, obviously picturing the whole thing in his mind. "Victorio and Lozan it is."

"Could be," Roman mused. "But we have other business."

"Well, I'm glad to hear that." Clay gave an exasperated sigh. "I got no real desire to go up against an army of Apache who would roast what little brain I got just to get their daily entertainment."

"Let's get some dirt pushed up over the bodies," Roman said, walking to his horse for a hand shovel. They'd brought with them two of the Rice-Chillingsworth trowel-style bayonets the Army had experimented with. Roman wouldn't allow them on the end of a rifle, said it was too much temptation to stick the muzzle in the dirt, but he did find them useful as digging tools and easy to pack on such a mission where space was at a premium.

"Poor souls deserve a decent burial, whoever they are." Never one to leave the distasteful work solely to his men,

Roman started for the bodies with his trowel. Trap joined him while the other two stood watch. Sweat dripped off both men by the time they had a sizable pile of dirt and rock piled over the bodies.

Trap knew it might keep the birds away for a while, but would never discourage scavengers like wolves or coyotes. He reckoned that out in the desert like this, decent folks like Captain Roman buried the dead so they could look at something neat and tidy as they rode away. If vermin and turkey buzzards dragged the bones out later, at least a man could know things were in order when he left. Burial was a luxury on the wide-open plain: peace of mind more for the living than for the uncaring dead.

A cool wind kicked up while Trap repacked the trowels. When he turned, something in the scrubby branches of a creosote bush caught his eye.

At first he thought it was a desert cottontail scurrying for shelter. Then, the wind moved the bush and he could make out straight edges, angular like something man-made.

Trap gave Skunk a reassuring pat on the rump and went to investigate. The others were already mounting up.

"What is it?" Clay asked, trotting over to see what Trap had found. It was a light brown envelope, half-burned. Scrawled in block letters, the ink smeared by an unsteady hand, was the word *URGENT!*

A single sheet of tan paper folded lengthwise down the center slid out of the envelope and into Roman's gloved hand. More than half of it crumbled into parched ashes when he tried to open it. He read what was left slowly to himself, then passed it back to Trap.

"Gentlemen, we can stop wasting our time feeling sorry for those men. It looks as though they were part of the group that kidnapped Señorita de la Cruz. I am assuming they were on their way to deliver these ransom instructions when they had the bad fortune to run into this little band of hostiles."

Trap read over the notes twice to make sure he got it all, then handed it up to Clay.

"It instructs the Army to build a fire on top of Kill Devil Mesa as soon as this message is received and the money is ready." Roman rubbed his tired eyes. "Further instructions follow, but they are burned away. Whatever their plan was, it may have changed since the message never got delivered. It's dated two days ago. The signal fire should have been set by now."

Clay's mouth dropped open and he began to fidget with his catch rope. "You think they might spook and kill her?"

"It's possible," Roman said. "More likely, they would send out another note since these two never returned. Sergeant O'Shannon. Can you pick up the dead men's back trail?"

Trap nodded, spinning Skunk. He was already on it. The track of two shod horses moving across the desert was easy enough to find and follow.

"Very well," Roman said. "We'll follow the tracks right back to the men that sent them—and hopefully to the girl. We need to move quickly. . . ." Roman's voice trailed off. He motioned with his hat toward a cloud of dust billowing on the distant horizon.

Someone was coming.

Clay turned in the saddle to slide Clarice out of her scabbard. "Apache?" he said under his breath as he lowered the block a hair to be certain he had a fresh round in place.

A growing red cloud boiled over the hills to the east. Whoever it was, they were getting closer.

Roman dismounted and stood quietly. He scanned the area around them, thinking. At length he looked up at Clay.

"Sergeant Madsen, see that patch of rocks?" He pointed to a long hill a hundred yards away.

Clay grunted. "Yessir."

"Take your long gun and set up a position of cover amid those rocks. Stay out of sight until I take off my hat. Don't rejoin us until I put my hat back on."

"How will I know if I should fire?"

Roman patted Madsen's horse on the rump. He smiled.

"Clay, if we start shooting, you go ahead and feel free to join in."

"Aye, sir." Clay put the spurs to his blue roan and loped up the steady incline to the pile of boulders. It was big enough to hide both horse and rider.

Roman stood by in silence as the dust cloud boiled ever larger on the horizon.

Trap was surprised that he felt no fear. He found himself too worried about letting Captain Roman and the others down to have any time to be afraid. He repeated Clay's earlier question. "Do you think it's Apaches? Victorio coming back, maybe?"

"They're coming in from the southeast." Roman shook his head. "It's almost sunset. That means the light is shining directly in their eyes. No self-respecting Apache would launch an attack unless the sun was to his back."

"Maybe they don't know we're here," Webber offered. His gaze too was locked on the horizon, the Winchester in his hands.

"Could be," Roman said. "But I doubt it. That cloud of dust has United States Cavalry written all over it. We horse soldiers are generally the only breed of human around these parts with enough hubris to let everyone and everything in the country know we're on our way. No, that's cavalry all right. And if it's who I think it is, I'm afraid he could pose nearly as much of a problem as Apaches."

CHAPTER 36

D Troop was under the command of Captain Fredrick Paul Lyons; Fredrick to the few friends he had, not Fred, not Freddy, or even F.P. He'd been known to correct generals if they attempted to call him anything but his proper given name.

A tall man with gray circles under matching eyes, he stood firmly on all points of formality and expected all those around him to do the same. The joke around the Army was that he required his wife to address him as Captain Lyons when he was in uniform and Your Highness when he was not.

A normal company was comprised of about a hundred men including officers, but with sickness, desertion, and other manpower shortages, D Company was lucky to have a complement of fifty. They breasted the sandstone ridge in columns of four, with Captain Lyons out front on a stodgy white horse. His aide rode next to him, followed by a mustachioed bugler. The swallow-tailed company guidon snapped on its nine-foot lance in the freshening breeze above the next trooper in line. Each man's face was set in a sort of grim, pinch-faced annoyance, as if he was being pestered by a fly but was unable to shoo it away because his hands were busy.

"The whole lot of them looks like they're marching off to Perdition," Trap muttered, moving up next to Roman.

Webber flashed a knowing smirk. "The poor bastards. You'd look that way too if you had to ride with Lyons. The man's an ass who can't . . ."

"That'll do," Roman said, his voice sharp but not un-friendly. "Explain to Mr. O'Shannon about Captain Lyons and his many idiosyncrasies another time. Just be certain you don't do it in front of me."

"Aye, sir." Webber winked at Trap, confirming he'd fill him in later.

Approaching, Lyons raised his bony arm to the square and gave the command to halt in a loud if somewhat nasal voice.

"The Lyons roar," Webber whispered, blank-faced.

Roman shot him a sideways look.

"Sorry, sir," Webber said. "Won't happen again."

Lyons urged his mount forward. "Lieutenant Roman, you're out of uniform," he barked from the back of his sullen horse. "Leave garrison for a few days and you go to hell in a handbasket, eh?"

Trap had seen the type before. Some men, officers and enlisted alike, felt like they were invincible from the back of a horse—ten feet tall and bullet-proof.

Two Apache scouts, wearing red scarves around their heads to set them apart from any hostiles, slouched on their sullen ponies and watched the two white leaders. One rolled his eyes and gave Roman a quiet, conspiratorial grin.

Roman nodded to Lyons. "I am, but not without orders. We're conducting business for Colonel Branchflower."

Lyons rubbed his receding chin and sighed. "You're filthy—covered in sweat and dirt from head to boot. A shambles, Hezekiah, that's what you are." He peeled off his glove and held out a hand. "Let's have a look at those orders of yours."

"Afraid I can't do that," Roman said. "They're classified in nature."

Lyons puffed up like a toad. "May I remind you," he har-rumphed. "As long as I remain your superior officer, you are obliged to comply with my orders."

"While that's not entirely true"—Roman smiled—"it is

a moot issue. Colonel Branchflower brevetted me to captain."

The bugler stifled a snicker behind his mustache.

"Is that a fact?" Lyons looked down his nose in unmasked disgust. "In any case, I am still your senior." He gave his hand a dismissive flick. "You and your men are enlisted to ride with me against Victorio. The savage and his band have been spotted raiding near this very spot."

"I know." Roman gestured over his shoulder. "We just buried two of his victims."

"Then you also know I'll need every man I can get my hand on when we find him. My scouts say he's two days away, but my gut tells me he's within a day's ride." Lyons took up the slack in his reins, preparing to move out without further discussion. His horse fought the bits, and he slapped it on the neck with a leather shoofly that hung from his wrist. "Have your men fall in at the rear. You may ride up here with me."

Trap and Johannes both looked to Roman for guidance. He stood completely still.

"Request denied," he said at length, folding his hands in front of him.

"That was not a request, Captain. That was an order."

Roman kept his voice low and calm in contrast to Lyons' high-toned quiver. "I have my orders and I intend to see them through to the end."

"I am still the senior officer here," Lyons spit though gritted teeth. "I will decide what missions are important and which ones are not while we are in the field. You *will* fall in with my command. I'll sort it out with the old man upon our return."

Every man in D Troop eased up slightly, leaning forward in the saddle to try and hear how the standoff would play out. The air buzzed with tension. Hoarse whispers moved like a wave through the ranks. From the crooked grins on their faces, Trap decided few of these men were rooting for their commander.

Roman was calm as a summer's morning, his voice firm

and matter-of-fact, as if he was speaking to a small child who didn't understand the seriousness of the situation.

"Captain Lyons, with all due respect, I suggest you continue on your mission and leave us to ours."

Lyons's eyes blazed. Feeling the tension, his horse tried to charge forward, and the captain had to yank on the reins to keep the animal under control. He shook his fist at Roman. "I've had enough of you. Sergeant Collins, put Mr. Roman in irons. If his men give you any trouble, shoot them."

Trap and Johannes both stepped forward to flank their commander. He motioned them back with a faint smile. Trap had never seen anyone so cool under pressure.

"Sergeant Collins," Roman said. There was the slightest hint of fatigue in his voice. "Delay that order."

"Collins." Lyons glared at his subordinate. "Do as I say or I'll bring you up on charges!" His head shook on stooped shoulders. His bloodshot eyes bulged in their sockets and looked like they might pop out of his skull.

Roman's voice rose at once like a clap of rolling thunder. "Captain Lyons, dismount and speak to me privately and I'll explain my orders to you."

Collins looked back and forth between the two commanders and swallowed hard. He took half a step forward, but Trap sent him a look that kept him in his place.

Lyons climbed down from his horse and handed the reins to his blank-faced aide. He stepped forward, out of earshot of his troop, and shot a dismissive look at Trap and Johannes.

"I thought you wished to speak in private. Aren't you going to have your men pull back?"

"I don't care if they hear every word I say," Roman whispered. He was smiling, so the rest of D Troop had no idea what was going on. "I asked you down here so I didn't embarrass you in front of your command."

Lyons started to turn and go.

Roman stopped him with a hiss. "My orders are more important than you could ever imagine, and I am not about to let a self-important boob who couldn't command an army of pissants dissuade me in my duty just because he thinks he has some power."

Lyons was taken aback for a moment while he struggled to regain control of the situation. A sly smile suddenly crossed his seething face. "You forget, Hezekiah. There are only three of you. If you turn this into a battle of force, I have forty-seven men at my disposal."

Roman ripped off his hat and moved nose-to-nose with the other captain. "Now you listen to me, you arrogant bastard. You may have an entire company, but the fourth man in my unit, the man you didn't even know existed until now, is up in those rocks behind you. I'm sick of your bullshit, Freddy. I don't take orders from you. I take my direction straight from Colonel Branchflower."

Roman smiled. His voice softened again. "My rifleman takes his direction from me. I'll leave it to you to figure out what that direction is."

Lyons turned his twitching face slowly to look up at the rocks. Madsen stared down the glinting barrel of his Sharps and gave him a little wave for effect. He'd moved up slightly so he could be seen once Roman removed his hat.

"He's loyal as hell to Captain Roman," Webber said. "And his skill with that rifle of his is unmatched. Wouldn't you say, Sergeant O'Shannon?"

Trap nodded. "None better, Sergeant Webber. He could part your hair at this range, that's for certain."

Lyons's face flushed a deeper shade of red. A purple vein throbbed along his temple. "I'll see you busted back to mucking stables for this, Hezekiah. I have friends in high places."

"So do I, Freddy." Roman tossed his head toward Clay and his rifle. "So do I."

Captain Fredrick Paul Lyons wasted no time in mustering his troops away after Victorio, who he no doubt would find an easier customer to deal with than Hezekiah Roman.

"I'd hate to be assigned to Company D tonight," Webber

allowed as he mounted up. Clay skittered down the hill above them on his roan.

"Or ever," Trap agreed. He loped Skunk out a few paces to the east and studied the ground while the others married up and prepared to move. He shook his head and figured out another reason to hate Freddy Lyons: D Troop, with their sixty-plus horses and pack animals, had completely obliterated the outlaws' back trail.

"Can you find where they crossed?" Roman looked at the ground in disgust.

"Yessir," Trap said. "I can, but not with any speed. It'll take some time."

Roman sighed. "As fast as possible then," he said. "I'm sure the kidnappers are getting antsy since their companions have failed to return. Time is something that's in extremely short supply."

CHAPTER 37

All of the men were horrible, lewd things who melded together in the girl's fevered mind into one awful mass of putrid cruelty. Two of them took Straw's body by the heels and dragged it out of the sandstone cave to feed it to the buzzards while his blood still pooled fresh in the sand at her feet.

The big Indian had ended her torment for the moment when he stabbed Straw to death, but there was no mercy in his black eyes. To him she was nothing more than property— property he was paid to protect. If the one paying the bills gave the order, he'd stab her just as quickly as he'd killed Straw.

The short man with a cowlick and close-set eyes appeared to be the leader. In the beginning, when she was in pain, but still had some semblance of her wits about her, she'd watched the group, looked for a weakness to see if there might be a chance for escape. If the group had what could be termed a boss, this one was him. He was the one who had the plan. He seemed to be the one paying for any operating costs. The others deferred to him a tiny bit more than they did each other—and that wasn't much. Whatever hold he had on his filthy band of confederates, it was tenuous at best.

She studied him the first day, thinking him at times weak, at times just foolish. Though she was in tremendous pain,

it was easy for her to feel morally superior to a little
Napoleon who barely had a grip on his group of cutthroats. Then, he'd ordered poor Charlie Dolan killed.

The brutality with which the bloodthirsty group fell on
her poor friend had changed her. They seemed to her like
raging beasts more than men, lusting for violence the way
some craved a woman. She'd been unable to turn away as
Charlie, a strong, courageous man who had a wife and two
daughters, screamed and thrashed in horrific pain while
they cut off his head—slowly.

Now, with thirst and pain and terror eating away at her
fevered brain, she could only cringe when any of the men so
much as looked in her direction. She wanted to die, to be free
from the pain. But she didn't want to die like Charlie.

She shuddered uncontrollably when the leader staggered
to his feet and swayed over to her in the dark cave. The fire
behind him cast a huge shadow against the back wall.

"I aim to turn you in for the ransom," he said, assuring
her that if she cooperated she might make it home alive.
"I can't have you ruined by a fool like Straw. If the Army and
your papa don't pay, you'll still fetch a little money from my
contacts." His small eyes narrowed when he caught her looking at the entrance to the cave. "Don't even think about
trying to escape, Pilar. There's snakes and lizards out there
that would kill all of us here with just one bite."

"I wish one would then," she heard herself say. Her
teeth chattered when she spoke. It would serve the fool
right if she died in her sleep from fever and infection.

The man chuckled. He knelt in the sand beside her
and reached for her injured hand. He was gentle in an odd,
uncaring sort of way, as one might carefully check an injured horse to see if it was still fit to race.

"It's been a hard-fought battle to get this far. I'll not let you
run off and steal my fortune." The smirk on his pitiless face
caused her to look away. "I got an awful lot riding on you, little
girl. Don't you disappoint me."

She looked away, thinking she would rather brave a pit
full of the deadliest of vipers as listen to one more word this
man had to say.

It was as if he read her thoughts.

He grabbed her by the waist and pinched her hard in the tender belly just above her navel, hard enough to make her yelp. "Papago will cut two little slits in your skin right here; then he'll take the cord he uses to tie you up and run it through the holes." The man laughed. "Makes it hell tryin' to get away while you're rippin' your own guts out."

He gave her bare thigh a swat. "I don't want to mess you up, little girl. But I'm a businessman first and foremost. If you do anything bad for business, well, that would be an awful shame." Convinced he'd made his point, the man walked out of the cave into the darkness.

Her head drooped in despair.

A huge black fly, sticky from the rancid antelope haunch, buzzed up to investigate the crusted blood on her swollen lip. Four days ago such a thing would have sent her into a spitting frenzy to scrub her mouth with soap. Now, she couldn't bring herself to care.

Payton Brandywine hunkered against a lumpy boulder at the edge of the cave and watched his plan come unraveled right before his very eyes like a poor pack-knot. The rock dug into his back, but he pressed against it all the harder, letting the pain in his flesh keep him in the grim reality of his circumstances.

Since that idiot Straw had become too familiar with the merchandise and gotten himself killed, the group had begun to polarize. The Papago was still with him, not so much for the money as for revenge against the greaser girl's daddy. The sullen Indian didn't have much love for Mexicans in general, but he hated Colonel de la Cruz about as much as he hated Apaches—which was more than considerable.

Other than the Indian, he wasn't sure who was on his side. No one had killed him in his sleep yet. That was a mercy anyhow. He was pretty sure the one they called Bent Jim was with him, if only for his share of the ransom money. Bent Jim's partner was a quiet man everyone called

Grunt, because that seemed to be the only way he knew how to communicate. Brandywine figured Grunt would throw in with Bent Jim, whichever way he went. That's what partners did. And out here everyone had a partner. A body had to have one to survive.

The Indian agent calculated his odds. The Papago was scorpion-quick, with the dead cruel eyes of a rattlesnake. Grunt looked to be worth any two of the others in a fight, but a bullet would kill him as quick as it would any man. Bent Jim was no slouch, but he was among the smallest of the group. Well into his fifties, he was definitely the oldest.

The two Mexicans were too mortified of Papago to go against him. Every time he stood, the two idiots nearly pissed their pants. Still, they could shoot, and he needed shooters. Hell, even he was scared of the Papago.

Haywood and Babcock, brooding whiskey peddlers Payton had known off and on for over five years, had been friends of Straw. They were none too happy to see their partner stabbed by an Indian over a Mexican girl. None of them had challenged him directly, but Brandywine knew the look when he saw it. A dispute was coming. It was just a matter of time.

A wild-eyed lion hunter named Tug leered at the girl like she was the ultimate prize instead of the money. He would choose whichever side would ultimately give him a go with her, Payton was sure of that. Tug was happy with nothing but a pile of skins to sleep on and flea-bitten hides for clothing, and the ransom meant little to him.

Tug's partner, Joe Simmons, was a filthy creature almost as old as Bent Jim. His skin and clothing were so equally stained with sweat and grime, it was difficult to tell where one ended and the other began. He would side with Tug.

A pair of cackling, towheaded twins not yet out of their teens were the wild cards. They dreamt of the money, but the thought of a few minutes with the señorita made them giggle maniacally and punch each other in the arms in turn. They were young and untested, but both were handy with their guns. Hiram, the crazier of the two, looked up to Tug the lion hunter and was apt to follow him as far as he went in any direction. Hiram's brother, Lars, would certainly go the same way, so there was a chance that whole group would band together if it came to a mutiny.

Brandywine sucked air in slowly between his teeth while he thought. "You sure got yourself a handful this time, Payton," he whispered under his breath.

If only that son of a bitch Evans would get back. He and his kid brother were supposed to deliver the ransom note two days ago and come back with supplies. The fact that they hadn't returned had tensions rubbed raw in the little group. The plan had been working perfectly until now.

If Brandywine ever had a partner it was Ponce Evans. The Army sergeant knew his way around the military. He was the one who'd heard the Mexican colonel's daughter was on her way to Phoenix under U.S. escort, the one who'd suggested how much money both governments might pay to get such a girl back. At first, the two men had thought to attempt the kidnapping with only Papago to help them, but when Evans found out the escort would consist of eight troopers, not including the coach driver, they decided to recruit more men.

To easily overpower an army, they had needed an army, so they were forced to cobble together this group of killers and misfits. If he'd known how young and inexperienced the escort was, Brandywine wouldn't have hired half the men he did. Now, they all wanted their share of the money, even if all they did was sit around and play dice and scratch themselves.

Brandywine was not a big man. For some reason, his hair had decided to thin everywhere except the cowlick at his crown. His cookie-duster mustache made him look more like a schoolteacher than a kidnapper. What he lacked in size he made up for in greed and ruthlessness. He felt confident he could hold the conspiracy together for a little while longer with the promise of money. Either the girl's father or the U.S. Army would pay. He was positive. Evans had assured him the Army considered the girl precious cargo. He'd heard enough talk from the officers about how strained relations were between the two countries. The Mexican colonel would want his precious daughter back, and the United States would pay nearly any price to avert sinking further into a squabble with their neighbor to the south.

Brandywine pushed himself to his feet. He couldn't very well stand by and watch all his planning and hard work crumble down around his shoulders. He had to do something. He needed to send out more ransom instructions before the pitiful girl died of fright or one of the men got to her in the night and killed her for the fun of it.

He didn't want to send anyone that would be on his side in a fight. In the end he decided on the Mexicans. They were too scared of Papago to go against him, and too greedy not to come back.

"Ruiz! Cardenas!" Brandywine clapped his hands together. *"Venga aqui."*

The Mexicans stood and staggered over to Brandywine. Neither was very tall, but both were strong men, with big hands and small hearts.

The remainder of the group peered up from their gambling to see what was going on. Everyone expected that the others might cheat or kill them at any moment—and in most respects, that was likely to be the gospel truth.

"We need supplies," Brandywine said, nodding his head. "I want you two to ride into Agua Caliente and see what you hear about Ponce and Sammy. I'm afraid they didn't get through. Take another letter with you and deliver it so we can get our money. If you can find that giant friend of yours, bring him back with you in case we need reinforcements." He studied the sodden, bloodshot faces of Cardenas and Ruiz.

"Comprende?" he said.

The men gave grunting mumbles of agreement. They brightened at the thought of a little escape from the tension of the cave.

"Very well," the Indian agent said. He turned his attention to the rest of the men. "This will all work out, boys, I assure you. In a week's time we'll all be rich."

It was Tug who proved he was the one to watch. Brandywine had been right.

The lion hunter spit a greasy brown slurry of tobacco into the sand. "You ain't got a week. If we don't see some cash inside of two days, I reckon some of us are gonna divide up our share of the spoils as best we know how." A cruel grin etched his greasy face and his hungry gaze fell on the cowering girl. He spit again. "*Comprende,* Boss Man?"

CHAPTER 38

A blind man could have followed the wide swath Lyons's troop had cut through the rough desert country. Trap kept a sharp eye out for any intersecting trails that might have been made by the dead outlaws.

His thoughts constantly wandered back to Maggie. Madsen was right about one thing. Life had a funny way of turning out a heck of a lot different than a person planned. Less than six months ago, he'd been a contented student at his father's school for Indian children. Now, he found himself married and part of a secret military unit.

As was his custom when the trail was apparent, Captain Roman ranged ahead about a hundred yards. Clay and Johannes hung back with Trap, riding on either side of him helping him try and cut sign.

"You ever think about getting older?" The words escaped Trap's mouth before he had a chance to consider the ramifications of such a question.

Clay shot a grin and a wink at Webber. "Told you he was ponderin' on the missus."

"By getting older," Johannes mused, "do you mean maturing or just getting on in years? I only ask because I don't think Madsen will ever do anything but age."

"Hell," Clay scoffed. "I'm old enough, I reckon. I expect I'll get creaky and stiff when the time comes."

Trap shrugged, sorry he'd brought it up. "I guess I

meant settlin' down. You know, building a little house somewhere, raisin' some kids . . ."

Clay lifted his reins and the big roan stopped in his tracks. The other boys pulled up alongside him. "A body's got to have a roof over his head, especially if he wants to have a wife that'll stick around—and I reckon young'uns are a natural consequence of having a wife that sticks around—but I will tell you this, partner: I may be young yet, but hangin' around my papa's whores taught me a good bit about this old world. I've seen you in the scrap. You got a gift when it comes to settlin' the score—you're a damned dangerous man, Trap O'Shannon, and I can't see no dangerous man settling down too awful early in his life. Just because you up and got yourself married don't mean you have to stop fightin'."

Madsen clucked to his horse and they all three began to move again.

"Look at the captain," Webber said. "He's as married as I ever seen, and he's apt to keep doing this for as long as he lives. You've heard him. He thinks he's an instrument in God's own hands." Johannes put on a stern face and squinted into the sun as he tried his best Hezekiah Roman impression. "'When the right path is before you, gentlemen—never pause, proceed.'" Webber laughed and shook his head. "I wish I had his kind of ambition."

"Drive be damned," Clay said. "Anything else sounds plumb dull after all this." He looked across at Trap, who'd skirted a tall saguaro cactus that stood lonesome in the rocky soil. "Hell, partner, I don't see why you'd want to grow up now. We're just gettin' started with the good stuff."

Roman trotted back toward them about the time a sudden shift in the wind brought the new smell to Trap's nose: the sour scent of manure, sweat, and mescal—a town.

"Agua Caliente," Webber said, pointing ahead of them with the tail of his reins. "Been through here once on a patrol. Not much to it except for a little cantina, some goat herds, and a couple of portly women."

Clay threw his hat back and grinned. "Heavy don't necessarily mean homely. I prefer my gals to have a little hip on 'em if I have the choice."

"Well, Madsen," Webber mused. "You should be able to have your preference on this occasion. Because more-than-adequate hips are something with which every tortilla-eating beauty in this little burg are well endowed."

Madsen ran his hand through his thick head of dark hair. "I'm hoping what you just said means the girls here have nice rear ends."

The captain slowed his horse and let the others come up beside him. "If you men are finished, we'll ride in and nose around in the cantina." Roman squirmed at any talk of loose women and though he didn't come right out and stop it, he didn't encourage it either. That suited Trap just fine.

"I'd like to get a decent meal if they offer such a thing," the captain continued. "Webber, you listen to the chatter and see what you can pick up. Maybe we can get a little light shed on those roasted men back there."

The pink adobe cantina occupied the position most towns would have reserved for the courthouse. It was a long, slumping affair with exposed cedar beams, bark peeling in long feathery strips, acting as reinforcements against the periodic fall rains. A handful of rustic houses of the same material, each a sad little replica of the tavern, slouched in a loose circle around the larger establishment.

Three molting chickens, skin as pink as the sunlit adobe, pecked and scratched in the street. A black and white dog flopped in the shade with just enough energy to look hungrily at the birds and give a wide-mouth yawn.

A flimsy wooden door leaned halfheartedly across the opening to the cantina waiting for a good breeze to knock it down. Madsen and Webber wasted no time in shoving the door aside, and shouldered their way in like they owned the place.

Roman tied his horse to a split-cedar rail and stuffed his gloves in a saddlebag. Trap reined up beside him and slid to the ground. He loosened Skunk's girth a notch—not too much in case they had to leave in a rush. He wasn't in too big a hurry to go into a saloon. Growing up under the strong religious influence of his father gave him a healthy dislike for that particular kind of enterprise. He watched as Captain Roman seemed to hitch up his will to make the trip in himself.

"My poor Irene would cry her eyes out if she saw me in a place like this," Roman said under his breath.

"Beg pardon, sir." Trap wasn't certain the words were meant for him, but it didn't feel right to ignore them either.

Roman blushed a little—hardly noticeable on his already sun-pinked skin. He took on a familiar tone O'Shannon hadn't heard before—as if they were friends instead of officer and subordinate. "Nothing, Trap. I was just thinking how my dear, innocent bride would feel about me going into such a place. I think she'd like to believe we camp in the hills and fight the good fight every day we're away."

"I reckon a fight gets a little ugly sometimes," Trap said. He stepped up to the door. "Maybe we can get something to eat while we're here, sir."

It took a while for Trap's eyes to adjust to the dim interior. What little light there was filtered through the broken front door and tiny slit windows built to use as gun ports when the cantina came under attack from bandits or marauding Apaches. Two rows of upright cedar posts ran down the center of the wide building, supporting the flat adobe roof. Rough-hewn wooden tables zigzagged around the posts. Four of them had active card games and hushed conversations going. At two others, loners did their conversing with bottles of cheap mescal. All told, Trap counted fourteen men. He wondered how many were left to tend to business around the little town.

The bar was at located at the back, between two peeling cedar posts. A coal-oil lamp, its globe blackened by soot and dust, cast a flickering shadow across two Mexican prostitutes sitting on tall stools and leaning on the rail. Clay and Johannes went straight for the bar. Each ordered a beer and sidled up next to the girls. True to Clay's recent description of his preferences, he struck up a conversation with the chubbier of the two.

Trap and the captain took a table a few feet away so they could observe without being too obtrusive. It didn't really matter; they were the only white people in the place, so there was no doubt they were all together.

To be as young as he was, Clay moved easily around the women. Neither of them appeared to speak English, but the language barrier didn't slow Clay down at all. With a mixture of sign language and facial expressions, he managed to get the heavy girl giggling and flirting back in a matter of moments.

Johannes was more circumspect. He sipped his beer and chatted quietly with the skinny girl. She had a bit of an overbite and a sour look that turned Trap's stomach if he looked at her too long.

Roman cleared his throat and motioned the two men over after a few minutes.

"That's two beers," he said. "Make sure and keep your wits about you."

Webber chuckled and shot a glance at Clay. "I wouldn't worry about us getting drunk," he said. "The stuff they serve here is more water than anything else."

Madsen nodded. He threw a flirting gaze at the chubby prostitute to keep her on the line while he was away.

"Are you finding anything out?" Roman looked down his nose at the two like they were mischievous schoolboys.

Johannes shrugged. "It's all just flirtation and coarse stories so far."

Madsen let out an exasperated sigh. "Beggin' your pardon, Captain, but do you mind if I ask you what thing in this world you consider yourself the best at?"

"Well," Roman blustered, taken aback. "I suppose I'd have to give that some thought."

"Well, I don't, sir," Clay said. "If I'm good at anything it's talkin' to women in general, whores in particular. These sorts of things are touchy. They take a little time, but if anybody in this town knows anything it's these girls. They're the only two sports around for miles. They hear it all, I guarantee it."

"Go on back and talk to them then," Roman said. "But remember, you're working."

Clay grinned and gave Trap a wink. "So are they."

Madsen continued to work his magic on the girls while

the bartender brought two hunks of barbecued goat out to Trap and the captain. There were mashed beans on the side and red peppers. It was surprisingly good, and both men dug into the meal with gusto.

"I'm surprised you don't drink," Roman said across his fork. "Is it because your father is a minister?" He'd kept up the familiar tone, and Trap found him an easy man to talk to. In some ways he was like Maggie. There was nothing false about him. His life and his personality were out in the open for everyone to see.

Trap swallowed a mouthful of the tender meat and washed it down with a glass of water. "No, not really," he said. "He takes a drink now and then at the suttler's store. No, I promised my mother when I was still a small boy that I would never touch alcohol. Have you ever met my mother?"

"Chuparosa? I have," Roman said. "She is a fine, temperate woman. I can see her teaching you to stay away from strong drink."

Trap took another bite. "She told me she got really drunk once on *tizwin*—back when she first married my father. Said she almost killed him." Trap stared at his food while he spoke. He'd never told anyone else this story, not even Clay, but he felt like he wanted to tell the captain— to let the man know he trusted him with a confidence. "She's afraid I'd be the same way if I ever drank. I have a bit of a temper, so she's probably right."

"You have fine parents, O'Shannon," the captain sighed. "Heed your mother's counsel. It'll save you a belly-load of grief." He tipped his head toward Webber. "Take our friend Johannes there. I've never met a more intelligent man. His father was a hard drinker. Beat him nearly every day when he was child. My mother and his mother were friends. I promised the beleaguered woman I'd do what I could to look after her son." Roman rubbed both eyes with the palms of his hands. "I suppose it's not a question of deserving—heaven knows I don't deserve all the blessing I have in my own life—but it seems to me that no one deserves the kind of upbringing Webber had. Now, he enjoys his liquor a little too much. I'm afraid it could be his downfall."

"That would account for all the anger wellin' up inside him," Trap said, a hint of melancholy in his quiet voice. He sometimes forgot that not everyone had a kind father and mother like he did.

The girls at the bar suddenly broke into a chorus of oos and ahhs. Trap looked up in time to see Clay give the chubby one a little hand mirror and the one with the overbite a folding paper fan. They tittered and giggled and moved in closer to the beaming Texan.

"I have to hand it to him." Roman shook his head. "He does indeed know women."

It wasn't long before the girls began to speak in hushed tones of broken English. Webber watched as two saddle-weary and sullen Mexican men shouldered their way through the broken door and eyed the sporting women.

Roman followed his gaze to the newcomers.

"I wonder if Madsen realizes he's monopolizing the only other pastime in this little town besides drinking mescal."

"I wonder if he cares," Trap grinned.

A short time later, Johannes helped Clay peel the girls off him and the two took seats at the table with Trap and Roman.

"Those two yahoos that just came in haven't been around for a few days," Clay whispered, stealing a piece of barbe-cued goat off Trap's plate. "Before they left, they were trying to get Linda, that's the pretty one, to give them a little bounce on credit. Both said they stood to come into a pile of money very soon."

"Neither of them have any job prospects," Johannes chimed in. "At least as far as the girls know. I think these could be two of our kidnappers, Captain."

CHAPTER 39

The girls put up an awful fuss when Clay told them he had to go. Linda clutched her breast as if she'd been shot and broke down in a wailing fit. Esmeralda stuck out her bottom lip in a pout big enough to compensate for her overbite and sobbed until her shoulders shook.

It looked as though the team might have to mount a rescue effort just to drag Madsen away. Trap's jaw fell open when Clay got misty eyed at the parting.

"I just ain't no good at goodbyes," the Texan said, a slight catch in his voice as they he left the bawling prostitutes slumped at the bar.

Outside, Roman gathered his Scout Trackers beside their horses. "Saddle up, men," he said, pulling the latigo on his saddle to snug up the girth. He kept his voice low. "We'll move out to the edge of at a distance, sit back and wait. When those two make a move, we'll follow them. With any luck they'll take us back to where they're keeping the girl."

The plan was straightforward enough and likely would have worked had it not been for Linda.

She was a big girl and the flimsy wooden door flew off its remaining hinge when she hit it and staggered into the street.

"Claymadsen! Claymadsen!" She whimpered his name as if it was all one word. Her yellow peasant blouse hung from one fleshy shoulder. Blood dripped from her swollen nose and splashed across the front of her torn clothing.

When she saw Clay, her eyes brightened and she lumbered straight for him, dimpled arms outstretched in a plea for help.

Madsen gave the captain a sheepish look. "Sorry, sir, I . . ."

A squat Mexican man with a great, twirling mustache that covered most of his wide face crashed out seconds after the girl, his hand on the butt of his pistol. Another followed, shorter than the first, hiding behind a bulbous, troll-like nose. An instant later, a third man ducked his huge head, then turned mountainous shoulders sideways to fit out the doorway. His whiskey-shined face held wild eyes that appeared to look east and west at the same time. He bellowed like an angry bull and beat his chest, tilting his head this way and that to bring the gringos into focus.

"It's the Cyclops," Clay muttered as he tried to peel Linda off him. "And he's brought his two little runts with him."

"Hold on, boys." Roman put up a hand. "We mean you no harm."

"Claymadsen," Linda cried. "These men are murderers. They are the ones you look for. Please help us, Claymadsen."

The giant went straight for Roman. He was at least a head taller than the officer and twice as broad.

The mustachioed bandit went for his gun as the Cyclops made his move. Roman, Webber, and Trap had all retreated from the half-naked prostitute and stood in a tight group by the horses.

Madsen tried to draw, but found it impossible to bring his Peacemaker into action.

"Save me, Claymadsen," Linda bawled like a pestered calf. "They will keeeel us all!"

"I would if you'd turn loose of my arms," Clay spit.

The bandit's first shot went wide and smacked into the adobe building with a loud crack.

At the same time, the giant bowled into the other three members of the team, sending them all flying.

"Leave off hangin' on me, damn it! You're gonna

smother me." Clay peeled away one chubby hand, but she grabbed a fistful of sleeve with the other. Her fleshy thighs encircled his leg and she pulled herself in tight, sobbing against his shoulder and enveloping him between her enormous breasts.

"Oh, Claymadsen!"

Another shot split the air. Trap looked up in time to see the giant kick a smoking pistol out of Webber's hand. Señor Mustache pitched headlong into the dirt, mortally wounded.

Johannes went down with a giant fist between his eyes, hitting the ground so hard Trap could hear his teeth rattle.

Roman rushed the big Mexican, plowing into him with his shoulder, while Trap attacked him from the other side. All three collapsed into a squirming pile, kicking and gouging as they fell. Trap's head felt like it exploded when a huge hand caught him in the ear with a strong slap. He heard Roman grunt as he got the wind knocked out of him.

The troll with the wide nose grabbed Linda by the hair and yanked her cruelly back and away from Clay. He held a knife to her throat.

"Much obliged," Madsen panted as he drew his Colt and shot the ugly little man over his left eye. "I thought I'd never get her off me."

The giant knelt over Trap and Roman, who were both addled half out of their senses. He held a bowie knife in his huge fist.

Madsen sent a round into the dirt. *"Sueltalo!"* He snapped, putting another shot inches from the giant's knees. *Drop it!*

Trap regained enough composure to kick the blade out of the big Mexican's hand.

Webber pushed himself up slowly on one arm, rubbing his tender jaw. The front of his shirt and britches was covered in red dust. Roman hadn't fared much better, and he spit to get the dirt out of his mouth.

"Tie him up," the captain said. He was still panting from the fight.

Trap hobbled over to his horse and got a length of stout

cord out of his saddlebags while Webber held the giant at
gunpoint. Clay tended to a sobbing Linda before he turned
her over to Esmeralda, who'd wisely stayed inside and missed
the whole brouhaha.

"Glad you had enough sense to take him alive." Roman
nodded a short time later at the two dead bandits. "I hope
he can tell us something about where they have the girl."

Johannes knelt in front of the sullen giant, questioning
him in harsh, rapid-fire Spanish. The big man said little
more than an occasional grunt.

Webber stood with a disgusted groan and shook his
head. "He's not talking, Captain. He knows where she is,
I can tell that much, but he's keeping it to himself."

Roman rubbed his chin in thought for a moment, eyeing
the prisoner carefully. "Ask him his name."

"Como se llama?" Webber fired down at the prisoner.

"Tu madre," the man grunted.

"He wants to talk about my mother," Webber scoffed.
"He's not going to talk without some encouragement."

"Tell him he'll hang if he doesn't help us. Tell him I can't
help him if he doesn't talk to us."

"Aye, sir," Webber said, unconvinced it would do any
good. He knelt and looked the drooling giant square in the
eye, giving the man's wide face a slap to make sure he was
paying attention. *"Escucha!"* Webber said, and translated
Roman's threats.

In reply, the giant coughed up the contents of his throat
and spit them in the Webber's face.

"You son of a bitch!" The trooper drew his knife in less
than a heartbeat and slit the Mexican's nose down the
middle. With his hands tied behind him, the hulking man
could do nothing but wail and thrash in the dirt as blood
soaked the front of his shirt.

"Sergeant Webber," Roman snapped. "That is enough."

Johannes glared. The Mexican's spit still dripped from the
side of his face. His chest heaved with fury. He wiped his
cheek with the back of his forearm and put away his knife.

Trap and Clay stood by, holding their breath.

The anger slowly ebbed from Webber's red face. "I apologize, sir. I don't know what came over me."

"I don't either, son," Roman said. His voice was quiet, but flint-hard. "But I'd better not see it again. I'll not have you mistreating a prisoner while you're under my command. Do I make myself clear?"

"Yes, sir."

"Damn it, man, we don't have time for this. There's a girl out there who needs our help."

Webber swallowed hard, staring at the ground. "Understood, sir."

"Very well." Roman took on his usual relaxed tone again. He drew the Schofield at his hip. "Now, tell the prisoner I'll not let anyone cause him any more pain, but I intend to shoot him dead right now if he doesn't tell us where the girl is."

Webber hesitated. "Captain?"

"Carry on, Sergeant." Roman aimed the pistol at the wide-eyed prisoner. "It is, at times, necessary to kill quickly and as humanely as possible. That is the nature of battle. On the other hand, if we start to mistreat our captives, we're no better than they are. I'll not have it." He thumbed back the hammer. "Tell him the bullet won't hurt him at all, but he'll still be very dead. Tell him he's got ten seconds."

It turned out that the giant outlaw's name was Rafael Fuentes. He had a firm enough grasp of English that he didn't need Johannes to translate a single word. It took him no time to tell Roman and others exactly what they wanted to know.

CHAPTER 40

"This damned antelope's done soured to the bone." Tug sniffed a piece of meat through a curled nose, then pitched it out the wide mouth of the overhang. He picked up his rifle and walked over to the girl. Hiking up his skin shirt, he rubbed a greasy hand over the pale belly. "I got me a cravin' for some cat. You ever ate puma?"

She pressed her face against the sand. Her throat was so dry she could hardly swallow, let alone speak. When she tried, it came out as a gurgling, unintelligible croak.

"Brandywine!" the lion hunter shouted over his shoulder. His hungry gaze never left the girl. "I think she's gonna die before long. We should take what we can whilst there's still something left to take."

The Indian agent jumped up from his game and scurried over the check on his investment. He toed at her thigh with his boot. She recoiled at his touch and curled into a tight ball, protecting her swollen hand. "She'll be all right with a little water," he said. He dropped a canteen on the ground in front of her. "The Mexicans should have the letter delivered by now. They'll be back with Fuentes and supplies any time."

Pushing herself up on her good arm, she curled her legs around so she could sit against the stone wall. Water. She didn't want them to know it, but she'd have done anything for just one sip. She knew her shredded gown no longer covered her, but she couldn't bring herself to care anymore.

Death was a certainty now; it was only a matter of how painful it would be, how much torment and degradation she would be forced to endure with its coming. Thirst carried with it much more agony than she had imagined it would. Her tongue was swollen and stuck to the roof of her mouth. Crying had plugged her nose, and her breath came in ragged gasps over cracked and bleeding lips. Her vision blurred and the sickening thump in her skull mixed with the white-hot ache of her broken tooth and the dull throb of her stinking hand.

She vaguely remembered a warning—it seemed so long ago in her fevered brain. Someone had warned her that this sort of thing might happen. She pressed the canteen to her lips and let the water slide over her parched tongue. It was warm, but it was wet and she drank greedily until Brandywine jerked it away.

"Go easy, Señorita," the Indian agent snapped. "Too much will make you sick."

The lion hunter chuckled. "And we don't want her sick," he said. "She's sick as a hydrophobic dog as it is, you blind, baldheaded nit. Me and Joe gonna go hunt us up some lion meat. When we come back, if you ain't heard anything about the ransom, I aim to have me a little go with this young'un before she crosses over on us. I don't care what you or anyone else says about it."

Before Brandywine could react, Tug wheeled and shot the Papago in the face with his big-bore rifle. The roar of the gun shook the small rock enclosure. The big Indian's head evaporated and blood sprayed the cave wall behind him.

Brandywine's jaw hung open as he watched his fiercest ally slump in a lifeless heap to the sandy floor.

The girl looked at what was left of the dead Indian and threw up the water she'd just drunk.

Tug prodded her in the rump with the smoking barrel of his gun. "I'll be back, Señorita. You get yourself cleaned up and I'll go get us some fresh cat." He looked up and

CHAPTER 41

"Son of a bitch!" Madsen snapped as the Scout Trackers picked their way single-file up a rock-strewn trail. It was little more than a goat path out of their fifth canyon of the day. Acacia trees shredded their clothes and jagged rocks threatened to lame the horses every step of the way. A stiff wind picked up bits of dry vegetation and sand, driving them into the men's faces with enough force to blast off a layer of skin.

"This whole place looks like the Good Lord forgot where he buried somethin' important and spent a couple thousand years digging ditches in the rock trying to find it. I've heard some troops say this country's so rough," Clay continued, "you can't get through it without cussing your way up and down these damned gullies and mountains."

"I'm inclined to agree," Roman shouted into the wind. "But from the sounds of things, you're doing enough for the four of us." The captain held his hat down with his free hand and nodded ahead. "Terrain flattens out some after we top this next ridge. I'd rather wait out this wind inside the protection of this canyon, but we don't have the time. Fuentes said the kidnappers are expecting a signal fire on Kill Devil Mesa by this evening. According to him, the cave is supposed to be northeast of there, so we're not far from it now. With any luck, this storm will hide our approach and we can have the girl back by nightfall."

Though it was still early afternoon, dust filled the

blowing air and made it difficult to see more than a few hundred yards. Each man's face was caked red above the bandanna he wore to protect his nose and mouth. The horses walked with eyes half shut against the whirling debris, stumbling every other step in the uneven terrain.

Drawn forward by worry for the kidnapped girl, the men pressed doggedly on, braving the cold and biting wind. The howl became too great for conversation, so they rode on in silence.

It was a chance meeting. No war party could have possibly known the men were out on such a bitter afternoon. A dozen Apaches were returning from a hunt, on their way back to camp in the shelter of the slick-rock canyons. The two groups were almost on top of each other before either of them noticed.

It was Trap who realized what was happening first. He caught the hint of cedar smoke on the wind, an instant before he glimpsed a fleck of a painted horse as it ghosted through the dust cloud twenty yards in front of him.

The lead Indian saw him at the same moment and let out a piercing whoop.

Trap spun Skunk back and ripped the bandanna off his face. "Apaches!" he yelled at the group.

"Follow me." Roman shouted his clipped order and turned his horse to the right, spurring it toward a dark outcropping of rocks that was barely visible in the shadowed distance. "Make for those boulders. There's a canyon nearby so watch out."

None of them knew for sure how many Indians there were, but staying around to count heads was not a way to live very long in Apache country.

The four soldiers let their horses have their heads. The animals, half-crazy from the moaning storm, took off at a dead run, jumping cactus and thorn bushes if they saw them, plowing through if they didn't. Hoofbeats and piercing Apache cries carried behind them on the wind.

The sandstorm itself seemed to join in the battle. It grew in intensity, picking up small rocks and hurling them like bird shot at white man and Indian alike. The haven of boulders was invisible in the billowing red curtain, but the troopers pushed for it anyway, knowing it was somewhere out there, somewhere next to a sharp drop into a deep ravine.

Trap saw the rocks off to his left as he sped past. The others were somewhere nearby. Their shouting voices carried on the wind, but he couldn't see them for the blowing dust. It was impossible to tell where he was, and he pulled back on the reins trying to stop.

Skunk squealed as the ground gave way underneath him. Howling wind mixed with the clatter of rock and dirt as the canyon edge turned into a river of rolling gravel and loose dirt. The little horse scrambled to regain its footing, flailing wildly, pawing out at nothing. A sudden sinking sensation pushed Trap's gut into his throat.

They were falling.

He let go of the reins to give his horse the freedom it would need if it ever did get its footing. A jutting branch snapped under them as they half-slid, half-fell to the canyon floor below. The next second, another tree upended the little horse and sent Trap spinning, head over heels, from the saddle. Dirt filled his mouth and nose when he tried to breath. A harsh wind moaned and whirred in his ears. Then, something slammed against his head. A sharp pain screamed like a banshee behind his ear before the world around him went black and he heard no more.

"I can't find him, Captain." Madsen's voice was tight. His youthful face quivered with anxiety and tension.

The Apaches, equally afraid of an unknown number of enemies, had run the other direction in the blinding storm. They were nowhere to be seen by the time the wind abated an hour later.

When they realized Trap had become separated, Roman and his men began a frantic search. From the rocks above, they saw Skunk, bruised and battered but alive, in the bottom of the canyon fifty yards below them. The wall of the shallow ravine gave way gradually. It wasn't sheer, but it was treacherous nonetheless, and the men had to work their way down cautiously to keep their horses from losing their footing.

The sudden storm had left behind an eerie silence. There was not a breath of a breeze. Even the crows were quiet.

The canyon floor was a labyrinth of sandstone boulders as big as houses, their sculpted sides smoothed over time by water and wind.

"He's vanished." Madsen's frustration poured out in a bitter voice. Two hours of searching had yet to turn up anything but the little black gelding.

"He's around somewhere." Roman put a comforting hand on the Texan's shoulder. "We'll locate. . . ."

"Over here!" Webber shouted from a gap between two sandstone slabs. "I found his pistol."

Webber stood in a narrow side canyon, looking at the ground. He held a Schofield revolver in his left hand.

"The wind didn't get back in this little pocket enough to destroy all the tracks." He pointed the pistol toward the sand at his feet. "Difficult to tell, but I think there were three people here."

Clay dropped to his knees to get a better look. "Wish we had the little runt with us so he could tell us what to look for." He relaxed a notch, just knowing that his friend was alive for the time being. He took his hat off and scratched his head. "It does look like there are three sets of prints here, but it's impossible to tell much else about them."

Webber scanned the rocks above, while Roman took a linen map out of his saddlebag and spread it out on a flat rock.

"According to Fuentes, we're near the cave." He used his forefinger to trace the lines that signified mountains on the map. "We've got about three hours until dark. I'd wanted to make our move then, but if they have O'Shannon, we may not have the luxury of waiting."

Webber took a deep breath. "I hesitate to bring this up, but remember what they did to their last male hostage."

Roman let his fist bounce up and down on the map while he thought. "I know."

"Well," Clay said, slapping his leg with his hat, "I say we just bust in there and shoot everyone who's not Trap or Pilar." He shot a glance at the captain. "One thing's sure. If she's still alive, Trap can keep her company till we get there. She'll be happy to see a friendly face."

Roman took off his hat and held it in front of him. His brow knotted and he rubbed his whiskered jaw with his free hand. "Yes," he said. "About Señorita de la Cruz." His voice was a course whisper. "Mount up. I'll fill you in on the details as we ride. There are things I've not been able to tell you until now—things you have a right to know."

CHAPTER 42

A river of fire gushed through Trap O'Shannon's head. He jerked awake from a dream of Maggie, struggling in vain against the thick ropes that bound him hand and foot. Blackness surrounded him. He fought to control his breathing and get his bearings. A familiar smell hung heavy in his nose and stung his eyes. Someone had pulled a coffee sack over his head.

Voices echoed inside his skull, adding to the searing headache.

". . . not as good as a lion, but he'll do," a voice sneered nearby.

"Where did you find him?" This voice was higher, twitching with nervous energy. "He may have something to do with the ransom."

Another, more youthful speaker cackled. "L-Lars s-ays we should c-c-cut his head off, like we did the o-other one. He likes to listen to the sss-screamin'."

"Shut up, Hiram," the tense voice snapped. "You boys want your money or not? Let's find out a little more about him, and then you can finish him off however you want to."

"Oh, let the young'uns have their fun," the first voice said. "I only brought him back so they could have a little sport killin' him. Maybe it'll toughen 'em up a little. He don't have our money."

Trap heard shuffling in the sand around him. A girl

whimpered somewhere nearby. The pitiful sound made him think of Maggie and filled his belly with anger. He pulled and tugged at the stiff ropes until they cut into his wrists and ankles. At length, he lay back in the dirt panting, waiting.

The soft hiss of footsteps on sand approached from his left. A boot crashed into his ribs before he could protect himself and drove the wind from his lungs. Powerful hands grabbed him by the shoulders, arching his back, while someone yanked the coffee sack off his head.

He blinked to clear his eyes, trying to focus in the scant light of the cave. The gray glow of evening barely spilled in from outside. Inside, the small fire cast more shadow than it did light.

"I know you from somewhere," the small man in front of him said. Trap was able to put a face with the tense voice. "I've seen you before at Camp Apache. You're that preacher's boy. What's your name?"

"Trap O'Shannon." He saw no reason to lie about something the man would surely work out on his own in a short time. Trap recognized him as Payton Brandywine, the Indian agent from San Carlos. His father had had more than a few run-ins with the corrupt official. "I know you too." He had enough of his mother in him that he would never stoop to begging for his life.

"Ohhhh, preacher boy." A greasy man wearing buckskin clothing shook his head back and forth. "Maybe you can say us all a prayer before my compadres cut your guts out and feed 'em to the buzzards."

This brought a chuckle from the other men in the group. Trap counted nine, including the agent.

Brandywine held up a hand to quiet the noise. "What brings you all the way out here?"

"You." Trap kept his face passive, though he seethed inside. It wasn't in his nature to lie or bargain with men like this, but he needed to stall. It would take time for Captain Roman and the others to work out a solid plan now that they were a man short. "We got the note in Agua Caliente. My

friends and I have the ransom money. They should be light-
ing the fire on Kill Devil Mesa any time now."

Brandywine beamed, slapping his fist against an open
palm. "What did I tell you boys? I told you it would all work
out, but no, none of you believed me. Now, we'll all be rich
men. You just have to be patient now." He looked back at
Trap.

"Where are your friends now?"

Trap shrugged. "Likely looking for me. Apaches got
after us in the middle of a sandstorm and I got separated
during the blow. Don't worry, though, they've got your
money. As long as the girl is still alive, you'll get paid."

The man dressed in greasy skins jerked Trap's head
back by the hair and held a long knife to his throat. "If you
got the note, what happened to the two Mexicans? How
come they ain't back yet?"

Trap couldn't move. He tried to relax, but found it impossible with the sharp blade already digging into his
flesh. "The last time I saw them, they were sidled up next
to Esmeralda and Linda back in town."

Brandywine put a hand on the other man's arm. "Hold
on for a minute, Tug. We got time to do that later. We're
talking thousands and thousands of dollars now. Let's not
throw it all away." The Indian agent's eyes gleamed in the
firelight. The men around were silent now at the thought
of such an enormous payday. "You'd better be telling the
truth, O'Shannon. If I so much as smell a whiff of a double
cross, I'll let the boys cut your head off like they're itchin'
to do already."

"No double crosses," Trap assured him. "As long as the
girl is still alive."

"She's fit as a fiddle," Brandywine said. He grabbed
Trap by the shoulder, dragged him across the cave floor,
and threw him next to the girl. He had no way to catch himself and slammed against the rock wall.

The men jeered.

When his head cleared again, Trap looked over at the girl.
She was an awful sight. Naked except for the flimsy remnants
of a tattered gown, she lay in a bruised stupor, cowering in

her own filth. A young outlaw with a maniacal face and an unruly blond mop stooped down next to her and grabbed a fist of matted black hair. He jerked her head backward, exposing the girl's face and delicate throat.

She moaned, drawing a purple hand close to her chest. Her eyes rolled back in her head, then fluttered open to fall on Trap. They were dark, pleading eyes, void of all but the last shreds of hope.

"Help me," she croaked. "Please help me." Her head lolled to one side.

Trap gasped when he saw her, not so much because of her swollen face, broken teeth, or bleeding lips—but because this girl was not Pilar de la Cruz.

Chapter 43

"Inez Hinojosa?" Clay frowned. The men were riding now, working their way along the canyon bottom. "Why all the secrecy? Why not just tell us we weren't coming to rescue the colonel's daughter? We were bound to find out anyway."

Roman looked ahead as he rode, thinking out his answer carefully before he spoke.

"Inez Hinojosa is an American citizen," the captain began. "Have either of you ever heard of the Secret Service?"

"Fake money and such?" Webber asked. He was leading Trap's gelding and urged it to keep up with a cluck.

"Exactly." The trail widened into a dry creek bed, and Roman motioned the two men to ride up next to him. "Treasury has had its hands full since the war. Some people estimate that a full third of the paper money circulating in U.S. border states is counterfeit. Miss Hinojosa is a government agent. She sent word two weeks ago that she and her partner had uncovered a major counterfeiting operation in Mexico. Her partner was murdered and she fled north. She is friendly with the de la Cruz family and knew she could trust him. He agreed to let her pose as his daughter and contacted us to arrange a military escort.

"Unfortunately for Miss Hinojosa, someone in her escort believed the colonel's daughter was worth a substantial ransom. They have no idea who she really is, or that she knows the whereabouts of millions in counterfeit currency." Roman stopped his horse and looked intently at both men. "If they did, she would surely be tortured until she gave up her secret. I don't have to tell you how badly that much money would hurt the government if it was put into circulation.

"Colonel Branchflower put me under strict orders to keep these facts from you until the last moment. The fewer people that knew the better—but our mission hasn't changed."

"We still need to save her," Webber shrugged. "No matter what her name is."

"I don't know about you." Clay urged his horse forward again. "But I'm going to save Trap. I don't give a hoot in hell about any counterfeit money." He eyed Roman warily. "I know you only had to do what you were told, Captain. It just takes a minute to digest all this new information. None of us hold it against you." He paused. "Well, Trap might."

"He might at that." Roman smiled. "And I wouldn't blame him."

The clatter of small stones above them sent every man to his sidearm. Clay relaxed when he saw three desert mule-deer does bounding up the steep slope.

"When they stop," Roman whispered to Clay. "Shoot one."

Clay was already returning his Colt to the holster. "Captain?"

"Shoot the deer, Sergeant!" With that, the captain gave a shrill whistle that echoed off the high rocks.

The does stopped in their tracks and looked back, big ears twitching, curious at the unusual nose.

Clay took careful aim with his Peacemaker and dropped the lead doe thirty yards away. She fell instantly and tumbled down the mountainside, almost at the horses' feet. The other two deer flagged their tails and bounded out of sight in an instant, evaporating from view.

"Wish it was always this easy to retrieve meat," Madsen said as he put his pistol away. "Don't know what you have in mind, Captain, but the kidnappers may have heard that shot. They're likely to know we're here now."

Roman nodded slowly. "Pistol shots don't carry far in all

these canyons. I doubt anyone heard it. In any case, they have O'Shannon. I imagine they know we're here already. In fact, I hope they do."

Webber chuckled softly. "I can tell you have a plan—and I want you know I'm behind you no matter what—but at some point I think you're going to have tell us what it is."

Roman nodded at the jumble of cliffs and piled rocks ahead. "It's difficult to make a concrete plan when we don't know what's around the next bend. The cave is nearby if Fuentes was honest with us. With a few minor changes to stack the odds a little more in our favor, I'm inclined to proceed with the plan as Sergeant Madsen presented it."

Clay jerked back in surprise, startling his roan. "Me? I don't know what you're talkin' about, Captain Roman. I never laid out any plan."

"Oh, but you did." Roman dismounted and walked over to the dead deer. "We're going to kill everyone who isn't Trap or the girl. Now, let's get this deer gutted and slung over O'Shannon's horse."

By dark, Trap's headache had fallen off to a dull thump behind his left ear. It was bothersome, but he could live with it. One look at the poor girl slumped beside him was enough to make him feel guilty for worrying over his own pitiful pain. It was nothing compared to hers.

She shivered in her fitful sleep, whimpering like an injured pup and pulling her knees up tighter to her chest.

Impotent fury welled in Trap's chest, pressing at his gut, until he thought he might be sick. He couldn't help but think of Maggie lying there in such awful circumstances, and supposed it would always be that way. If he saw a woman in trouble, he would always think of what he would do if it was his sweet Maggie.

Trap shook his head to clear the thought, and attempted to calm himself by taking careful stock of the situation. A cold throbbing in his toes drew his attention to his feet. His boots and socks were gone. A quick glance around the chamber revealed one of the blond twins had himself a new set of Army-issue brogans.

All the men but Brandywine cussed and laughed at each other while they huddled over some kind of game. The Indian agent sat alone, staring out the cave mouth.

Trap wiggled his fingers and found his struggles had loosened the ropes—not enough to escape—but enough to be able to twist his hands some. If given a chance, he might be able to pull his arms under and bring them in front. Roman and the others would be coming soon. Trap wanted to be able to fight when they did.

Five hundred yards away, Hezekiah Roman pulled a dry tuft of bunchgrass, crushed it in his hand, and let it drift away on the night breeze. Only the faintest sliver of a moon cut the night sky, but a white curtain of countless stars provided enough light to navigate.

Once he got a fix on the wind, the captain began to heap dry brush, sticks, and anything else that would burn into a large pile.

Johannes pushed a sharpened cedar stave, as big as his wrist, lengthwise through the skinned mule-deer carcass. Clay took one end and helped him position it over two boulders to one side of the wood.

"This ironwood will burn hot and long," Clay said, pulling a match out of an oilskin bag in his shirt pocket. "We were lucky to find it."

"I don't believe in luck, Mr. Madsen," the captain said. His voice was reverent in the darkness. "Change out of your boots and into moccasins before you light the fire. We'll need to be as stealthy as we can for this to work. We'll leave the horses here. By the time the meat starts cooking good, we should be in position."

Haywood, the whiskey peddler, scooped up the yellowed bone dice and held them in a grimy hand. He slowly turned his head toward the cave mouth and sniffed through his pug nose. His sagging eyes relaxed and he gave a fluttering sigh. "You boys smell what I smell?"

Brandywine tilted his head and drew in a lungful of

night air. He could smell something—something sweet and delicious floating on the gentle breeze—just a whiff at first, tickling the nose and pulling the men to their feet. Moment by moment the savory odor grew stronger. Stomachs used to canned goods and stale coffee began to growl. Mouths began to water.

"Venison," Bent Jim moaned, licking his lips. "Who the devil would be cooking venison hereabouts?"

Brandywine slapped his thigh and shot a gleeful look at O'Shannon. "You say your friends have the ransom?"

Trap nodded. The girl flinched in her sleep when he spoke. "They're prepared to meet you tomorrow like you instructed in your note."

A crooked smile spread over the Indian agent's round face. He smoothed his thinning hair and smacked his lips, bouncing with energy, hardly able to contain his excitement.

"What the hell's the matter with you, Brandywine?" Tug spit a slurry of tobacco juice through the gap in his front teeth. "You look like you're about to catch fire."

"Don't you see?" The agent slapped his knee again. "This is just perfect. Those fools have the money with them. I say if they're stupid enough to cook their meat where we can smell it, we ought to go help ourselves—to dinner and the cash."

Realization rippled slowly over the men, each catching on at different speeds. The twins were the last to figure it out.

"If we go ahead and take the money tonight, we won't need to turn the girl over tomorrow. You can keep her at no extra charge. We win the whole damned pot."

"What about the preacher boy?" Hiram sneered, his voice twitching with anticipation. "C-c-can we go on a-h-head and k-kill him?"

Brandywine held up a hand. "All in time, Hiram. Let's make sure we have the money first, then you can have your fun." He walked to Trap, looking down at him. "How many friends do you have out there?"

"Twenty," Trap said.

Brandywine kicked him hard in the side, doubling him over in pain. "I never expected you to tell me the truth anyway. It doesn't matter. They don't know we're coming.

"Hiram," the agent said, spinning on his heels. For the first time in a week he thought he might live to spend his money. "You and Lars stay here and guard these two. Don't do anything to them until we get back. The rest of you boys get your guns ready. Those men out there have our money and I'm ready to go take it from them."

"Y-you better bring us b-b-back some meat." Hiram stood, unhappy at being left behind.

Tug elbowed the boy in the ribs, hard enough to make him flinch and touch the spot gingerly. "We'll bring you meat back, don't you worry about that. Just do like Brandywine says and take care of the prisoners."

Hiram grinned, showing a mouth packed full of crooked, yellow teeth. "Oh, we'll t-t-take c-care of them all right." He began to cackle and his brother Lars joined in.

Tug grabbed him by the collar and hauled him off his feet with a powerful arm. "Listen, you stutterin' little bastard. I don't care what you do to the runt, but you leave that girl be till I get back, you hear me?"

"I h-hear you, T-Tug." Hiram swallowed hard.

Lars nodded his agreement. "Do what we want to the runt."

Hiram and Lars sat poking the campfire for some time after the others left. They whispered to each other, giggled hysterically, then whispered some more. Every now and then they'd leer at the girl or look at Trap and draw a finger across their throats.

Trap scooted up next to the wall next to the girl. He didn't want to startle her.

"Can you hear me?" he whispered.

She opened her swollen eyes and stared at him. There was a sudden wildness there, as if she'd been awakened from a nightmare, but it subsided when she realized who had spoken to her. She gave a slight nod. "I hear you." Her voice was hoarse and frayed.

"I don't want to frighten you," Trap said. "But those boys are working their courage up to try something any time now."

She sighed. "I know. I've been waiting for this time.

Maybe it will all be over." Her head fell sideways, so she looked Trap square in the eye. She was young, not too much older than him. She had the broad-hipped build Clay thought so much of, and could have been pretty if not for her present condition. "I'm Inez Hinojosa. What's your name? Since we're about to die, I think we should at least introduce ourselves."

Trap pulled at the ropes behind him, gritting his teeth at the effort. "Trap O'Shannon, United States Cavalry. I came to rescue a girl named Pilar de la Cruz."

The girl gave a halfhearted chuckle, but winced and the pain it caused her raw throat. "They think I'm her."

"Inez, listen to me," Trap said. "We don't have much time. They'll try for me first. But I'm going to need your help."

"Okay," she said, sounding tired and unconvinced.

"My hands are tied, but yours aren't. They will underestimate us because they believe we are helpless."

Her face was expressionless, but she held up her injured hand. The ring and little fingers jutted out at right angles to the palm. They were purple and swollen to twice their normal size. "I'm afraid I won't be much use to you."

Hiram was already on his feet. He threw another armful of branches on the fire and stood for a minute, staring with gleaming eyes at the prisoners. Lars stood behind him, a little to the left.

Trap watched them carefully out of the corner of his peripheral vision, knowing that if he made eye contact they might sense his determination. He wanted them to believe he'd given up.

When Hiram started to move toward him, creeping in for the kill with a wood-handled butcher knife, Trap let his head fall sideways next to Inez's ear. "Do what you can," he hissed. "I can't do this without you."

"It's good to meet you, Trap O'Shannon," the girl croaked as Hiram made his move.

CHAPTER 44

Trap rolled away on his back, kicking up at Hiram's hand. He connected and felt the white-hot pain as the blade sliced the ball of his foot. Hiram yowled in surprise and the knife spun away, clanking off the cave wall.

Lars moved in to help, but Inez threw herself into him, screaming like a spirit of the damned. All the rage from her long hours of torment and suffering boiled out of her and overflowed onto the startled boy. She wrapped her arms around both legs and pulled him to the ground, sinking her teeth into the tender flesh of his thigh.

"Turn aloose of meeeee!" he squealed, beating her on the top of the head. She held fast.

Trap kicked out again, as Hiram descended on him. He caught the boy a glancing blow in the midsection, knocking him sideways but not doing much damage.

Quickly, Trap pushed his arms down as far as he could and brought them up in front of him. He was still tied hand and foot, but he was far from helpless. He knew Inez wouldn't be able to hold out for long; he had to finish this fast.

When Hiram fell on him again, Trap let him come, rolling to the side at the last possible second. He delivered a powerful haymaker with both fists to the back of the other boy's skull. Reaching over Hiram's head, Trap pulled the cord that bound his wrists tight against the stunned twin's throat. He wrenched back with all his might, feeling the windpipe collapse as he twisted and pulled.

Hiram flailed wildly, both hands clawing at Trap's wrists. It did him little good. In a matter of seconds the gurgling stopped and the boy lay still.

Trap pushed him aside and rolled toward the knife. He had it in an instant.

Lars had been so busy with Inez he'd not noticed his dead brother lying in the sand. When he finally knocked the girl out and wrenched himself free from her grasp, he turned to face Trap and a butcher knife in the belly.

He groaned and slumped forward, his mouth open, gasping for air like a suffocating fish.

Trap pushed him aside and let him finish dying in the dirt beside his filthy brother. He held the knife in his teeth to finish freeing his hands, then bent to cut the cords around his ankles. When he was free, he dropped to his knees to check on the girl.

He put a hand to her neck. She had a pulse, but not much of one. She was a fighter, though, she'd shown that. He carried her to a clean spot by the fire and put her carefully in the soft sand, taking care to watch her injured hand, then took off his shirt and draped it over her shivering, twitching body. He gently brushed a lock of hair out of her face.

One eye was swollen completely shut; the other only opened a crack. She smiled. "I'm glad to meet you, Trap O'Shannon. Could I please have a drink of water?"

"What the hell do you think you're doin', preacher boy?" Tug stood at the mouth of the cave, his rifle in his hands. The lion hunter's chest heaved from anger and the exertion of a long run. His face glistened with sweat in the firelight. "You gone and done it now, haven't you, boy." He nodded at the dead twins. "Well, I don't care about no money. I aim to get me a little of that sweet thing there and there ain't a thing you can do to stop me."

Trap scrambled to his feet, casting his eyes around for a weapon of any kind. In his haste to take care of the girl, he'd left Hiram's knife on the ground beside Lars's body.

"You're an awful brave man," Trap said. He heard Inez moan softly behind him. "Killing an unarmed man and molesting a half-dead girl . . ."

Tug spit and gave a long belly laugh. "Aw," he said. "You're gonna make me get all weepy." He raised the rifle to his shoulder and aimed at Trap's belly. "This'll be slow. That way, you can watch—"

A boom like a clap of thunder rocked the inside of the cave. Trap flinched, knowing he was mortally wounded. When he opened his eyes he saw Tug had fallen to his knees. The lion hunter's face twisted, his jaw hung open in a mixture of shock and outrage. A dark and ugly stain spread across his chest.

"Damn it," he spit and fell face-forward into the sand. His rifle hit the ground an instant before he did.

A moment later, Clay Madsen stepped into the cave. "Bad hombre like that shouldn't stand out in a silhouette if he don't want to get shot."

"What took you boys so long?" Trap suddenly felt heady and collapsed back into the sand next to Inez. "I thought I was going to have to kill all these outlaws myself."

"With what, your teeth?" Madsen knelt down in the sand beside his friend and shook his hand. "I was worried about you, compadre." He grinned, blinking moist eyes. "Most of all, I was afraid you'd get all sad and despondent without me around to tell you stories."

Roman and Webber came in the cave with pistols drawn. Both men relaxed when they saw things were under control.

Webber toed the bodies of the dead men, kicking weapons out of their reach to be on the safe side. "How many were there?"

Trap counted in his head, trying to remember faces. "Nine, I think. You got Brandywine?"

Roman slid the Schofield back in his holster. "Juan

Caesar won't have to worry about him cheating the Apache anymore."

"This is all of them then." Webber smiled smugly and nodded his head. "This cave is a fortress. I don't care how determined we were; if we would have attacked this place head-on, we'd have been slaughtered. Captain Roman, I have to hand it to you. Your little plan saved the day."

Clay and Inez had already formed a tight kinship by the time they reached Camp Apache. He didn't seem to mind her broken tooth, and she appeared genuinely interested in hearing lots of stories about Clay Madsen and Bastrop, Texas.

After two days of rest and reuniting with their respective sweethearts, the three sergeants sent a special invitation, penned in Lieutenant Fargo's flamboyant hand, to Captain Hezekiah Roman, asking his presence at a ceremony in the Camp Commander's office. The Reverend and Mrs. O'Shannon, Maggie, Inez, Mariposa, Webber's sweetheart, Lieutenant Fargo, and Colonel Branchflower were all in attendance in the cramped, but tidy room.

Dressed for the first time in the blue kersey uniform of a cavalry trooper, Trap O'Shannon did the honors.

"Sir!" The entire room came to attention when Roman walked in, hand in hand with his beautiful Irene. Trap held a shining saber out in front of him in both hands. He offered it to Roman. "The men—your men—wish to make you this gift."

Irene Roman gave her husband's arm a squeeze. He snapped to attention and accepted the sword. His eyes glistened as he drew it from the metal scabbard and held the polished blade up to the light. "I am deeply honored, men." He coughed to clear the catch in his throat. "I . . . I don't know what to say."

Colonel Branchflower harrumphed from behind Fargo's desk. "Don't keep us in the dark, Captain. Read the blasted thing."

Roman swallowed and took a deep breath. As strong as he was, he leaned against his wife for support and read haltingly the words engraved on the blade.

"TO CAPTAIN HEZEKIAH ROMAN—A MAN WORTH FOLLOWING. THE SCOUT TRACKERS. OCTOBER 1878. SANGUIS FRIGITIS!"

CHAPTER 45

1910
Idaho

"Do you reckon the good captain would mind a little toast of some good hot coffee over his casket?" Madsen sniffed, using a red bandanna to wipe a tear out of his eye. "I miss the straitlaced old son of a bitch." He tipped his hat. "Pardon the language, ladies."

Trap smiled and helped Maggie out of her seat. "I imagine he'd be happy to see us."

It was chilly enough to see their breath in the mail car, and everyone but Maggie buttoned their coats up around their necks.

Clay raised his cup above the simple pine casket. He started to speak, then seemed to think better of it and changed course. "If we haven't said it yet, it's too late, I reckon."

"Forgive me." Hanna Cobb reached up to touch Clay gently on the arm. "I know I'm an outsider, but from what you've told me, Captain Roman knew full well how you felt about him."

"I hope so," Trap said, raising his cup next to Clay's. "I sure hope so."

A muffled grunt from behind a stack of bags interrupted

the toast. Clay's eyebrows shot up and he set his cup gently on top of Roman's casket. "If you don't mind holding that for a minute, Captain," he said, drawing his Colt.

Trap followed suit and pulled the Schofield from under his coat. He motioned the ladies back toward the door.

"Who's there?" Clay snapped. He pointed the pistol at the boxes. "Come out and show yourself."

A head full of disheveled black hair poked warily over the top of a steamer trunk. Two eyes as big as pie pans looked back and forth from the Colt to the Smith & Wesson. "What have I done to make you boys so mad?" the man said. He slowly raised two rough hands above his head.

"It's the sick passenger I was telling you about," Hanna said.

"What's your name?"

"Reed," the man said in a hoarse voice. "My friends call me Big Mike."

"You sick, Big Mike Reed?" Clay kept the pistol aimed in.

"No, sir," the wobbly man said. "Leastways, not anymore. Got a hold of some bad whiskey back in St. Regis. Thought it was gonna rot my guts out for a while there. The swayin' of the train nearly did me in, I don't mind tellin' you."

"So you don't have the smallpox?"

The man's mouth fell open. "Smallpox? I don't know what you're talkin' about, mister."

Blake O'Shannon arrived a short time later and after a short conversation with his father through the window, boarded the train with Dr. Bruner from Wallace. The doctor took one look at Reed and declared him hungover, but as of yet not infected with smallpox.

There was a sudden commotion outside the mail car door as the doctor helped the queasy miner to his feet. The portly conductor eased in backward, shoved into the cramped and narrow confines of the mail car by Birdie and Leo Baker.

Leo's eyes were swollen and blue. A bandage crossed his pink nose. Birdie's piled hair had fallen a good six inches.

Her black boots were scuffed and the tail of her linen blouse was untucked and trailing behind her. Nostrils flared on her prominent nose. Her squinting eyes burned with revenge.

"Get out of my way, you incompetent imbecile. This is all your fault for letting that filthy Indian woman on the train in the first place." The beefy woman beat at the conductor's raised arm with a rolled-up newspaper.

"Ma'am," the pestered man said. "Please, let's work this out like civilized adults."

Leo weighed in at that. "Are you implying that my wife is uncivilized? Why, she's the most civilized person on this train."

"No." The conductor frowned. "Mr. Baker, I must insist—"

"Insist this, you ignorant bastard." Leo Baker took a wild swing at the conductor. Maybe it was his lack of spectacles, maybe he was just a poor pugilist, but his punch missed completely.

The conductor stepped to one side and Leo, along with his wife, who'd crowded in behind him, both fell headlong into a wide-eyed Big Mike Reed. The postmaster's balding head hit the queasy miner square in the gut, causing him to throw up all over Birdie's coiffure.

Birdie wailed in outrage.

Leo pushed himself back to his feet and fumed. "I am the postmaster of Dillon, Montana. I deserve a little respect around here."

Clay attempted to step forward, but Blake raised his hand and winked.

"Oh, this is bad, sir," he said. "Very bad."

"And just who might you be?" Leo tried to console his screeching wife. "You look as though you are part of the problem."

"Blake O'Shannon, deputy United States marshal." He plowed ahead before Leo could make any more comments about him looking like an Indian. He turned to the doctor. "Doc Bruner, I believe it would be prudent to quarantine the Bakers for a few days since they've had

such close contact with someone who may be infected—
for their own safety, that is."

Bruner grinned, then caught himself. His brow creased
and a serious look crossed his face. "You are right, Deputy."
He found a packing blanket and draped it around Birdie's
sobbing shoulders. "This is extremely sensitive. We don't
want to start a pandemic. Afraid we'll have to keep you here
in Idaho for a while."

Leo looked up at him, suspicious. "How long? I have a
conference in Phoenix in a week."

"Not this year, sir." Doc Bruner herded his three patients
out the door. "You'll be fine. We just need to watch you a
while." He looked over his shoulder as they crowded out
the narrow door. "We'll take special care of the postmaster of Dillon, Montana."

"So this is your son," Hanna Cobb said when they were
all seated in the dining car again and Blake had a hot coffee
in front of him to warm his shivering bones. Trap hadn't
had time to notice it before, but the boy was drawn and trail-
worn. His clothes were damp from a hard ride and he was
soaked to the skin. Dark circles hung under weary eyes.

He downed his steaming coffee like it was water.

Hanna filled his cup again with a porcelain pitcher at the
table. "Your father and mother have been telling me so
much about their youth—the Scout Trackers and all."

Blake's eyes suddenly widened. He slapped the table. "I
almost forgot, Pa. I have news."

"I thought so," Maggie said, giving Blake a sidelong
look. "You seemed to be carrying a heavy burden."

"It's about Mr. Webber," Blake went on. "He was recuper-
ating in a hospital in Phoenix under the name of Johannes
Fargo. He was in pretty bad shape and wasn't expected to
live. One of the local deputies recognized him from a
poster I sent down and put a guard on him." Blake took a
sip of his coffee. He'd finally stopped shivering.

"There's more, isn't there?" Trap sighed, knowing, sens-
ing what his son was about to say next.

"There is. Webber killed the man guarding him and slipped away last night."

"I knew it was too good to be true." Clay pounded his fist on the table. He fiddled with the end of his mustache while he stared, blank-faced, out the window. The train was moving again. "Johannes is too wily to be cooped up in some hospital."

"I can't believe he murdered the captain." Hanna stirred a spoonful of cream into her coffee. "From the sounds of things, Roman was the one who watched over him the most."

"Some folks fight because they're angry," Maggie said. "Or because they hate Indians or some other such thing. Johannes Webber fights because his brain is on fire. He resents what he was, and he grew to despise Hezekiah for trying to help him."

"I know I wasn't as close to him as Trap or the captain," Madsen said. "And it will likely fall on me to kill him someday. But, there's one thing I know for sure. I would have died for him all those years ago."

"Anyone of us would have," Trap said. "Without hesitation—and he would have done the same for me."

Hanna Cobb took a drink of her coffee. "To go from a devoted comrade at arms to hateful killer—that's quite a leap for anyone. There had to be something. Something had to happen to make him hate you all so much."

The train picked up speed now, rocking the dining car gently. Snow-clad firs and spruces rolled by outside in the chilly blue shadows of evening. It was beginning to snow again.

"That, my dear Mrs. Cobb," Clay said, "is a very long story."

Hanna pushed her cup away. She put both hands flat on the table and leaned forward, spellbound with anticipation. "I'll bet it's interesting." Her green eyes sparkled.

Madsen looked at Trap, then at Maggie. They both shrugged. The big Texan sighed. "Oh, darlin', you have no idea."

THE LAST GUNFIGHTER SERIES BY
WILLIAM W. JOHNSTONE

Available Wherever Books Are Sold!

Visit our website at www.kensingtonbooks.com